THE
CORD

THE CORD

A NOVEL

JIM O'LOUGHLIN

bhc press™

Livonia, Michigan

Edited by Jamie Rich
Proofread by Tori Ladd

THE CORD

Published by BHC Press

Library of Congress Control Number:
2021944536

ISBN: 978-1-64397-295-4 (Hardcover)
ISBN: 978-1-64397-296-1 (Softcover)
ISBN: 978-1-64397-297-8 (Ebook)

For information, write:
BHC Press
885 Penniman #5505
Plymouth, MI 48170

Visit the publisher:
www.bhcpress.com

To my father

THE CORD

THE CORD
FAMILY TREE

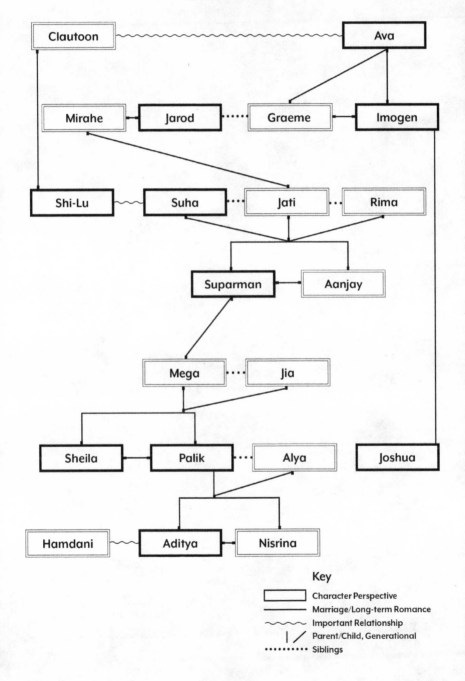

THE CORD

BOOK

III

Leap Second

Imogen

Now was as good a time as any. Imogen blinked, and when she opened her eyes, she was sitting in a polished aluminum room staring out a viewport into the vastness of space. This was Station, the stop at the end of the space elevator. Imogen was here, circling the Earth and surrounded by a universe of stars far brighter than what could be seen from the surface of the planet.

There was a knock at the door, then the door slid open and a doctor entered the room, smiling warmly at her.

"*Halo*, how are you feeling, Ms. Martin?" he asked. The doctor strode over and sat down in the chair next to her. The chair no longer shined silver; now it was embroidered with dark, rich leather, and it was not unlike the doctor, who was handsome with broad facial features and eyes that shone with promise. The doctor was now all she could see. He blocked out the rest of the room and even the view of the universe beyond them. When he spoke, he looked right at Imogen—right through her—and she had to fight an impulse to turn away.

Instead, she stared back into his deep brown eyes and replied, "Please, call me Imogen. I've not been well, Doctor."

The doctor's face deepened with concern. He carefully took her hands in his. His hands were large, and his touch was gentle. He enveloped her palms with his fingers. She was glad she had worn her long sweater, one of the nicest pieces of clothing she owned.

"You take care of others, Imogen, but who takes care of you?"

The doctor pushed up the sleeve of her sweater and pressed his fingers against the inside of her wrist.

"Your pulse is racing," the doctor said. His face was very close to Imogen's.

"Ms. Martin, it's time now."

"I said, call me Imogen."

Suddenly, gravity stopped working. The doctor floated toward the ceiling. Imogen gripped the arms of her chair so as to stay seated.

"Well, Imogen, then. It's time. He's ready for you."

Imogen was confused. Her legs kicked out to stabilize her, and she realized the voice speaking to her was not the doctor's. She blinked quickly, and the image of the floating doctor disappeared along with the room and the entire space station. She was no longer in space. Now what she saw in front of her was on Earth, a starkly furnished waiting room—all bright primary colors and stain-resistant carpet—and an annoyed nurse who flipped up a SenseVisor to glare at Imogen.

"Is everything okay there, missus?" the nurse asked in an irritated tone.

"Yes, everything's fine," Imogen replied, her face flushed and her legs spread awkwardly in front of her. Imogen quickly sat up and double blinked to close the file with the doctor. "Sorry, I was distracted."

The nurse didn't say anything. She flipped her visor back down and turned toward the door that led into the facility. Imogen knew to follow her, so she said nothing as she felt redness rise in her cheeks. How embarrassing to be caught screening a fantasy on her lenses in public like she was an adolescent! How could she let herself do such a thing? What was wrong with her?

Imogen tried to get ahold of herself as she followed the nurse into the facility and down a familiar hallway, keeping a couple steps behind.

They stopped at one of the visiting rooms, and the nurse swiped a code into the keyscreen next to the doorway. Then she placed a sensing device into Imogen's hand.

"Okay, Ms. Martin, you know the rules. If the device detects any distress, we will send someone down immediately. But the patient is restrained, so even if he does become agitated, you will be in no physical danger. Do you have any questions or concerns?"

"No," Imogen replied. She had heard these directions many times before. She placed the device into the pocket of her sweater.

"Then I would like to thank you again on behalf of the Commonwealth of Australia for your participation in this research project. Your willingness to give of yourself is essential to its success. Please have a nice visit with your great-grandfather. *Sampai jumpa lagi.*"

Great-great-great-grandfather, Imogen thought, but she didn't want to quibble. "*Kembali,*" she replied. Imogen opened the door, stepped inside and closed the door behind her, glad to be out of the nurse's sight.

Her great-great-great-grandfather, Joshua Martin, sat in a chair facing the window on the far side of the room. He was dressed in gray hospital pajamas that were about the same hue as the skin that hung loosely from his face and arms. His remaining wisps of hair grew at odd angles, but he sat straight upright, and his hands gripped the arms of the chair forcefully. All things considered, he did look like he could be her great-grandfather.

"Hello, Joshua. It's Imogen."

Joshua jerked his head to the side to look at her and grunted an acknowledgement before turning back to the window.

"It's a nice day out. The UV's a little high, but there's a breeze coming in off the ocean."

Joshua mumbled something, but the only word Imogen could make out was "ocean." She took a seat in the chair across the room from him. She could have moved the chair closer, but she felt more comfortable with some distance between them.

Then she started talking. She told Joshua about the incident that had just happened in the waiting room and how it was humiliating to be fantasy screening in public like that. It wasn't even a particularly good fantasy. What could be less sexy than a space station? But she found herself doing that kind of thing more often, calling up daydreams and viewing them on her lenses. She found it hard to stop. Doctor fantasies were a favorite, but they weren't the only ones. She also regularly screened a scene in which she protected a group of orphaned infants from a rampaging cyborg, and there was another where she was taken hostage by a handsome but unstable terrorist. She didn't want to get into the others. The point was she knew this couldn't be healthy.

The problem wasn't the fantasies—she had as much right to hers as anyone—but her inability to stop screening them. There was a time when she would have just popped a sugar pill to relax. She should have been able to manage this. After all, she was a trained placebologist. She was someone who helped others. She wasn't someone who needed help.

Did this all start when she quit her job? There would be a comfort in thinking her problems began when she left placebology to care for her husband, Graeme, but it had been happening when she was still employed, when the stress of work drove her to fantasize between clients, sometimes screening right through scheduled appointments. If she hadn't left her job, she probably would have been fired. But as long as Graeme was collecting his severance and disability, they didn't really have to worry about money for a while, at least not until Ava was old enough for university, and that wouldn't be for a few years.

"Years," Joshua grumbled. He sometimes repeated the last word Imogen said in a sentence. It wasn't quite conversation, but she appreciated the effort, even if speaking seemed more an impulse than a conscious mental act on Joshua's part.

Imogen had been shocked when she was first contacted by the researchers and told about Joshua. She never would have imagined that she had a relative who was a—well, she hated to even use the word to describe him. Her parents had died a few years prior, and they had never said anything about Joshua. She doubted they even knew about him. After all, people like Joshua weren't something a family would brag about, and he had been institutionalized long before her parents were even born. The researchers had only found Imogen through a DNA match.

The research program aimed to establish connections between people like Joshua and relatives, in hopes that regular social contact might have an impact on their condition. She had begun visiting Joshua, hoping that she would coax him into conversations and find out something about his life. The researchers didn't know much more about him than his birth date. But she had studied history in university and envisioned getting a firsthand account of the period when Joshua was young. She wanted to find out about her family's past, so much of which was lost now, or at least stuck on storage devices buried in land-fills somewhere. She had shot hyperview footage of their initial discussions, with vague ideas that she would create a Personal Experience Program about the experience. She could see her PEPod becoming a huge success, perhaps the beginning of a second career for her.

But the visits had not turned out as she had hoped. She quickly realized that Joshua was not really able to have a conversation. The hyperview footage just consisted of her asking questions that went unanswered or received a grunt in response. Eventually, she blinked her camera off and gave up on the whole idea.

Still, she had to believe that there was something comforting for Joshua in having someone speak to him, and, over time, she came to realize that the visits were good for her as well. She wasn't sure what it said about her, but she enjoyed visiting Joshua because she got to talk all about herself under the guise of helping him. Every couple of weeks, she stopped by for an hour and babbled on about whatever was on her mind—her marriage to Graeme, the challenges of raising a teenaged Ava, the most recent episode of *GRON.inc* she had screened. She shared all her fears and desires with Joshua, telling him things about herself she had never before spoken out loud. It was for the best that he didn't seem to understand anything she said.

Today she told Joshua about Graeme's latest crazy plan. Suddenly, after not having seen his brother, Jarod, in more than a decade, Graeme had decided he wanted to go visit him on Station. Yes, with all of his medical issues, not to mention being out of work, Graeme wanted them to go on an expensive holiday and take the space elevator into orbit where they would spend two weeks essentially living in a big metal box that was tethered to the planet by a thin cable. He wouldn't stop going on about it, and now the idea of visiting Station was even interrupting her fantasies.

She had learned over the course of their marriage contracts to respond to Graeme's plans by just nodding and listening. Most of Graeme's enthusiasms were temporary, like getting a biodog for a pet or investing in an algae farm, and nothing came of them. Then again, sometimes he acted on his ideas, like with the deep-sea trip they took, which also meant spending weeks in a big metal box. What did Graeme have against beaches or wide-open space? Why couldn't they take a trip she would enjoy for once?

But all that was beside the point. They really couldn't afford an extravagant holiday until Graeme was back on his feet and able to get another job. And with Ava's schoolwork taking up so much more time, they couldn't just take off on a moment's notice like they had in the past. But Graeme needed to have some adventure or scheme that he could look forward to. It was part of his personality, and she had to admit, it was part of what had initially drawn her to him.

She still remembered that time in university when Graeme had gotten his hands on a hydrohover and they had taken to the water at night so that they could get to Motuhoa in New Zealand by dawn for the sunrise. She didn't ask how dangerous the trip was at night or how many customs laws they broke, but she remembered waking up just as the night sky was beginning to lighten and seeing Graeme on the bow, his shirt off and his muscles all his own, wind whipping his hair back across his face. It was an image that was as vivid to her now as it had been then. Graeme could be exciting to be with when he wasn't infuriating. It was just one of the paradoxes of her life.

"Life." Joshua growled, nodding his head forward.

Imogen checked the time and saw that the visit was almost over. She had almost forgotten about what she had brought.

"Joshua, I have something to show you." Imogen rose from the chair and crouched down between Joshua and the window. "Now, I know I'm not allowed to give you gifts, but I thought you might like to see this. I was in the Melbourne Museum where there was a wonderful history exhibit on the era when you were a young man, and the gift shop had the cutest thing in the children's section. I thought of you immediately when I saw it."

Imogen reached into her pocket and pulled out a small metallic sphere. It looked a little like the sensing device the nurse had given her earlier, but when Imogen pressed a button on the sphere, it opened up and transformed into a tiny automaton with generally human-looking features, except that instead of legs it had a sphere that allowed it to roll around on Imogen's palm.

"See, Joshua, it's a robot. It's a re-creation of the kind of robot that would have been used when you were—that you should recognize. And look, it responds to basic voice commands. Robot, clap."

The robot moved its miniature hands together, making a surprisingly loud, tinny clank.

"Isn't it cute?"

Joshua had ignored it at first, but the sound of metallic clapping drew his attention, and his eyes focused on the object in Imogen's hand.

"Robot!" Joshua shouted. He tried to yank himself out of his seat, only to be forced back by the restraints.

Imogen pulled back in surprise and slipped to the ground. The automaton fell from her hand and slid to the floor, where it kept clapping as it lay on its side. Imogen struggled back to her feet.

"Robot!" Joshua screamed again. He wrenched against the restraints and snapped the one holding his right arm in place. Then he lurched toward Imogen and grabbed the bottom of her sweater. Imogen stepped backward and tried to pull the sweater out of his hand, but Joshua's grip was firm. The sensing device fell out of her pocket and clattered to the floor. He yanked on the sweater, drawing Imogen a half step toward him.

"Let go! Let go, you—zombie!"

Imogen screamed as loud as she could and lurched away from him, pulling the sweater over her head and arms. She wiggled out of the sweater, then reached down to the floor and grabbed the sensing device, squeezing it hard. Joshua had stuffed her sweater into his mouth and was trying to chew it.

"Robot!" he shouted, his voice muffled by fabric.

Suddenly the door flew open and two orderlies ran in, followed by the nurse that had brought Imogen to this room. They immediately grabbed Joshua's free arm and pulled it back down to the chair. It took all three of them, but they were able to apply a temporary restraint, and then the nurse gave Joshua an injection of some sort so that he stopped struggling. Imogen's sweater fell from his mouth.

"Are you okay?" the nurse asked Imogen.

"I'm fine. I'm fine."

"What happened?"

"I don't know. All of a sudden, he started shouting, and then he grabbed my sweater. He's never done anything like that before."

"Did you provoke him?"

"No, of course not. I just—I had shown him…" Imogen gestured toward the floor.

One of the orderlies picked up the robot and held it up.

"This?" the orderly asked. "This toy?"

"I thought he would like it. It's a re-creation of an automaton. From when he was, you know, really alive."

"We're going to have to fill out a report on this," the nurse said. "Are you okay to give a statement?"

"Can I—can I just have a couple minutes?"

"Sure, *kekasih*, come on over to the lounge. Let's get you some water." The nurse's voice had dropped into what Imogen recognized as a sympathetic tone. Imogen calmed down enough to feel self-conscious that she was standing in front of the small crowd in her bra. She folded her arms over her chest.

The nurse reached up onto a high shelf in the room. She grabbed a towel and draped it around Imogen's shoulders. Then she took Imogen's arm and led her out of the room. Imogen didn't look back at Joshua. They went down the corridor to a larger room with cushioned chairs and reclining self-massage machines. Imogen sat down on a chair, and the nurse got her a cup of water.

"Let me get you something to put on," the nurse said. "I'll be right back."

The nurse stepped outside and quietly closed the door, leaving Imogen alone. Imogen reached into the pocket of her slacks and pulled out a sugar pill. She put it in her mouth and swallowed it with a sip of water.

"And now, the tension will leave my body," Imogen said out loud. "I feel relaxed. I feel relaxed."

She did not feel relaxed, but she believed in the power of persuasion. It was her job, or at least it had been when she was working. She tried to take deep breaths, but she knew her hands were still shaking.

For the first time, she understood why people like Joshua were called "zombies." They really were a kind of soulless undead. Whoever Joshua had been, he was now just a collection of mindless physical impulses with brief flickers of memory. He would have eaten her brain if he had had the chance.

So much for immortality. In Joshua's time, they had had such faith in bioengineering. They were so sure they had figured out all the mysteries of the world. "The death of death" they had called it. But eventually everyone who took the immortality treatment had wound up like Joshua. For some it happened immediately, for others it took years, but they all wound up with broken brains that told them to turn on those around them. Most had been killed, and those who were captured and kept alive languished in institutions from generation to generation, as hopes for anything resembling a cure all but disappeared.

But why had Joshua reacted that way to a toy robot? Something about robots must have imprinted on him so strongly that it survived his zombification and still meant something even after generations of time had passed.

There was a knock at the door, and the nurse stuck her head in the room. Her SenseVisor was down, so she was probably able to tell that Imogen's heart rate had finally slowed.

"Ms. Martin, do you think you'd be able to give a statement now?"

Imogen looked up at the nurse and nodded. The nurse handed her a shirt to put on, and Imogen removed the towel from her shoulders. Suddenly, she felt self-conscious in the presence of this nurse. How foolish did Imogen appear, a middle-aged woman living life in a daze of fantasies who thought she could help a zombie? Wouldn't it have served her right if Joshua had eaten her brain? She'd been warned about introducing items that had not been preapproved. She'd violated the protocols of the research project. There was a risk involved. Joshua was, after all, a zombie.

The nurse clicked two fingernails against the brim of her visor, activating a recorder.

"I'm required to keep a transcript of your statement," the nurse said.

"Of course," Imogen said. She really was done. This would be her last visit with Joshua Martin.

• • • • •

WHEN SHE GOT back home, all Imogen wanted was to talk to someone about what had happened with Joshua, but of course she couldn't. She hadn't told anyone that he even existed, and how could she now? Besides, even if she had decided to confess all that had gone wrong, Graeme was following doctor's orders, for once, and taking a nap. Ava had netball practice after school and wouldn't be back until dinner. And what if they had been available? Graeme might just laugh at her, and Ava's current means of communication seemed to consist entirely of eye rolls and sighs. No, she was on her own.

Imogen stood in front of the console in the kitchen while it scanned her retina. When she was recognized, the home account came up on her lenses and she saw that Graeme had left the credit file open. She was about to close it when a line item jumped out at her. A purchase, a hugely expensive purchase, three tickets for a trip to Station! She scrolled through the whole file. She couldn't believe it. He had gone and booked the whole holiday without even telling her. They couldn't afford this! The more she looked, the worse it got. Graeme had gotten all sorts of nonrefundable "deals" on the dirigible flight to Labicittá and the space elevator passage up the Cord. She went on QuikChat to try to cancel the tickets, but it couldn't be done. They were stuck with this trip.

She was so angry, she wanted to wake Graeme up with a hurley stick. This was worse than the deep-sea trip, even worse than the RoBro! How could he do such a thing? Then she realized that her birthday was next week. He was going to present this awful trip to her for her birthday. That's exactly what he was planning to do. He was going to say that this was for her!

In a rage, she blinked and her private files appeared. She scrolled to her profile on the hookup app, the one she had time and again revised and fine-tuned, yet never activated. But she didn't have to put up with Graeme. There were other options. Taking a breath, she activated her profile.

It only took an instant. Avatars of available men began popping up in her kitchen one after another. First a pair, then a handful, soon more than a dozen. It was as if they had just been waiting for her to activate. Some were tall, others short. Clean-shaven, bearded. All were smiling as they delivered a canned introduction. The voices overlapped and began to overwhelm her. She left-winked to try to clear the crowd, but the more of them she closed, the more seemed to appear. Her kitchen was crowded with men, and they seemed to be closing in on her.

"Deactivate!" she shouted, and the avatars evaporated before her. She was alone again in her kitchen. Imogen sank into a chair, defeated and deflated. What had she been thinking? She didn't want her life to become more complicated than it already was. What she wanted was peace and a little serenity.

She returned to her private files to close them down, but on the far side of her field of vision, an advert appeared. "Do you want peace and serenity?" it said. Imogen had learned to ignore most adverts that came into view, but she couldn't stop this one from catching her attention. Yes, she did want peace and serenity. She blinked on it and read.

A few minutes later, Imogen closed up all of the files and programmed in some bangers and mash on the auto dinner, leaving a message with the RoBro to say that she had to run an errand. In a way, that was true.

A short time later, she was downtown and standing in front of the Australian Technological & Metaphysical Institute, a converted warehouse that didn't quite live up to its impressive title. She thought about turning back, but then a wave of despair swept over her again. She just couldn't bear to go home feeling like this. Something had to change.

So, taking a sharp breath, she strode through the front doors and walked up to a glistening metallic reception desk. She caught the eye of one of the tall, slim men wearing the saffron robes of the order.

"*Halo,*" he said with a smile. "*Selamat datang di* AT&M Institute."

"*Selamat siang,*" Imogen replied. Then she got right to the point. "I would like the Holiday Retreat Package." As unlikely as it was that someone she knew would see her here, she didn't want to spend any more time than was necessary in the public reception room.

The man at the desk apparently had seen this response before because, without another word, he led her right into a nearby private room. Though the room was furnished with only a desk and two chairs, it was mood-sensitive. Immediately, the wall near Imogen reflected the gray of her tension, and the blue of the man's serenity appeared on the wall behind him. The colors soon combined into a dull yellow-green that surrounded them like ancient wallpaper. The man looked at the walls and frowned.

"This is your first time?" he asked, although his tone indicated that he knew it was.

Imogen nodded yes, and the man launched into an introduction that was more concerned with legal liability than with any services being offered. He was handsome in the same way that the doctor of this morning's fantasy screening had been, but she was not at all drawn to him physically. Maybe it was his vow of chastity.

When he was done with his explanation, the man smiled. "I'm sorry I have to begin that way. It is *nécessaire*." He took a towel from a basket on the desk and draped it around her neck. The SmartFibers gently massaged her shoulders. Then he rolled out a screen and placed it into her hands. He swiped at his desk surface screen. The ceiling lights lowered, and her chair molded to meet her body's contours. The man asked her to close her eyes, breathe deeply and just let the screen rest on her palms. She did as he asked.

"Just concentrate on your breathing. One more minute. Now exhale. Let the tension leave your body."

Imogen exhaled, wishing she had taken another sugar pill before coming here. She tried to focus on her breathing, to blow out the anxiety and uncertainty that gripped her chest. After a minute, the lights went up in the room. She opened her eyes and saw that the walls around her had changed to a soothing aqua color. She felt a little better. The man took the screen from her hands, rolling it back up into a tube.

"Will you need me to sync in so you can get my preferences?" Imogen asked.

"No, the screen you were holding registered them."

"But I didn't say what they were."

"The screen was able to sense them. We get a more accurate reading this way. Sometimes people don't know what they really want."

Imogen considered that. More than sometimes, she thought.

Again, the man swiped at his desk surface screen. It flickered with light, and he informed her that her ideal retreat would be a small tropical island. Imogen laughed, and the man gave her a quizzical look.

"Next month, my family and I are taking a blimp from Sydney to Labicittá."

The man continued to look puzzled. "I understand the island of Labicittá has some beautiful beaches," he said.

"But then we're taking the space elevator up to Station."

"To Station!" The man seemed truly surprised. "That is a once-in-a-lifetime opportunity!"

"Yes, so my husband says. He's always wanted to go into space. But as you can see, I would prefer a beach."

The man smiled again and continued. He scheduled her for an appointment later in the week for the brain wave transfer, and he explained the process to her. After the DNA sequencing was complete, a temporary body could be grown relatively quickly. She would have her choice of several of today's most notable celebrities, of whichever sex, for the temporary body. Then her avatar would be implanted and provided with resort accommodations on the institute's private island for two weeks. And no, the man said with a smile, she could not go to the island herself (many people apparently asked this). Only avatars were allowed on the island, for legal purposes, since the institute was, of course, legally responsible for all of the avatar's actions. She would be able to access a live feed of her avatar's actions through an EarthWeb connection. At the end of two weeks, the avatar's memories would be transferred, the avatar would be decommissioned and the body would be recycled.

"Does the avatar have to be decommissioned?"

"I must emphasize that the recycling is mandatory. The host body for your avatar has an extremely limited life cycle, and it could not exist beyond the scheduled experience time."

Imogen nodded. After the morning with Joshua, she didn't have to be told twice about all the ways bioengineering could go wrong.

The man described how, upon Imogen's return, there would be a Reuniting Session, and she would have to make a decision. After a private review of the avatar's memories, she could choose one of three packages. The Replacement Package allowed the avatar's memories to replace her own for the period in question. Her own experience would be transferred to external storage so she could still access it, for legal purposes, but her own memories would be otherwise wholly forgotten. It would feel as if the avatar's experience had, in fact, been her own.

The Parallel Package would place the avatar's memories next to her own. She would be able to access the avatar's memories, but they would not replace her own experiences. The man indicated that many customers who had purchased this package reported that the avatar's experiences felt much like a daydream. Other Parallel Package customers said it felt like an actual dream, something that involved you but had not quite happened to you.

She could also choose the External Package. In this package, the avatar's memories would be placed in an external storage device, which she could choose to access at her leisure. However, because the experiences in the External Package would not be implanted, they would not be felt with the same intensity of memory. Those occurrences would feel closer to a computer simulation or a Personal Experience Program. The man asked if Imogen was familiar with PEPods. She said she was, because her daughter, Ava, very much enjoyed creating them. This was not entirely untrue.

Finally, the man noted that Imogen would be responsible for all charges if she chose to destroy the avatar's experiences altogether, and that would apply whether or not she found out what those experiences were.

"Do many people choose to destroy the avatar's experiences without knowing what they are?" Imogen asked.

"Some do. Some people prefer to leave the avatar's time at the resort...at the resort. Of course, sometimes simply knowing that one may choose which memories to keep frees individuals to enjoy their own experiences more fully. It is impossible to predict in advance. That is why we do not ask you to choose until the Reuniting Session. Our institute fully supports whichever choice you make. Our goal is to help you find your own path to serenity."

Imogen felt herself start to choke up. A path to serenity? At this point, she couldn't envision one. At home, hidden at the bottom of her sock drawer, Imogen had a PEPod she had made when Ava was just an infant. Imogen had been on maternity leave, though she did some remote consulting during Ava's naps just to keep her hand in things, and all things seemed possible. On this particular day, she had taken Ava out in the pram for a walk, and it was such a nice day that Imogen had decided to shoot some hyperview footage. The trees were in bloom, and birds were lightly chirping in the background. Ava squirmed and wanted to be picked up, and Imogen took her out of the pram, looking into the face of this creature who represented all of Imogen's hopes and desires. When she looked at Ava, it was as if she saw an image of herself, and Imogen knew exactly what her daughter wanted and needed.

Imogen had held Ava tightly in her arms, knowing that she was doing precisely what she should be doing at this particular moment in her life. And then Graeme appeared, home from work early. He jogged over to them, gave them both a peck on the cheek and started pushing the empty pram. He asked her how Ava had eaten that day, and she had eaten well, so they were both pleased about that. Ava shifted, and Imogen could tell she wanted to face forward so that she could see everything that was ahead of them. Imogen rearranged Ava. Imogen understood. She wanted to see everything that was ahead of them as well.

Later, when Imogen had synced into that PEPod, the intensity of the experience was overwhelming. She could smell the blooming trees and the light perspiration on baby Ava's head. The chirping birds and Graeme's deep baritone voice seemed like a symphony. And the colors! Vibrant greens and a rich blue sky. It was all so much.

It was too much. That was why the PEPod was in her sock drawer. It physically hurt her to screen it now. She could only contrast that moment with where she was now and where she was heading, to be stuck in space with an unhappy husband and a jaded teenaged daughter. It brought her no comfort. She could only hope this Holiday Retreat Package would truly allow her to escape rather than remind her of what she no longer had.

The man was staring at her. She realized that he had said something to her and was waiting for her response.

"What?" she asked.

"I said, 'Are you ready to journey down the path to serenity?'"

The man smiled, and his deep brown eyes showed kindness, perhaps even concern. He did not take Imogen's hand, nor would she have wanted him to. Path to serenity? She didn't expect all of that. She'd be satisfied just to make this horrible holiday trip up the Cord to Station an experience to forget.

Imogen held out her wrist and tapped the keypad tattoo on it. Her billing information came up.

"Scan me, and let's make this real."

Jarod

Outside the viewport was a silent galaxy of stars and the Earth below. But inside Station, things were abuzz. Jarod tapped in and felt the anticipation. Two new babies were due on the next shuttle coming up the Cord. Station had a good medical clinic, but the better maternity facilities were in Labicittá, so couples cycled down to Earth for the last month of a woman's pregnancy. That meant when a new baby was brought back to Station, everything stopped. Relatives turned out in droves to greet the shuttle, and since almost everyone on Station was related in one way or another, it made for a crowded arrivals gate.

But Jarod had his own anticipation to share, so he cast that into the mix and felt it ripple out. The next shuttle to arrive would also have his brother Graeme and Graeme's family, and he couldn't help but be pleased that Graeme had gone through the effort and expense to visit him on Station. After their parents passed away, he and Graeme had gone in different directions, and they hadn't even seen each other since Graeme and Imogen got married. Jarod had only ever met their daughter, Ava, via vidchat, and she was fourteen now. So when Graeme first floated the idea of a visit, Jarod didn't think it would really happen. Everyone says they want to go into space, but most people don't actually make it. However, Graeme was persistent, though it was literally out-of-the-world expensive for three people, even when Jarod got them every available discount he could through the tourism bureau where he worked. He was eager to have this visit go well.

He tapped in and let his anxiety flow out. Reassurances came back to him, and he was reminded once again of how much he liked living here. The attraction wasn't being in space; it was being in space with the people on Station.

As he looked around the waiting room, he could feel the warmth and kindness without even tapping in, though maybe it was also the charge of energy captured from the floor. Though the room was packed with people pacing in various directions and talking to one another, no one seemed put out by the crowded conditions. Jarod tried to match the crowd's equanimity, though he found the design of this waiting room a little too clever by half. He understood that the oscillations in the uneven floor and the occasional blasts of air from the wall vents were supposed to keep him on edge and alert, but, really, all he was doing was waiting around. Would it be so wrong if he just paced the floor aimlessly or even stopped to stare out the viewport down the Cord at the swirl of clouds, oceans and continents on the Earth below?

A gust of air from the wall vent caught the back of his head, and Jarod instinctively drew up his handgrip. He chuckled at himself. Score one for the room designer. He was now on edge and alert again. A glance at the dynamometer on his handgrip revealed that he had generated more joules than he would have guessed.

He continued pacing the floor and soon fell into stride alongside a man with hyperadaptive eyes who wasn't quite up to the pace set in the room. The man wore an anti-goat, one of those beards with the goatee shaved out of it, which was popular in Europe now. Jarod guessed the man was an astronomer visiting from Earth. With so many people in a small space, they had to choreograph their paths along the floor so as not to bump into one another. Jarod, having worked on Station for almost ten years, was used to generating power and building muscle mass at every opportunity, but the astronomer seemed to have trouble coordinating his walking with his handgrip.

Then, to make matters worse, the astronomer bumped into a woman passing in front of him. She lost her footing and stumbled toward Jarod. Jarod dropped his handgrip and grabbed her so she didn't fall to the floor. The woman shouted in alarm, and Jarod saw that he vaguely knew her. She was an engineer and a distant cousin of Mirahe's. He and Mirahe had been together for a decade, but he still couldn't keep track of the names of all of her relatives on Station.

After the collision, everyone paused for a moment. Then Mirahe's cousin righted herself and flashed the astronomer a bewildered look. The astronomer smiled back sheepishly. He picked up Jarod's handgrip and returned it.

Crisis averted, everyone in the room began pacing again.

"*Mi dispiace*," the astronomer said to Jarod. "I don't quite have the hang of this yet."

Jarod pumped his handgrip and smiled back. "It all takes some getting used to. I'm just glad these handgrips are pretty sturdy now. I broke these grips *hàng tháng* my first year on Station."

As they walked side by side around the room, Jarod tapped in and learned that the astronomer's name was Alessandro. He was Italian, which wasn't that unusual on Station, but he was also transhuman, which was a surprise. Transhumans might not have been that unusual in Europe, but there weren't many on Station. He tried not to be rude and stare, but he couldn't help but wonder what parts of Alessandro were robotic.

"So, your *familgia* is from Australia," Alessandro said. Apparently he had tapped in to find out about Jarod as well. "I've always wanted to visit Australia, but the closest I've come is watching it down below. *É molto bello*, I am told."

Alessandro gestured through the viewport toward Earth and the wedge of western Australia they could see below them. Jarod had grown up near Melbourne in the east, and he'd only been to western Australia a couple times when he was a kid. But he tapped into his video archive and forwarded some of his personal footage of the trip to Alessandro. Alessandro smiled and stayed silent, and Jarod could tell he was screening on his lenses in translucent mode while walking. That wasn't what Jarod would have recommended, as it was a good way to bump into someone, but they continued pacing unimpeded until there was an announcement that the shuttle passengers had cleared quarantine and would be arriving soon. The floor stopped oscillating, and people in the waiting room crowded toward the gate.

Mirahe's cousin walked up to the wall console and swiped the screen. She announced to the room that they had generated 297.36 joules of energy according to the floor measurement. "This many people and we couldn't break three hundred? You people have babies on the brain."

Everyone laughed, and Jarod remembered her name. Benvolese. Mirahe had introduced them at a party over in Observation last summer. Jarod considered giving Benvolese a hard time and telling her to include the joules on the handgrips in the energy totals, but the moment passed as a hydraulic hiss sounded and the quarantine door opened.

The parents with the babies were the first ones off, following tradition. They were welcomed with a round of applause and a burst of joy that was cast widely. Jarod let it wash over him as he strained for a look at the tiny bundles cradled in the parents' arms. Jarod knew one of the parents in passing, a systems engineer who was another distant cousin of Mirahe's, of course. The other couple was unfamiliar, so Jarod tapped in to see what he could find out. The two women worked in Administration. They were originally from China, and their sperm donor was on Labicittá. The baby was a girl. Her name was Lijuan. There was already an image album available. Information traveled fast up here.

The parents and their babies moved to the center of the room for the joining ceremony. An old woman in a transit chair, whom Jarod had only ever heard people refer to as Grandmother, was brought over to them. The children were lowered to her level, and she placed her hand over each child, speaking too softly for Jarod to hear. Then the couples brought out small, identical blankets, which they unwrapped. Jarod couldn't quite see through the crowd, but he knew that each blanket contained a section of each child's umbilical cord that the parents had preserved. The grandmother took a decorative strand of carbon nano-tube and wound it around each of the sections of umbilical cord before refolding the blanket. Then she spoke in a voice that was louder than Jarod would have expected.

"We welcome these children to Station. Let us take them into our hearts and bind them to us with the strength of the Cord that ties us to our brothers and sisters on the Earth below and allows us to live here on Station in a world of our own making. *Selamat datang,* children!"

"*Selamat datang!*" the people shouted. There was more cheering and a rush of conversation. People circled around the new parents and took hands with them. In the shuffle of confusion, a wave of passen-gers from the shuttle began to enter the waiting room, adding to the crowd. There looked to be the usual crowd of tourists, scientists and regulars cycling in for the term on Station. Jarod noticed another one of Mirahe's relatives, Samir was his name, emerge and take hands with Benvolese. Like most of Mirahe's relatives, Samir was lean and a head shorter than Jarod. Samir also had those great cheekbones that were a dominant trait in Mirahe's extended family. From across the room, Jarod caught his eye and waved.

Meanwhile, a somewhat peaked-looking traveler made her way into the waiting room. Alessandro offered a formal bow and took a small suitcase from the woman who had come up to him. A quick tap told Jarod that this was another astronomer, but Jarod would have guessed that anyway when the two astronomers each tugged adaptive eyeballs out of their sockets and synced them together. He had heard that this was just a form of greeting, but it was kind of uncomfortable to watch, so Jarod was glad when Samir came over to say hello. Jarod and Samir often crossed paths when Jarod gave tours of the agricultural sector where Samir farmed. Jarod took hands with him and tapped in to send welcome.

"Is that your family I traveled with up the Cord?" Samir asked.

"Yes, my brother and his wife and daughter. Are they behind you?"

"They are behind. They were not moving quickly. They found the trip…taxing."

"I find the trip taxing, Samir. And I've done it almost a dozen times now."

Benvolese interrupted to hand Samir his gauges. Samir took out the decorative ones he was wearing and inserted the Station gauges in his earlobes. Benvolese made a joke about Jarod having saved her from falling earlier. Samir pressed the gauges into place and smiled at Jarod when they were activated.

"Thank you for your welcome, cousin. After your family acclimates, bring them to see the bamboo fields. I will show them the bounty and the beauty."

"Thanks, Samir. That would really be *hebat*."

Samir and Benvolese soon left, as did the rest of the passengers eventually. Jarod found himself alone, staring down the long hallway that led into quarantine. He resisted the temptation to go down and see what was holding them up. Instead, he paced and watched, and he felt like a little kid again, waiting for his big brother, Graeme, to come out of the locker room after a match. Graeme had been a great footballer, a natural midfielder, and, when Jarod was a kid, Graeme had seemed like some kind of superhuman giant, hurtling down the pitch with huge strides. Even though Jarod grew to be a couple inches taller than Graeme, Graeme would always seem big to him. And right now it was hard to kick the feeling that a teenaged Graeme would soon emerge, hair wet from a shower and surrounded by teammates all talking about the match.

But when the family made their way down the hallway, Jarod didn't think it was them at first. Instead of a cluster of happy, young athletes, he saw an exhausted trio hauling way too much luggage. Jarod had warned them that magnalev bags wouldn't work on Station, and he told them to pack light, but that message didn't seem to have made it through. Graeme was struggling to carry a bag with a broken strap under one arm and pulling another behind him, bumping it into the wall as he walked with an erratic gait. His wife, Imogen, had only one piece of luggage, but it must have been almost as heavy as she was, judging from the way she had to heave it behind her. Only Ava, bringing up the rear, seemed to have a reasonable-sized bag, a glowing pull-pack with stylized graffiti written on it in a language that Jarod didn't recognize. Jarod waved and watched.

He realized why Graeme seemed to have trouble moving. Graeme was apparently undergoing extensive body modification and was only midway through the process. It was all Jarod could do not to stare at him in his tank top and shorts. His arms and left leg were muscular and sculpted like a bodybuilder's. But his right leg was flabby, and he had a belly on him that reminded Jarod of their father in his later years.

Finally, Graeme made it across the threshold. Jarod put out his hand and grabbed Graeme's wrist.

"Take my hand, brother," Jarod said, offering the traditional Station greeting and realizing that it had never had this literal meaning for him before.

"Jaysus," Graeme said, throwing his arms around Jarod in a bear hug. "Look at you! You haven't changed a bit. You look *fabuleux*."

"It is so good to see you," Jarod said, patting Graeme's newly muscular shoulders. "It's been too long." Jarod wasn't sure what you were supposed to say to someone mid-modification—you're looking halfway great?

Graeme pulled back and swept his arm toward his family. "You remember Imogen, and here's Ava."

Jarod turned to Imogen and grabbed her wrist. "Take my hand, sister." He'd only met her the day of the wedding, and aside from hair that was a slightly different shade of red, kind of a reddish purple, she seemed much the same, though also harried from the trip.

Imogen grabbed Jarod's wrist back and let herself be pulled toward him. She had apparently studied up on Station etiquette. Jarod similarly extended his hand to Ava, but the girl hung back.

"Take my hand, sister."

"I'm your niece, not your sister," Ava said in a high-pitched voice that made her sound younger than fourteen. She looked like her mother, with the same big eyes and sloping shoulders, though her hair was a bit lighter than Imogen's, at least lighter than the current color of Imogen's hair.

"It's just a saying, my niece," Jarod said, smiling. He gave her wrist a friendly squeeze, then let go. "Welcome to Station."

"I had begun to wonder whether there was any end to that elevator," Graeme said. "That's a hell of a long trip, a real *turas fada*, you know?"

"Forty thousand kilometers from Earth. There's nothing else like it, that's for sure."

Graeme shared details of their travels up the Cord, the initial nausea and how Ava had been scared to look down through the ports at first. Ava objected, saying that she hadn't been scared, she just didn't like the view. Graeme said he'd hardly been able to get Imogen to take her eyes away from the port.

"What about you, Jar? Do you just take the view for granted now?"

"I try not to. Giving tours helps. I have to try to see things the way someone new to Station sees them. But I'm sure there are some people up here who don't even look down anymore."

"It's hard to imagine," Imogen said, looking out through the view window. Jarod wasn't quite sure what she meant. That statement covered a lot of territory.

Imogen rifled through her pockets and pulled out a vial. "I almost forgot. We have to do this." She poured three pills into the palm of her left hand, then placed her right hand gently against Graeme's cheek. "Say, 'Now my stomach will settle.'"

"Imogen, do we have to do this right now?"

"The sooner the better; you know that. Now say it."

"Now my stomach will settle," Graeme said reluctantly. Imogen placed one of the pills into Graeme's mouth.

Imogen repeated the process with Ava, and then she made Graeme place a hand on her cheek as she said the same phrase.

"What's that you're taking?" Jarod asked.

"Don't worry. Nothing contraband," Graeme assured him, popping a pill onto Imogen's tongue. "It's just a sugar pill."

"What do you mean 'just?'" Imogen said, swallowing.

"Nothing, *petite amie*, nothing."

Jarod knew that Imogen was a placebologist, but he had never seen one in action before.

"But will it work if you know it's a sugar pill?" Jarod asked.

"It's not the pill that matters. It's the fact of caring. And the touch." She placed her palm against Jarod's cheek, and he felt a surge that he knew didn't happen.

"So, Jarod, what do you say we get these bags stashed?" Graeme pressed the keypad tattoo on his wrist but nothing happened. He jabbed at his skin to no avail.

"Oh, come on! I was told my converter would function up here."

"Graeme, I said not to bother. Those things never work. Here." Jarod took three earrings out of his pocket. The serrated lanthanum setting glistened silver in the overhead light. "Clip this onto your earlobe. They're not as fast as a gauge, but they'll let you tap in while you're on Station. And here are some lenses. They'll let you record, but don't forget that StationWeb has storage limits. If you try to shoot your whole day in hyperview, you'll be full up around lunchtime. We always recommend shooting in standardview."

"So, there's no EarthWeb connection with these?" Graeme asked as he clipped on the earring.

"Nope, not while you're on Station."

"That's what that Samir told us, *pobrecito*. It was the funniest thing." As Imogen spoke, she opened her eyes wide to pop out her EarthWeb lenses and pop in the StationWeb ones. She kept speaking like someone who had been popping lenses in and out her whole life, which was likely the case. "All the way up, Graeme keeps fiddling with his tattoo, and he says to this man sitting next to us, 'I've got no EarthWeb connection, no audio link, no video capacity. If it wasn't for the built-in clock, I wouldn't even know what time it is.' And the man—"

"And he says to me, if you can believe it, 'Cousin, you need to turn off your clock.'"

• • • • •

OVER THE YEARS, Jarod had come to understand what people wanted from a tour of Station. First-time visitors weren't really concerned with the mechanics of how a space station operated. They wanted to see gorgeous views, and the recent renovations featured full-viewport decks with video-friendly vistas both Earthside and starside, as well as lush plant beds of medicinal herbs and decorative flowers. After that, some visitors would want to explore the more cramped inner core section or hear about the precise chemical makeup and production process for carbon nanotubes, but there was no reason not to let people just revel in the experience of being in space.

So, after giving Graeme and his family the standard warning about the give in the floor—"Each step you take produces energy that is circulated back into Station's energy grid."—and the vertigo—"Just close your eyes if you start to feel dizzy."—he chose a path back to his rooms that took them through Artsutanov Plaza, the premiere open space on the periphery. It was midshift, so there weren't too many people walking around, which was a good thing, since all the luggage made it hard for anyone to pass them in the opposite direction.

Jarod grabbed Imogen's suitcase with one arm and picked up Graeme's biggest bag with the other. Then he led everyone through a series of narrow hallways that opened up into the plaza. Artsutanov Plaza was adjacent to the school and recreation center, and the ceiling had a latticed viewport that offered an unimpeded look into deep space. Right now, there was a Tai Chi seniors group meeting on the near end, and kids from the grade school were climbing playground equipment on the far end. Jarod put the luggage down and let Graeme and his family roam. He could tell that they immediately ignored his earlier warning and started shooting hyperview footage. Jarod took a few standardview shots, trying to make sure to get images of his brother's family with stars in the background. He had learned by now that though it was irresistible to take lots of footage of space, all the stars would start to look alike after a while. It was only the footage with people in it that would matter over time.

Ava was the most excited. She was shouting out constellation names and pointing to favorite stars. "Look, Mum, that's where Vela is, the one with the Goldilocks planet. Over there must be where the Virgo cluster is. Take footage of me with Orion." She apparently had studied up on her astronomy.

Ava had her face pasted against the side viewport as she shouted to her mother, who tentatively stuck to the center of the room. Imogen's reluctance to stand close to the edge was not uncommon among new visitors. While Ava continued calling out constellation names, Graeme had Jarod take a forced perspective shot where it looked like he was drinking out of the Big Dipper. They were all having a good time, and the flow of people walking through the plaza made the whole scene vibrant and exciting. Jarod tapped in and cast his pleasure.

But when he tapped in, he realized that a message stream had been flagged. He blinked over to check it out. That was a mistake.

TO: All Tourism Sector Members
SUBJECT: Today's Tourism Sector Meeting

Alexey: All, I see that Jarod has taken today off though a tourism sector meeting is scheduled. Since the work of the tourism sector is vital to the success of Station, I am willing to step forward and chair today's meeting. I've attached an agenda.

Jarod sighed and messaged back.

Jarod: The meeting has been rescheduled for the same time next week. There is no meeting today.

As Jarod expected, Alexey responded immediately.

Alexey: There are many vital, time-sensitive discussion items that need immediate attention, Jarod. Those of us who are able will step forward and carry on in your absence.

Jarod: I appreciate your concern, Alexey, but the meeting will be held next week. I should note that none of the items on the agenda you wrote up are new. All have been discussed extensively at previous meetings. That said, as time permits, we can return to them at next week's meeting.

Alexey: These items are time-sensitive because they have not been resolved at previous meetings. We are missing huge opportunities by devoting so much attention to the solar arrays and astronomy and not increasing tourism from New Caucasia.

Jarod: As time permits, we can return to those issues at next week's meeting. Alexey, if you'd like to discuss this further, please private message me.

Alexey: Jarod, you can't private message your way out of addressing the challenges that the tourism sector is failing to address. A refusal to be responsive is a classic failure of leadership, and, as someone with a background in leadership studies, I can offer many suggestions as to how—

Jarod tapped out. Was it too much to take a couple days off to spend time with his family? But he didn't expect any less from Alexey, at least not anymore. Alexey had worked in the tourism sector for many years. He was very bad at his job, more concerned with showing off how many arcane details he knew about Station than he was about considering the needs of a first-time visitor. Jarod had learned to tolerate Alexey's monologues and condescending "tips," a skill the rest of their coworkers had also developed.

Then, last year, Jarod was promoted over Alexey, and suddenly Alexey became his nemesis, attempting to undermine him and the whole tourism sector, which Alexey now began to speak of as "hopelessly backward-looking" and "hostile to change." Of course, the only change Alexey was interested in was change that would give him power to implement his pet project, which was to give preferential treatment to visitors from the New Caucasia region, where Alexey was originally from. This was a really stupid idea, as everyone else realized. One of the primary goals of the tourism sector was to give all the countries on Earth an experience with and connection to Station. If the Marsite Occupation had taught them anything, it was that Station needed to be valued for many reasons by many people, so that no single interest group or country could colonize it again.

But that was a reasoned, logical argument and therefore of no use when dealing with Alexey, who was unable or unwilling to listen to other people. It wasn't that Alexey was a sociopath, exactly, but when Jarod dealt with him as if he were a sociopath, Jarod was not disappointed. Jarod expected attempts at manipulation, he expected subterfuge to cover up an obviously self-motivated desire, and he knew he could never persuade Alexey of anything.

When Jarod had been promoted, he found himself with more responsibility but no more authority. He couldn't fire or transfer Alexey. All Jarod could do was tolerate him and try to keep him from being too disruptive. Jarod wasn't sure he was doing a good job at that.

He needed to shake off Alexey and not let work interfere with his family's visit. He walked over to where Imogen stood, examining the plants growing along the walls. Jarod picked some cinnamon basil and gave it to her to sample. He explained how Station grew almost all of its own food and pointed out how almost every exterior room had plantings that took advantage of natural light.

Imogen chewed on the basil and nodded. "You should have ginger. That's helpful for nausea."

"We do, just not here. Once you get acclimated, the nausea shouldn't be a problem. The artificial gravity control is excellent now."

He would have offered Imogen an antinausea pill, but he knew that would have been an insult to a placebologist.

The combination of exhilaration and anxiety reminded him of his first trip up the Cord to Station. He had wondered at the time if the ride up the Cord would feel like a long transoceanic dirigible trip, but it was nothing like that. Passing up through the atmosphere and watching the planet slowly recede was incredible and a little terrifying. Even when he had to huddle under a lead suit during the ascent through the Van Allen radiation belt, it had all been part of the adventure. Then when they burst through the atmosphere into space—well, he still didn't have the words to describe it. And then to see Mirahe, looking more beautiful than ever, and to be led around by her in this place that still seemed half a fantasy. He would never forget that feeling, and he knew his brother's family was experiencing something similar now. He went through his archive to find his footage of that time, and he cast it to Mirahe so that she could reexperience it again, too.

The family easily could have spent the rest of the afternoon at Artsutanov Plaza, but Jarod wanted to get them settled in, so he moved them along another stretch of twisting hallways. The varied colors of the thermoplastic walls were replaced by bamboo-lined passages as they neared the main residential complex.

"Jarod, are we going to get to see Mirahe tonight?" Imogen asked.

"I'm not sure about tonight. She has a double shift on the solar arrays. But she has an off day coming up, and she's really looking forward to spending time with you all. And she'll be able to give you all the scientific explanations I can't."

Mirahe really was eager to meet Graeme's family, and she was even okay with putting them up in their rooms after they realized it was too expensive to get separate lodging for them. But in order to afford the oxygen credits for the visit, Mirahe had to work extra hours practically the whole time his family was here. It was the only way. Jarod could work twenty-four hours a day and not earn enough credits with his lower rating in tourism. But since Mirahe was in the solar section, her hours counted for more.

When they got to the rooms, Jarod keyed in and was glad to see that they had turned to face sunside. The prisms Mirahe had installed by their personal arrays refracted flashes of rainbow throughout the living room, and the poppies had fully opened in the sun. It was a nice time of day to arrive. As Graeme, Imogen and Ava took in the room, Jarod hauled in their luggage and tried to find space for the bags. It was going to be a tight fit.

"Well, why don't you all relax for a little bit," Jarod said. "I can put together something to eat."

"Jar, is there someplace we can sit down?" Graeme asked as he leaned against a wall. "My new leg could use a break."

"Sit?" Jarod asked, confused at first. All the furniture in the common area where they now stood was designed for energy capture. There were treadmills and weight machines, but no actual chairs. They even stood to play chess. "Just a moment. I think the exercise bike converts into a recumbent."

Jarod played with the settings until the bike saddle reclined into a kind of rocking chair.

"Sorry, that's the best I can do. We don't do much sitting around here, what with energy and muscle atrophy concerns and all."

"*Tidak ada masalah*, I'm all for keeping on the move, especially while I'm breaking in this new leg. I just need to pace myself," Graeme said, huffing as he maneuvered into the seat.

"Is there a place we should put our bags?" Imogen asked.

"Well, this is the place, but don't worry, all this equipment will automatically store in the ceiling, and I've got beds that will fold out of the wall consoles. The luggage may be a little tricky, but I think we can make it all fit."

"You don't waste any space, do you, Jar?"

"We don't have any to waste. It's kind of an obsession up here. I guess there are a lot of obsessions on Station."

"Well, we just want to thank you for all you did to make this trip possible for us," Imogen said. "We know how much we'll be putting you and Mirahe out."

"I'm the first person in my school to go both up into space and down into deep sea," Ava said. She had hopped onto a treadmill and was striding with assurance. "See, Mum, the sun is white in space without the atmosphere filtering it, just like I told you."

"Deep sea, that was a couple years back," Graeme said. "We ate great fish, but I only recommend visiting if you don't have claustrophobia."

"Fish are big here on Station. Wait until you see the Big Bowl."

"And Suha's room? And the Dead Zone?" Ava all of a sudden got animated and had to put her hands on the guide bars to steady herself on the treadmill. "And I've got to interview Mirahe for my school newsfeed."

Imogen reached over and lowered the speed setting on Ava's treadmill. "Ava is going to be working on some special assignments to make up for the school time she's missing, and she did a project last year on Suha's video diaries, so she's very excited to meet Suha's grandniece."

"Mirahe will be glad to share what she knows, but it's mostly just stories her grandfather told her. It may be possible for Ava to interview Shi-Lu. He's the last of Suha's friends still on Station."

"Mum, I have to! Can I?" Ava stopped walking on the treadmill and was almost jettisoned off the back of the machine.

"One thing at a time, Ava," Imogen said, grabbing Ava's arm and steadying her on the machine. "One thing at a time."

Jarod wasn't sure which one thing Imogen meant.

• • • • •

THEY HAD A nice evening together, though an unusual one from Jarod's perspective. While they got caught up, Jarod's visitors were also acclimating themselves to StationWeb. They'd be having a conversation when all of a sudden something would pass over their lenses, and the whole family would get slack-jawed and silent. Apparently, this was now acceptable etiquette on Earth. Jarod had always found StationWeb more intuitive than EarthWeb, and he knew that soon enough it would adapt to Graeme's family and stop distracting them so much with new information.

Still, after the third time that conversation came to a standstill, Jarod left them alone and went over to the terrace to pick some herbs and tomatoes for dinner. He had gotten some skipjack tuna earlier over at the Big Bowl. If he had been making the tuna for himself and Mirahe, it would have been much spicier, but even though it was pretty mild, the fish would go well with lime rice. While Jarod cooked, the smells caught Imogen and Graeme's attention and snapped them out of their trance (though Ava remained glued in). Imogen unpacked the suitcases while Graeme got Jarod caught up on a lot of news from Earth that Jarod already knew. It wasn't as if Station was completely isolated from the planet. He tapped in to tell Mirahe that everyone had arrived while Graeme spoke. Eventually, Graeme went into detail on his body modification. He had one more operation left, and then he'd be "built like a brick shithouse." Jarod wasn't too sure about the whole process, but at least it seemed safer than those operations that created all those zombies. Still, the whole process seemed a little wank.

By the time dinner was ready, everyone was eager to dig in, though the family was clearly thrown off to realize that they'd be standing at the dining table. Imogen drew Ava into the conversation by asking her to talk about school. It was amazing what kids were doing at her age now. He had been in university before he took his first astrophysics class, and here she was already with a whole year of quantum mechanics under her belt. And he hadn't realized how much she knew about Suha. Apparently, Station history was in the Australian curriculum now. Ava had watched all of Suha's vidiaries and had done her own hyperdocumentary on Suha. Jarod was surprised, but he could get the appeal of doing a project on Suha. After all, how many teenagers in history had been the direct inspiration for a revolution?

When they finished eating what Graeme described as "better than any fish they had deep-sea," Jarod suggested another walk closer to the core where they could see the moonset. Graeme begged off, claiming dinner on his feet was enough for him. But Imogen and Ava were excited to go, and it was a nice time of night to stroll. The route to the core went through another bamboo section, which was always a good place to walk even though it was crowded in the evening. Ava kept falling behind them, stopping to gaze out of each port or to read each historical marker, recording everything as if storage space was infinite, which Jarod supposed was pretty much the case for her generation on

Earth. He tapped in and transferred some of his daily storage allotment to Ava. He'd hate for her to fill up on her first day on Station.

Jarod asked Imogen to tell him more about their trip from Australia. She had a lot of complaints, and Jarod guessed that she was just one of those people who didn't like to travel. The blimp ride from Australia had taken longer than scheduled because of the headwinds. They had actually seen a military plane at one point, which was the first airplane Imogen had ever laid eyes on outside of a history text. She wished they had been able to spend more time in Labicittá and hoped they'd get to see some of the island after they went down the Cord.

Imogen had a lot of questions about what life on Station was like. Jarod would have liked to have made their lives sound glamorous, but they both worked a lot of hours, as almost everyone on Station did, and there were a lot of meetings. He supposed that most of the time their lives were a lot like anyone's on Earth, only they were thousands of kilometers over the planet. Of course, when they cycled down to Labicittá, they had a lot more free time. He was still a surfer at heart, after all.

"*Oui*, Graeme told me about your surfing," Imogen said. "According to him, you 'feared no wave.'"

Jarod said he wasn't sure about that. Maybe he should have feared a few more.

They got to the core just in time for moonset, finding an open spot on an old-style porthole. Jarod passed out some goggles and handgrips. A group was already stepping in place next to them, generating joules while they waited by pumping their handgrips. Maybe the goggles weren't necessary, but the tour agency made him hand them out. Now, if it had been the end of an equinox, then goggles would have been required all around due to the sunclipse. The sunclipses were really something to see, and it was too bad they wouldn't be here for one of those. Jarod pumped his handgrip and pointed out eastern Australia below them to Ava.

"Right there, that's where you live. It must be around teatime now."

Ava pressed her glasses against the port. "I see it. Can I record through these goggles?"

"You can try, but the light filter might make the image too dark. Go ahead and try. We can edit it later."

"Why would I edit?" Ava said with a tone of disgust. "Oh, right, I forget that standardview is still the norm here. That's so weird."

"Well, if you really need to use hyperview, there are a few transfer stations where you can cast—I mean send—footage back to Earth."

They marched in place, though Jarod could see Imogen and Ava were just holding their handgrips. Jarod felt himself pumping his harder, as if to make up for their lack of concentration. Finally, the crowd quieted as the moon slowly slipped behind Earth. Jarod still found the moment when the last of the orb disappeared somewhat unsettling, as if they were all a little less anchored in place now. The automatic lights gradually rose up in the room, and everyone in the crowd started to applaud.

"Clapping?" Imogen asked.

"It's a tradition." Jarod shrugged. "It's not because of the moon. It's because the lights came on."

• • • • •

BY THE TIME they got back, Graeme was already asleep. Imogen explained that they all still had some blimp lag, never mind the nausea. Jarod said maybe they should call it a night since Mirahe wouldn't be back until the end of the shift, and she would see everyone in the morning. Jarod got the other beds out of the wall storage and set Imogen and Ava up for the night. Then he went into his bedroom and tapped in to discover that the tone had taken a turn. People were never as happy under artificial light. Mirahe had left him a message that she'd eaten at work and needed to check in on one of her uncles on her way home. He sent thanks and warmth. There was also a flagged message from Alexey, but that could wait until tomorrow. Jarod wasn't used to going to sleep this early, and it felt odd to be just lying in bed instead of walking the treadmill. His legs were kind of antsy. He bicycle-kicked for a while even though there was no way of storing energy from it. It was silly, but it made him feel better.

Jarod half dozed, but he roused himself when Mirahe arrived. He started to sit up, but she put her finger to her lips while she closed the door. Jarod put his head on his pillow and watched her undress. There was nothing intentionally seductive in the way she undressed, but she couldn't help but be alluring, and by the time she crawled into bed next to him, he was wide awake.

"How'd it all go today?" Mirahe asked quietly. "No one stirred when I came in, which is either good or bad."

"I think it went well. Graeme was tired, but, yeah, it went well."

Jarod ran through the visit, and he cast Mirahe footage of the welcoming ceremony. Mirahe said her uncle was feeling better, and then she told him about work. There were always problems with the mobile rectennas near Labicittá, but the arrays under Mirahe's control were all functioning, even if the replacement schedule was still inadequate. She was already looking forward to the next equinox, when the Earth would block the sun and everyone in the solar section would get a well-deserved break. But that was a ways off.

Jarod and Mirahe had first met when Mirahe had taken some vacation time during a cycle down and hopped a blimp to Karimunjawa, where Jarod had been a surfing and scuba instructor. She took her first scuba lesson with Jarod, and he was amazed at how fast she picked everything up. That and she was gorgeous. Only later, when he found out she was from Station, did he realize that most of her free time as a kid was spent in weightlessness, so scuba diving was no big deal. He offered to teach her how to surf, but that didn't come as easily to her. Still, surf lessons were a good excuse for Jarod to get to know her while showing off his board skills. He found out she was a solar scientist, which was both intriguing and intimidating (it still was), and he found himself fascinated by what she said about life on Station. He didn't think he had many good stories of his own to share, but Mirahe had this way of drawing details out of him. She knew the questions to ask so that he described himself in ways that made him seem more interesting than he felt. He had basically been a surf bum since dropping out of university, but when he talked to Mirahe, he felt like an adventurer.

He asked her out to dinner, and she wore a set of ear gauges that he recognized right away. The gauges were decorated with the same figure as the tattoo he had on his hip, a spiral with a kind of hook coming out of it. Mirahe didn't believe him when he said that he had the same figure as a tattoo. She said it was an old Indonesian symbol. He had just thought it was an interesting design when he got inked in New Bali. But Mirahe was impressed that he had it—at least that was how she acted when she saw his tattoo that night.

By the time Mirahe's vacation was over, Jarod was head over heels for her. He quit his job and moved to Labicittá where he spent six months in a cramped apartment on the island giving swimming lessons to kids while Mirahe tried to work out a visa for him from up on Station. They communicated by Personal Experience Programs sent up and down the Cord. Courtship by PEPod wasn't the same as being there, but it allowed Jarod to find out so much about Station that by the time his visa was worked out, he felt like he was returning to an old haunt. Mirahe also managed to find him a job in the tourism sector.

So Station became the place he spent nine months out of the year, and he and Mirahe were happy. There was something about the way Station took you in. Once you tapped into StationWeb, you mattered. People cared about you, and they expected you to care about them. It was an easy place to belong, and he hadn't felt like he belonged anywhere since his clutch in university had broken up. Five of them had lived together in the clutch and even got registered, but then after graduation two couples emerged and he was left alone. He swore off plural relationships after that and spent most of his twenties drifting from one resort gig to another. He didn't know what he was looking for until he found Mirahe and the community on Station. If only there was a way to surf in space, he would have nothing more to ask for. Well, he could also do without Alexey.

Mirahe lay with her head on her pillow and her eyes only half-open while she asked about his family. Her questions were all framed in that

Station way that wasn't about individual people but about social relations. "Characterize the mother/daughter relationship?" "What is the kinship model?" "Explain Ava's projector/receptor balance?" Mirahe would never ask a question like, "How does Ava like school?"

Jarod could have talked all night, but he could see that the double shift had worn Mirahe out and she was ready to sleep. She drifted right off, but Jarod wasn't tired anymore, so he read for a while until he found himself scanning the same sentences over and over again on his lenses. He decided to just pop out his lenses and gauges. They only needed to come out once a month for cleaning, but Jarod had never quite gotten used to sleeping with them. With the gauges and lenses by his side, and Mirahe noiselessly breathing beside him, everything felt still. He thought that if he concentrated really hard, he could feel the rotation of Station at times like this. Mirahe told him that wasn't true, but part of him still thought it was.

• • • • •

MIRAHE GOT TO meet everyone at breakfast. Their kitchen was crowded with five people all standing around the counter, but after hugs and handshakes and a round of omelets, everything started to seem comfortable. Mirahe had taken a class in placebology as an undergraduate, so she could talk about Imogen's work. And she promised Ava she would share all the stories she knew about her great-aunt Suha when she got home tonight. Mirahe was even able to ask a few good questions about Graeme's work, even though brand therapy was about as far from Mirahe's sphere of experience as you could get. Graeme detailed his efforts to resuscitate a once-popular type of vacuum pump, and he would have chewed Mirahe's ear off if Jarod hadn't made her leave for work so she wouldn't be late.

Then the four of them stood around drinking tea, and Graeme and Jarod swapped tales about when they were kids. Graeme shared his favorite story about the time he had slipped their dog's collar onto Jarod and gotten him to go over the electric borderline. Everyone, even Jarod, had to laugh when Graeme imitated the young Jarod getting shocked and trying to jump out of his skin. Jarod recounted the trip the whole family had taken to Uluru, and he cast some original video to everyone. They couldn't access the audio track with their earrings, but they could see the endless horizon from the plateau.

"Hey, I've got more great views to show you today," Jarod said.

"Why are we looking at old video from Earth? Let's move on."

Jarod cleaned up from breakfast and was good to go, but it took the family an impossibly long time to get ready to leave. Finally, when everyone was set, they were off to StationLand.

If you lived on Station, you got sick of StationLand pretty quickly. It was as if someone took your life and turned it into a cartoon, removing all the nuances of how you actually lived. But it was the most popular attraction on Station and a must-see for all Jarod's tour groups. And, as he had guessed, his brother's family loved it. Ava went right for the Space Junk game, which simulated the thrust lasers on Station that forced old satellite debris down into Earth's orbit, where it burned up harmlessly. Imogen played Life Support Balance, a game that mirrored the efforts to maintain the oxygen and energy levels on Station while minimizing supplies coming up the Cord. But what really got Jarod was how much Graeme loved the Dead Zone feature in Suha's World. It was a room that replicated the weightless conditions in the original dock where Suha had shot so much of her vidiary footage. Jarod had to admit that they had done a great job on the design. You really felt you were in an abandoned space dock, and when you took that first plunge off the ledge and fell toward the glass port with nothing but open space in front of you, it was really terrifying. And then, once you got used to the shifts from pure weightlessness to partial gravity, it could be a lot of fun.

But Jarod was still surprised to see Graeme acting like a kid, rolling around from one side of the room to another, pushing off the walls into somersaults and taking swan dives off the ledge. Graeme would have stayed there all day if there hadn't been a limit set on how much time anyone was allowed out of full gravity. Jarod wondered if part of Graeme's pleasure came from being able to forget about his mid-modification body for a while.

They all loved the Centrifuge. It was modeled on the original Station design, which created artificial gravity through rotation. The Centrifuge was attached to Station's outer hull, and it was off the main gravity plates, so once you were out there, it was just the spin that kept you in place. Jarod had been on rides like that at amusement parks as a kid, and he didn't like them then, so he sat that one out.

This gave him time to check in at work and make sure that Alexey wasn't causing any more trouble. And aside from a message titled "Current Administration Inadequacies," things seemed to be okay. He scanned the message, and it seemed to add nothing beyond Alexey's usual rant, so he was able to ignore it and tap out by the time Graeme's family stumbled off the Centrifuge and into the gift shop.

But the trinkets they wanted to buy! Jarod tried to dissuade them since everything could be bought for half the price down in Labicittá, but to no avail. They bought a nanotube yoyo, a model solar array, a moonrise hologram projector, a framed excerpt of Suha's vidiary narration on bamboo paper, even a fake asteroid pillow, the last of which made no sense at all since Station had more in common with Venus than an asteroid. Jarod didn't know how they were going to fit it all into their luggage, but he didn't want to dissuade them from enjoying StationLand.

On the walk back to Jarod's rooms, they couldn't stop talking about all they had seen and all they still wanted to do. Jarod would take them on the official tour tomorrow, and they'd get to see the real-world equivalents of the games they had played today.

On the way back, Imogen and Ava wanted to take a long route so that they could shoot some footage of the Suha memorial near the original Dead Zone. Jarod could see Graeme was pretty wiped out, so he suggested they split up. Imogen and Ava went off ahead, and Jarod set a leisurely pace down the hallway.

"I'm sorry to be such a bludger," Graeme said. "I'm slowing everyone down."

"Do you want me to call for a transit chair?"

"No, I'm supposed to be walking on the new leg as much as I can. It's just going to be hard until I get rid of this original one."

"When's the surgery set?"

"Oh, it's coming up not too long after we get back. Hey, how about that there. *Que bonito.*"

Jarod looked around for a viewport, but they were in an interior section, surrounded by metal and some hardy dracaena plants that could grow in low light. Then he realized that Graeme was referring to the women that were passing them in the other direction. Jarod vaguely recognized them as the daughters of one of Mirahe's aunts. He nodded as they passed. Graeme gave him a look.

"They're Mirahe's cousins, or maybe nieces; I'm not sure."

"I guess you've got to keep your eyes to yourself around here. It seems like almost everyone's a relation. Anyway, you've been a brick, putting us up like this and taking us around. I don't know how it got to be so long since we've seen each other."

"I hear you, mate," Jarod said. "I wish I'd made more of an effort to get back to the continent when it was just a short blimp ride away. Who knew I'd wind up on Station? But it's great you are able to be here."

"It was quite a row with Imogen, to be honest. She wanted to see you and Mirahe of course, but she was scared to death about the whole elevator at first. And then she just changed her mind. I don't know why. She's been fine since we've been here. I'd like to think I understand her after all these years, but sometimes she's a mystery to me. *Grande mistero.*"

"Now, how long have you two been together?"

"Well, we're on our second contract now, and I guess we're up for renewal in a couple years. I suppose we'll sign on again. We haven't really talked about it, but it's a whole lot easier to renew than not, especially with Ava. But it's you I want to hear about. I never thought a surfer boy would wind up in space. And what about you and Mirahe? Are you two ever going to sign a contract?"

"Well, we're engaged, but that was just to make it easier to get rooms for two on Station. We haven't really talked about it. Contracts aren't really that big here."

And things went on like that, two brothers catching up, talking just like they were back in Melbourne rather than forty thousand kilometers above the planet.

· · · · ·

THAT NIGHT, EVEN though Jarod was officially not working, he needed to go into work and set up next month's tour schedule. It should have been something he could just tap in to take care of, but he had learned that people's available times weren't always when they were actually available. In the end, he had to go find Alexey in person during a twilight tour.

Alexey's tours tended not to run on schedule because he talked too much, but this was not the time to address that. Instead, Jarod staked himself in a position by the bamboo fields, knowing he would catch Alexey at a time in the tour when visitors went off on their own for a while. This way Alexey couldn't complain about an interruption.

Well, at least Alexey couldn't reasonably complain. But he did anyway when Jarod found him sitting on a bench as visitors wandered through the bamboo.

"Jarod, what do you want? Can't you see I'm working?" Alexey sighed as he swiped his big mane of hair off his forehead.

"It will only take a second. You didn't confirm your schedule for the month. I just need you to sign off."

"Can't this wait?"

"No, you're the last person to confirm. Just give it a quick look." Jarod rolled out a screen and put it in front of Alexey.

"I can't do this without checking my residence calendar."

Without speaking, Jarod swiped at the screen so that Alexey's residence calendar popped up.

"Fine, fine. Here you go." Alexey pressed his thumb to the screen, accepting the schedule. "You know, Jarod, if I wasn't in the middle of a tour, we'd have a lot to discuss."

"You're right, Alexey. We would."

Jarod took back the screen and rolled it up. Then he saw Mirahe's cousin, Samir, who had ridden up the Cord with Graeme's family, and he used the excuse to walk away from Alexey. He and Samir took hands, and Samir re-extended his invitation to have the family take a tour of the bamboo fields. They made tentative plans for later in the week, and by the time he and Samir had finished talking, Alexey's tour group had moved on.

Jarod tapped in and saw that Ava was interviewing Mirahe about her great-aunt Suha. He didn't want to interrupt, so he pulled up a privatecast on his lenses and made his way over to his residence section's exercise track. He really missed using the treadmill now that his common space was all beds and suitcases, so this was a good excuse for a brisk walk. Translucent screening while walking was never a good idea, but things were pretty quiet on Station this time of night, and at least Jarod could generate some joules while watching the interview.

Jarod punched in on the wall monitor so the track would capture energy and started walking. It was clear that Ava was really up on the subject. There were none of those "what kind of person was Suha?" questions. Ava got right to the heart of things. "To what extent was Suha involved in the Resistance?" "Do you believe she intended her vidiaries for the public?" "Do you believe any of the conspiracy theories about Suha?"

They were, of course, impossible questions to answer definitively. The revolution had happened two generations ago, and no one during the Marsite Occupation kept careful records about anything that happened on Station. There was no StationWeb then, and the Marsites intentionally tried to put as little on the record as possible. All there really was to go on were oral histories and, of course, Suha's vidiaries.

But Mirahe was used to talking about the subject, and she answered Ava's questions as well as she could. She thought Suha was sympathetic to the Resistance though probably not formally involved. No one does creative work—novels, games, vidiaries—without some sense of an audience. Mirahe didn't pay much attention to conspiracy theories. No one knew for sure what had happened. All one could do was surmise.

Mirahe also shared stories that her grandfather had told her about how Suha wanted to go into astronomy and how easily math came to her. Suha could solve difficult problems in truly unique ways. There were also stories about life during the Marsite Occupation. Many people on Station did not like to reflect on that period, and Mirahe cautioned Ava to be discreet if she spoke about it to anyone who had lived through that time, as it was associated with feelings of shame and humiliation. However, it was difficult to understand Station today without knowing what life was like then. StationWeb was different from EarthWeb because of that period. The sustainability initiatives and the investments in the solar arrays, which caused much disagreement among Earthlings—people on Earth, Mirahe corrected herself—were vital to Station. Such things were necessary for a people who had been treated like afterthoughts, who had been told they didn't even deserve the scraps and "donations" the Marsites gave them. The educational system on Station and Labicittá only made sense once you knew that the Marsites had discouraged education and closed all the existing schools. One could not know the pride of sufficiency without having experienced the shame of deprivation.

Mirahe had gotten pretty worked up by that point, and then she smiled, as if in apology.

"Ava, I am used to having to argue on behalf of the solar arrays. There are still those who would like Station to function as simply a launching pad to different planets."

Ava had some questions about the solar arrays, which Jarod definitely did not need to hear described again. Between what he needed to know as a tour guide and all that he learned from Mirahe, Jarod felt he could operate an array himself. So he archived the rest of the interview and punched out of the track. 24.38 joules.

• • • • •

THE NEXT MORNING, Jarod took the family on a behind-the-scenes tour with a group of potential investors from the Sahara Oasis. He would have thought solar power was plentiful in the middle of a desert, but it wasn't his deal to negotiate.

The behind-the-scenes tour could get pretty technical, but Graeme's family all seemed up for it. They started in the Tsiolkovsky

Facility, where you got to see all the inner workings that made life on Station possible: the paragravity generator, the cryogenic distillation system, the space debris detection center. It made you appreciate how many things had to go right, and go right all the time, for Station to function.

Ava was a sponge for details. She wanted to know why Station didn't use centrifugal force for its gravity anymore, and she questioned the accuracy of the space debris-clearing lasers. Imogen was similarly full of questions, though most of hers had to do with the redundancies built into the atmospheric systems.

The investors were not the most inquisitive bunch. They weren't particularly interested in the functioning of the space station, and they didn't interrupt Jarod once until they got out to the solar arrays. Then they were all questions. How many watts per square meter? What was the collection rate? How much was lost in microwave conversion? Fortunately, Jarod had reviewed the specifications and was able to answer their inquiries.

After lunch, they were free of the investors, and they picked up a group of teachers for the history tour. This was a challenging tour to give, since many of the older sections had been renovated over the years and a lot of history had been lost. But recently, work had been done to recondition important revolutionary-era sites, and there was still a lot to see in the old gathering hall where the Marsite surrender had taken place.

It was always a powerful experience to visit the Old Quarter to see where Suha had lived. If one thought the current residential space restrictions were tight, it was hard to envision that three people lived in Suha's rooms, which were the size of most people's closets back on Earth. Graeme joked about that, saying they must have slept in shifts or let the toilet double as a kitchen chair. Both he and Jarod had to be careful not to bump their heads at every doorway, and they had to watch out for the old-fashioned hinged doors that constantly got in the way.

The visitor center next to Suha's rooms had a good, augmented reality tour. They tapped into a program that screened on their lenses throughout the Old Quarter, superimposing the look and feel of prerev-olutionary Station onto the current quarter. It made Jarod appreciate how awful it must have been when Station was all steel and sharp edges with only minimal lighting. Almost all the postrevolutionary design decisions on Station were a reaction to the aesthetics of that earlier period. It was hard to find a piece of exposed metal now, and plants grew in just about every available nook.

Visitors weren't allowed into the original Dead Zone anymore. The Dead Zone had never been properly shielded, and the radiation levels were too erratic, but Jarod's pass allowed him to bring people to the observation booth that the crane operators once used. From there, you could see into the dock. By itself it wasn't anything special, but it had been the setting for most of Suha's vidiaries and for so much else. The Dead Zone was still a kind of sacred space on Station, and no one needed to be told to treat it that way. All the visitors were quiet as they looked through the observation booth window, staring at the space where Suha had floated and recorded so much, and suffered so much as well.

People remained subdued as they left the booth. This was the end of the tour, and Jarod liked to leave people a little time to reflect and walk along the basin at the edge of the Old Quarter. The teachers thanked Jarod and stepped into a café. Imogen and Ava went into a gift shop. That left Graeme and Jarod surrounded by the ghosts of the past.

"So, that Dead Zone dock, was that one the Marsites used to launch colonization drones?"

"No, the Dead Zone is even older than that. It was used for a couple planetary probes and some satellite repair missions, nothing special. All the Marsites' docks were over where StationLand is now."

"Now, don't take this the wrong way. The Marsites were awful, and I don't deny all they did to Mirahe's people, but some days when it seems like nothing is going right down on Earth, I wonder if they were onto something about colonizing and terraforming Mars."

"Graeme, are you gammin me? The Marsites were deluded ideo-logues that destroyed everything they touched. Terraforming was a fantasy, and the price paid for even attempting it was too high. Besides, that kind of fatalism about Earth is what led to the rise of the Marsites anyway, and none of their doomsday predictions played out. Climate change has plateaued, resource sustainability has worked, even the coral reefs are coming back."

"Well, sure, for now. But none of those things are guaranteed to continue. Everything could still fall apart. I'm just saying, I understand wanting to start over on Mars."

"Graeme, I don't think we're going to agree on this one. And, really, don't let Mirahe hear you talk like that. Those are fighting words here on Station."

"Don't worry, I'm no chook, bro. It's just that there's a lot of space, and I can't believe something better can't happen out there. I think maybe you've spent too much time in this tin can here."

"Well, I guess this is my home now."

"So, you think this is it? You going to live the rest of your life in space with your earlobes all stretched out with those gauges?"

"It's not like I'm trapped here. We cycle down to Earth on a schedule. I can even still surf on Labicittá." Jarod thought the dig about the gauges was a bit much coming from someone with half a new body.

"Don't you ever worry?" Graeme continued. "You don't own anything. The flat's not yours, you don't get a salary and you don't even control your time. Look at you, even when you're off, you're working that handgrip all the time."

"You've got it all wrong. I get paid."

"In money?"

"Well, not when I'm on Station. What would I do with money here? But I have an account on Labicittá."

"It's just that I'd think you'd need more for yourself." Graeme stopped, and a smile came to his face. He patted his still large belly. "Sorry, that must be my stomach talking. *Ik heb honger.*"

Jarod wrapped an arm around Graeme's newly muscular shoulders. "You're still the old Graeme, even if you're on your way to looking like an action hero. Let's get a bite."

• • • • •

DURING THE AFTERNOON they spent in the Old Quarter, Ava met Clautoon. Clautoon was pretty hard to miss. Though he was only a year older than Ava, he was tall for his age, and he had a shock of dark hair that he wore straight up on his head. When he walked through the Old Quarter's narrow corridors with his stand-up bass, you had no choice but to step aside. The bass was kind of ridiculous, but Jarod understood that that was the point. In a place where every square centimeter of open floor seemed spoken for and where personal space was kept to a minimum, what better way was there to thumb your nose at those restrictions than to devote yourself to playing an enormous, impractical instrument?

Besides, acoustic music was big on Station. At first, that had seemed an odd throwback to Jarod. There was nothing stopping people from playing instruments on Earth, of course, but the entire sonic spectrum was digitized now. Anyone on EarthWeb could start out by humming a tune and turn it into a symphony in no time at all. But during the occupation, when the Marsites monitored and limited all power use, people on Station had begun fashioning instruments out of scrap objects and playing for one another during those long, cold nights. After the revolution, all those instruments suddenly became national treasures. The PVC flute and the oxygen tank bagpipe were now as much identified with Station as the space elevator and ear gauges. Clautoon, with his stand-up bass, was as much a traditionalist as he was a rebel.

But as interesting as Station musical history was to Jarod, that wasn't the main draw for Ava. When she had first seen Clautoon performing for tourists in one of the Old Quarter's pocket-plazas, she had made all of them stop and watch him play his bass for a while. Clautoon began showing off a little bit, walking lines up and down the bass. Ava picked up a power stick that was lying next to the bass and broke it down so that she could play triple stick against the outside of the case. Clautoon smiled and started improvising. Jarod was no musician, but he could tell that Clautoon was changing up the rhythm and pace, seeing if Ava could keep up with him. She could, and Jarod was impressed. A small crowd had gathered to watch their duet.

The song ended with a furious finish. Clautoon was slapping at his strings, and Ava's triple sticks were a whirl of action as she matched his pace and even pushed him to step it up. After the final crash of sound, the crowd burst into cheers, and Clautoon had a huge smile on his face. He stepped over and began speaking to Ava.

"That was excellent. You were *sangat baik*. What is the name of my new collaborator?"

Ava tried not to blush, unsuccessfully. "My name is Ava."

Then Clautoon began to sing "Ava Ever," which was a song Jarod remembered from when he was a kid. Clautoon had a great voice, and when he got to the line "*Je serai toujours amoureux d'Ava*," Ava and Imogen both got all teary-eyed. Clautoon stopped and asked if they knew that song. Imogen said she had sung it as a lullaby to Ava when she was a baby. When Clautoon heard that, he insisted that he would custom cast Ava a performance of the song. He pulled a locket from his case and switched it with the gauge in his left ear. Then he performed "Ava Ever" again, this time accompanying himself on bass. It was a beautiful rendition. When he handed the locket to Ava, she said she would wear it forever. Imogen tried to pass Clautoon some credits for it, but Clautoon refused, though she was able to persuade him to come out to dinner with them that night.

They all met later at one of the restaurants on the Big Bowl. It was a favorite place to take visitors. The fish was fantastic, of course, but the view was even more memorable. The dining area sat below the huge glass tank that served as both ceiling and fish farm. While you ate, you could stare up through the convex bottom of the tank like it was a giant aquarium, watching dozens of varieties of fish swimming in the water above, and beyond them was deep space, serving like a dark canvas for a sparkling tropical painting.

It made for a unique dining experience. The rules of etiquette changed to allow people at any point in a conversation to crane their heads upward to gaze at a passing swordfish or a darting school of bluefish. Graeme and Imogen were mesmerized by the bowl and hardly said a word at dinner. Mirahe, of course, knew Clautoon's family, so she was able to draw him out about his music and school. Clautoon's family had recently cycled up, and his sister wasn't thrilled about it. Apparently, she liked the school on Labicittá better and had wanted to stay. But the rules about family separation were unbreakable when it came to cycling on and off Station, so his sister was here and unhappy.

Ava and Clautoon enjoyed a lot of the same music, and they started talking about bands Jarod had never heard of before, so the conversation divided off. Jarod pointed out to Graeme and Imogen how the tanks were segmented so that predator fish wouldn't eat everything in the Big Bowl. Mirahe knew details about the water filtration system as well. But once the food came, they all dug in eagerly and took their eyes off the ceiling to talk as a group. Well, except for Ava. She only had eyes for Clautoon.

Pretty soon after, Ava and Clautoon had become inseparable. It all seemed to Jarod to happen a little fast, but Graeme and Imogen were happy to see Ava infatuated instead of alienated. To be honest, Imogen seemed half in love with Clautoon as well. He was a sweet kid, and he had a gentle way about him that made him easy to like. But things got louder in their rooms. It seemed that every second Ava was apart from Clautoon, she was practicing on the triple stick.

· · · · ·

"THOUGH WHAT YOU see before you looks like a field of separate bamboo stalks, the root system of all these stalks is joined together in the water running below our feet. While each stalk is separate, as a plant it is connected below the surface, like all of us here on Station, where we pursue our individual goals while joined together in bonds of family, of friendship and of comradery. Please take a minute to enjoy the field."

Samir gestured to the plants behind him with a florid sweep of his hands. Jarod got a kick out of it. Samir had a dramatic flair. Jarod wasn't used to being on the receiving end of a tour, but Samir knew as much about the bamboo as anyone else on Station, so it was a pleasure to have him show Graeme's family around.

The initial section of stalks was slightly raised off the floor in an enclosed planter so that visitors could examine them up close. But the majority of the bamboo was grown in rows, stacked one on top of the other, making use of every available meter of space. It was an impressive operation, but calling it a "field" seemed a bit of a misnomer, though the name had stuck.

As they wandered through the field, Samir explained that this project had been controversial at first because of the space taken up by the fields and because only a small part of the bamboo was grown for food. "But bamboo is a traditional building material among many of the peoples who now reside on Station, and it has become our preferred renewable resource. If you look down toward the base of the bamboo, you will see the irrigation system below it. This section of bamboo is hydroponic, grown entirely with wastewater via a growing process that doubles as a water purification system. The water running below our feet will eventually be suitable for drinking."

Ava crinkled her nose, and Imogen laughed. Graeme was impassive. He didn't seem like much of a plant person. The bamboo field was the most impressive part of the agriculture section simply because of its size. The rest of the crops were grown in smaller greenhouse rooms, some in natural light, some in artificial light. Jarod had led many tours through the narrow hallways of the greenhouses. Though the experimental stations were interesting for the variety of flowers and plants in them, he always found the tomato rooms a little disturbing, what with little red orbs floating in fishbowls.

Ava and Imogen both shot lots of footage, and Jarod followed them around in case they had questions. Graeme stuck with Samir, and they drifted off in a different direction. By the time everyone met up again, Jarod found Graeme and Samir in a heated discussion over whether the agricultural section was truly sustainable. Graeme argued that it would have been cheaper to bring bamboo and food up the Cord than to transport all the soil and water that was necessary to make the agriculture section function. Samir countered that Graeme was only taking into account the cost of freight per kilo on the elevator. If Graeme had used the full extraction-to-use cost (both financial and environmental), he would see that this method was much more efficient.

These were not unfamiliar arguments. Jarod had heard versions of them at section meetings, but Graeme seemed a little more animated than was necessary, and Jarod didn't want Samir to be offended, so he intervened with a joke about one person's sustainability being another person's frugality. It wasn't a very good joke though, and it didn't take the feeling of animosity out of the air. Jarod gathered everyone up and thanked Samir. He cast his gratitude, but he could feel Samir's return was lacking in warmth. He couldn't blame Samir though. What was with Graeme?

Graeme had seemed erratic the past few days. When Jarod had arranged a tour of the astronomy section, all Graeme did was complain about it. Admittedly, the astronomers were a quirky bunch. They tended to ignore visitors, and they did most of their work without even looking up at the stars, huddling over screens and analyzing data. The tourism sector had had to push for an optical scope just so visitors would be able to look into space during the tour. Jarod had seen Alessandro, the astronomer he had met while waiting for Graeme's family, and Alessandro had been nice enough to come over and explain his work. But whether it was the anti-goat or Alessandro's accent or maybe the fact that his shirt was buttoned up unevenly, Graeme ended up laughing right in Alessandro's face. It was an uncomfortable moment.

In fact, the whole family was acting in ways that didn't make sense. After Jarod had to go back to work and couldn't guide them around every day, they had all gone off in different directions. Graeme had become a regular in the recreation center, floating in the weightlessness of the rubber room and chatting people up in the sauna (when he wasn't insulting them). As far as Jarod could tell, Imogen was now spending most of her time in the common area viewing privatecast programs on her lenses. At least Ava seemed to be having a good time with Clautoon. Clautoon had introduced her to the slideboard slopes, which to Jarod was nothing like surfing, but kids seemed to enjoy it. As soon as Clautoon got out of school each day, Ava was off slideboarding or playing music with him and his friends. She said she and Clautoon were recording some songs together, but they hadn't finished anything yet since, according to Ava, Clautoon was a real perfectionist when it came to music. Jarod suspected Ava wasn't getting much work done on her project for school. Jarod spoke to Mirahe about how odd they all seemed to be acting, but she said he was misreading the situation.

"You're beginning from the assumption that they should spend time together because that's what happens here. But perhaps for them what was unusual was all the time they were together those first few days. What's happening now probably feels more normal to them."

Maybe she was right. He was wrapped into a tight social world, so he worried that Graeme and his family would feel abandoned when he went off to work. He had kept them busy each evening with visits to meet people in Mirahe's family, and they had eaten some great Indonesian food at friends' rooms. Maybe that was more socializing than Graeme's family was used to. Maybe they needed more time to themselves. But that didn't explain Graeme's outbursts or why Imogen seemed withdrawn. There were only a few days left in their visit. Jarod hoped they were enjoying themselves, but he just didn't know.

The next day, Jarod's work schedule meant he wasn't going to be able to spend any time with the family, but as it turned out, they had all made other plans anyway. Individual plans, of course. Ava went with Clautoon and some of his friends to a bounce lounge. Imogen was off to the transfer station to check in on Earth, "to see how a friend of hers was doing," she said. Graeme had been invited out for lunch by Samir, which Jarod thought was particularly nice of Samir considering how rude Graeme had been to him previously.

Maybe this was for the best. It could have been that they had gotten comfortable enough on Station that they didn't need him to make plans for them. Maybe he just needed to stop acting like a tour guide all the time.

So, after breakfast, they all dispersed in different directions. Jarod had tours to give in the morning and then a late afternoon meeting. There was a break in between, so Jarod decided to take a leisurely walk to his meeting, or at least use the time to generate some joules. He wasn't eager to get there early, since it was a meeting of the IUPC, the Interagency Uniform Policy Committee, which he had nicknamed the Intentionally Unachievable Plan Committee. It was a long-range planning group that was supposed to make consensus recommendations, though few of any consequence had emerged during the many monthly meetings he had attended. He was really only there because Alexey was a member, and he didn't trust Alexey not to undermine the rest of the tourism section.

He pulled out his handgrip and chose a route that took him planetside with a great view of the Earth. Through the cloud cover, he could make out landmasses below, and it was clear over southern Indonesia, where Mirahe's family originally had come from as refugees from the Great Floods. He had read that archeologists were beginning to recover some of the lost islands. There were a whole series of mini-Atlantises to be studied. At one point, he had screened some of the footage, scouting for a good scuba vacation, but Mirahe wasn't interested. It wouldn't have been just scenery to Mirahe, and he could understand that. To her it would just seem like walking on her ancestors' graves. Still, he wished he knew more about the past, if only so as to understand how the world got to where it was today. Sure, he could read about the history of the oceans' rise and the Resource Wars, and right now he was living through the Solar Transformation and the oceans' recovery, but understanding what someone else's experience of the past was like, that was a completely different, and more involved, thing.

Jarod had gotten lost in his head as he walked, and by the time he realized it, he was late for the meeting. He hurried over to a conference room lined with treadmills and covered with ferns except for one wall with a giant screen that had a connection to Labicittá. A half dozen representatives were there, including Alexey, who was in the front of the room helping to adjust screen settings, so Jarod hoped he could just hop onto a machine in the back of the room without anyone noticing. He tapped in to see when he was scheduled to discuss a proposal to retrofit a display of solar arrays to make it more tourism-friendly, but he could see that Alexey had deleted the item. Jarod added it back as Alexey stepped onto a treadmill across the room from him.

"Jarod," Alexey said in a voice loud enough to stop all the other conversations in the room. "I wasn't sure you would be here. I thought you might still be entertaining relatives."

"Thank you for your concern, Alexey," Jarod said through a forced smile. "I think the original agenda will work fine."

But even that was untrue because the first item on the agenda was the next leap second. It was all Jarod could do not to audibly groan. Why would anyone make an impossible issue the first thing to be discussed?

With the main screen settings adjusted, the images of the Labicittá representatives appeared on the view screen. They were dressed in that odd combination of tropical print shirts and dress ties that counted for businesswear down on the island. Things were more casual on Station. Jarod wondered if he could still remember how to tie a Windsor knot.

Discussion began on the Leap Second Initiative, and the acronyms started flying—IERS, CUTA, CGPSSIC, HMNAO. Jarod called up his acronym list. International Earth Rotation and Reference Systems Service, Coordinated Universal Time Authority, the Civil Global Positioning System Service Interface Committee and Her Majesty's Nautical Almanac Office. It was hard to keep the names straight, even though the issue never changed.

The issue was that no one could agree on what time was, which, historically speaking, was not a new problem. The lunar calendar had never lined up perfectly with the solar calendar. The Gregorian calendar used extra days during leap years to keep the seasons in order. Then, once atomic clocks were invented, Coordinated Universal Time could be measured without the loss of a second in millions of years. But atomic clocks measured time more closely than the planet did. A leap second was needed every few months in order to keep time on Earth in line with time as the atomic clocks measured it. For most of life, a second here or there didn't matter. But some satellites were on CUT while most GPS devices ran on a different time model, and everything had to be recalibrated every time a new leap second was announced by IERS. After the revolution, Station went onto solar time and refused to recognize leap seconds, which were derided as an Earthbound standard. Even a few milliseconds separating Station Standard Time from Coordinated Universal Time was enough to make it impossible to link StationWeb with EarthWeb, which was fine as far as most of Station was concerned but a continual headache for Labicittá.

The whole discussion was migraine-inducing for Jarod. Alexey said that visitors complained about not being able to access EarthWeb. Some did, even Jarod's own brother, but Jarod pointed out that most tourists came to appreciate being off EarthWeb. It was one of the things that made Station a unique destination. That earned Jarod a scowl from Alexey, but their disagreements were minor next to the squabbles between the administration, astronomy and communications sections, which then took over the meeting.

Jarod could follow the flow of the conversation by the speed of the treadmills. The communications rep started pacing faster when he complained about the antiquated transfer stations. The astronomy rep slowed down as she detailed new theories about the limitations of atomic time as a universal measure, since it assumed that the universe itself was not moving. You could see the Labicittá reps roll their eyes at that one, and he half suspected they fantasized about cutting the Cord and letting Station drift off on its own. Jarod himself had to cringe when Alexey weighed in with his uninformed view on the latest research in physics. Wow, did Alexey like to hear himself talk.

What was interesting was how little agreement there was, and how little there always had been, about time. You would think that the world couldn't function like that, but here they were, going on about their lives, understanding each other and mostly working well together, without agreeing on something so fundamental as the nature of time.

Suddenly, an alert sounded, and it was as if a balloon popped inside Jarod's head. He bolted upright and practically fell off his treadmill. His first thoughts were of a disaster, a rupture in an exterior wall or an undetected meteor, but then he looked around the room and realized that everyone else was pacing on their treadmills normally, though now staring at him with looks ranging from puzzled to disturbed. Jarod had been the only person to receive the alert, which meant it was just a personal emergency.

Jarod switched off his treadmill and stepped off. He apologized to everyone but said a personal emergency alert had come through. He would have to leave. He asked to reschedule his agenda item, and when Alexey offered to take his place, Jarod cut him off with a shout of "no!" and then darted into the hallway.

He tapped in and saw that an alert had come from the medical clinic telling him to come over immediately. Jarod began running through a narrow passage. Something awful must have happened.

At Artsutanov Plaza, the first place he had brought Graeme and his family, he had to weave through a crowd of tourists and other midday wanderers. He told himself not to jump to any conclusions. He didn't know anything yet. But by the time he neared the clinic, his mind had scrolled through any number of awful tragedies. Was it Mirahe? Graeme? Imogen or Ava?

Jarod had considered such a full range of horrible possibilities that he was frantic as he ran the last few meters, and it took him a while to realize that Mirahe was shouting his name. He stopped and turned, panting for air, to see Mirahe running up behind him, similarly short of breath. His first response was just to be grateful that she was okay, and he threw his arms around her when she approached.

"I got an alert!" she gasped. "What happened?"

"I don't know. I got one, too."

Mirahe pulled back and grabbed his arm tightly as they forged through the clinic doors and up to the reception desk. Jarod cast his alert information to the nurse at the desk, still trying to catch his breath.

The nurse calmly swiped at his desk screen and called up enough information to inform Jarod that his brother had been rushed to the clinic and his condition had stabilized.

"But what happened? What is the condition?"

"The doctor can give you more details. Please follow me."

The nurse led Jarod and Mirahe down a stark thermoplastic corridor and into a small room. Graeme was lying in a bed, and he had a huge white bandage in the center of his face. A doctor hovered over him with a handscanner. Imogen and Ava stood against a wall, looking on silently.

"Graeme!" Jarod shouted. "Are you okay? What happened?"

The doctor shot up. *"Arrêt!"* She pointed the handscanner at Jarod like it was a weapon. "Stay right there."

"He's my brother," Jarod said, more quietly and feeling kind of foolish.

"It's all right, Jarod," Imogen said, coming forward to pull him back toward the wall. "The doctor says he's going to be fine. It was just a heart episode."

Graeme looked pale and jowly, lying in the bed with his face obscured by the bandage and his body covered by a thin white sheet. He looked at Jarod but didn't say anything.

"We got an alert…" Jarod trailed off.

"All of you. Outside," the doctor said sharply. Her annoyance with Jarod hadn't abated.

They all stepped into the corridor, and Imogen said that Graeme had been at a café when it happened, and he had been brought to the clinic right away. He was resting comfortably now. Everything should be fine.

"Who attacked him?" Mirahe asked.

Imogen looked at her with a puzzled glare. "It was his heart."

"But what happened to his face?" Mirahe asked.

"Oh, well, that's the other part of it," Imogen replied. "That happened before the episode."

"He got in another bar fight," Ava interjected.

"Ava, stop," Imogen said. She turned toward Jarod and Mirahe. "Apparently, there was some kind of altercation. We don't have all the details. We really don't know what happened." She shot a look at her daughter.

Jarod wanted to ask more questions, but Imogen seemed shaken up and Jarod didn't want to make things worse. There was nothing for them to do but pace the hallways and wait for the doctor. The floor in the corridor was just tile, and it wasn't set up to collect energy, but Jarod took out his handgrip anyway and started walking back and forth. The women all leaned against the wall, saying nothing and staring at the door to Graeme's room.

Jarod tapped in to see if he could get any more details. There was already a lot of information about the altercation to scroll through. Reports were on the newsfeed, and a number of witnesses had recorded the fight. Jarod could choose from his choice of view angles.

Fights were pretty rare on Station. There was a lot at stake in having a minimum of disruptions here. And though alcohol wasn't banned on Station, it just wasn't all that common, partly because there were a number of practicing Muslims here and partly because alcohol's effects, even in controlled gravity, were unpredictable. People might have a drink or two with dinner, but bar brawls? That was new territory. Samir had apparently brought Graeme to one of the licensed cafés where they spent the afternoon drinking. Someone had already edited security footage of them sitting at an exterior table, smiling and chatting as the number of glasses on the table accumulated over several hours according to the time stamps.

Then, suddenly, the table was upturned and glasses had shattered on the ground. Graeme had his hands on Samir's shoulders, but Jarod couldn't tell if Graeme was trying to push him down or hold him back. The two men stumble-fought through the café, looking like a clumsy dance pair. Both men were shouting, but Jarod couldn't make out what they were saying. However, he recognized the sound of a pop when Samir took a swing at Graeme and broke his nose. Then Graeme fell to the floor. Samir shouted at him to get up and fight, only stopping when it became clear Graeme hadn't been felled by the punch, but by his heart.

• • • • •

GRAEME HAD TWO hearts, which was a surprise to Jarod, though it wasn't the only thing he didn't know about his brother. To be honest, Jarod didn't even know such an operation was possible, but Graeme had apparently gotten a supplemental pig heart a few years ago. The operation had been successful, but it should have disqualified Graeme from body modification surgery, and it should have put him on the "no ride" list, as far as taking a space elevator to Station went. There just weren't the kind of medical facilities here to deal with that kind of thing.

Fortunately, the pig heart was strong, and it had continued working when Graeme's own heart temporarily stopped beating. But Graeme was going to need more medical care than could be provided on Station, so as soon as he was able, the family would need to go down the Cord.

And that would be for the best, since there was a lot of fallout over the fight that Graeme had started. At first, Jarod had wanted to stick up for his brother. After all, Graeme had been the one who got his nose broken, and he was still recovering from a heart attack. But then more information came out about the fight. Additional camera angles, eyewitness accounts from people in the café, even transcripts of the exchange. Someone had even created an animated version of the fight scene.

All in all, it was clear that the fight was Graeme's fault, and being drunk was no excuse for the things he said. As far as people on Station were concerned, the history of the Marsite Occupation was very much alive. Graeme knew that, and it was unconscionable for him to have said the things to Samir that he did. It took gall to make jokes about Station being recolonized or to talk about how "the Marsites had the right idea" or to say "there's too much oxygen on Station, if you ask me." That last line was the one that had gotten his nose broken. Samir had lost two of his grandparents during the occupation when the Marsites had cut the atmospheric controls to their section.

Jarod might have hit him, too, if he had been there. He was angry with his brother, but that was nothing compared to the blast of fury that confronted him every time he tried to tap in. Yes, people on

Station seemed easygoing, but they were always very conscious of how vulnerable Station was. It wasn't just because of the Marsite Occupation. Station would always be a prize coveted by larger forces on the planet. It was as if people on Station could feel the greedy gaze from Earth. The unspoken goal was to make Station so popular for everyone that no single power could ever try and recolonize it. Tourism was designed to attract people throughout the world. There were no exclusive rights for energy captured by the solar arrays and transmitted to Earth. Astronomy slots were open to all scientists.

So it was a sore spot Graeme had touched, and people were unlikely to forget it, at least to judge by the discussion threads and mood collages that assaulted Jarod whenever he tried to cast an apology or offer some kind of explanation. The worst part was that Mirahe was perhaps the angriest one of all. She had refused to speak to Graeme or Imogen since the incident, and she barely spoke to Jarod, as if he was somehow complicit in all of this.

Imogen now spent all her time in the transfer station, apparently glad to have the excuse of setting up Graeme's medical care on Earth so that she could ignore everything else. Ava refused to leave Jarod's rooms. She and Clautoon had apparently had a big argument about Graeme, and Clautoon had stopped coming over. At least, that's what Jarod surmised, because Ava wasn't speaking to anyone. She just sat on the floor replaying demos she and Clautoon had recorded and stared out into deep space through bloodshot eyes. She wouldn't even visit Graeme at the clinic.

Jarod wasn't all that interested in visiting Graeme either, though he made a trip over each day just to see if Graeme needed anything. They hadn't talked at all about the incident. Jarod told himself he was going to wait for Graeme to apologize, but Graeme barely acknowledged him when he came in the room.

Things weren't any better at work. The incident had lit a fire under Alexey, who claimed Graeme's violence proved the importance of increasing tourism from New Caucasia. Of course, the two things had nothing to do with one another, but there were no objections when

"New Caucasia Initiative" appeared on the next meeting agenda, and Jarod wasn't in a position to shut Alexey down.

If it wasn't for having tours to conduct, Jarod wouldn't have been talking to anyone. Fortunately, Station was always new and exciting for first-time visitors, so Jarod threw himself into his work and tried to feed off the enthusiasm of the tourists, but when his shift ended, he would be back where he was, with a wall of silence awaiting him.

From what he had been able to gather from Imogen during a rare moment when she had been willing to converse, Graeme had been having problems for a while. He had stopped working full-time because of health issues, and he didn't exactly have a job now, though that had been because of his abrasiveness with clients and not because of his health. But Imogen was evasive about discussing Graeme's heart condition or the body modification surgery, perhaps rightly suspecting that Jarod wondered what her role had been in all of this. "He hasn't been easy to live with," she said at one point and then waved her hand dismissively and began streaming a show on her lenses, right in the middle of their conversation. That would have been considered rude anywhere. Jarod just couldn't figure her out.

One night, he couldn't bear the idea of returning to the silence of his rooms. Imogen and Ava had started eating on their own, further minimizing the need for contact, and Mirahe was slated for another double shift. He considered pacing over on the track, but he didn't want the awkwardness of running into one of his neighbors. He decided to go see Graeme and find out what had happened once and for all.

It was past visitors' hours, but the clinic wasn't particularly strict about that sort of thing. When he walked to the desk, he nodded and cast his intentions. The reception nurse shrugged his shoulders and turned back toward his work screen. Jarod made his way to Graeme's room and found the door open. He looked inside, expecting to see Graeme screening something on his lenses with that slack-jawed look he got, but Graeme was just looking up at the ceiling and noticed Jarod as soon as he approached.

"Well, little bro, wasn't expecting to see you."

"I was in the area," Jarod said. He sat down in a chair next to Graeme's bed. He had come to hate sitting in chairs. "I heard from Imogen you've got passage booked down the Cord."

"So she says. A couple more days and you'll be rid of me."

Graeme paused. Jarod said nothing.

"That's an old figure of speech. You're supposed to say you'll be sorry to see me go."

Jarod wasn't in the mood to joke around. "That fight never should have happened. What were you thinking?"

"I was wondering when you'd ask. Well, I don't suppose I was thinking much at all, which was the problem. You spend so much time here walking on eggshells, pumping handgrips and pretending it's all one big happy family. I just decided to speak the truth, *dire la vérité.*"

"The truth." Jarod scoffed. "You mean like you told the truth about your heart or about your surgery or about being out of work?"

"So now you, too. It's not enough I've got Imogen acting like she's already off in deep space and Ava not talking to me."

"Don't you think you brought this one on yourself?"

"Maybe." Graeme paused. He scratched underneath the bandage that still covered his nose. "I don't know anymore. I just wanted to get up into space. From everything you said, it sounded like a place to start everything over, and that's all I wanted to do. And for a while, when we first got here and I was in weightlessness, I felt like I was in control again, like my body was my own. But then... Now don't take this the wrong way, but you're more confined here than I am down on Earth. It's all rules and regulations here. And the lectures! I just couldn't put up with another one."

"Oh, so you're the victim?"

"I'm not saying that. Look at me. I'm a drongo. I've got a pig in my chest and a body that's half fake and half flab. And now I'll have a crooked nose to go with it. There, you happy?"

Jarod didn't know what to say. What was there to say? He hardly knew Graeme, it seemed. He wondered now if he had ever known him.

They were interrupted by a knock at the door. Jarod was expecting it to be a doctor who would kick him out of the room, but he was surprised when Samir stuck his head in.

"May I enter?" Samir asked.

"I should get this many guests during visitors' hours," Graeme replied. "Come on in and survey the damage."

Samir walked over alongside Jarod. Jarod cast a welcome. Samir nodded but did not cast back anything in return, which was rude, even under these circumstances. But then Jarod noticed that Samir wasn't wearing any gauges, and his extended earlobes flopped awkwardly on either side of his face. Samir asked Graeme how he was feeling, and Graeme gave him the update as if Samir had been his care nurse rather than the person who broke his nose. Samir listened thoughtfully, asking questions about Graeme's hearts. Apparently, the idea of having two hearts was new to Samir as well.

As they spoke, Jarod tapped in to see what he could find out about Samir. Samir hadn't fared too well either. There had been a lot of discussion as to what Samir's responsibility was for the whole fight and whether or not he should have just ignored Graeme. He scrolled through more. Wow, there was a lot of discussion about Samir, and a lot of back-and-forth over what it meant that Samir had thrown the first punch. Jarod realized that Samir had gotten much worse than he had. Most people didn't hold Jarod responsible for his brother's actions, or at least they excused him somewhat because he wasn't originally from Station. But Samir was a native, and for him the expectations were a lot higher. He could see why Samir might have decided to take out his gauges for a while.

This whole situation was one of those odd things about Station that Jarod wondered if he would ever fully understand. Punching someone who insulted you, while maybe not admirable behavior, was at least understandable to him. But pacifism was practically a religion up here. The violence on Station during the Marsite Occupation had led to such a strong counterreaction that he was surprised Labicittá was even able to staff its small navy.

Meanwhile, Graeme and Samir kept chatting away like two old friends. Samir even gave Graeme a beautiful bamboo print that he said his daughter had made. At the end of the visit, the two men took hands. Jarod made sure to take an image. He would cast it later in hopes of redirecting the flow against Samir, and maybe against Graeme. Samir departed, and Jarod and Graeme sat staring at each other.

"He's an all right bloke, even if he's a bit of a conch when it comes to bamboo."

Jarod smiled and shook his head. "Graeme, you mug. I think I may take a swing at you next."

• • • • •

BACK WHEN THEY were kids in Australia, Jarod had always walked in Graeme's shadow. One time he begged and pleaded to join in a hurling match with Graeme and some of his friends, even though Jarod had been almost a meter shorter than everyone else who was playing. The whining worked because they let him suit up and gave him a hurley, though the stick was almost as tall as he was. About five minutes in, he got hit in the head with the sliotar, and the ball knocked him to the ground.

He was a bit woozy and didn't get up right away. Graeme had been on the other side of the pitch, but he ran right over to Jarod and knelt down with a look of concern and panic in his eyes. The last thing Jarod wanted to do was to be the little kid who needed looking after, so he forced himself to stand up and pretend he was all right.

"Kidding," Jarod said. "It just grazed me."

Jarod never knew if what Graeme did next was truly because of anger or just as a response to Graeme's own momentary feeling of fear and impotence. Either way, Graeme slapped Jarod pretty hard, and Jarod started crying. Graeme's teammates, most of whom had seen that the sliotar really had given Jarod a whack, grabbed Graeme and started yelling at him, pushing him between them in a circle.

"Leave my brother alone!" Jarod had shouted from behind the pack. Jarod pushed into the scrum but got knocked over and stepped on. Then Graeme scooped him up and broke through the pack, carrying

Jarod like he was a rugby ball. Graeme ran with him until they were in the woods next to the field. Then he put Jarod down and walked away without saying anything.

Jarod hadn't known what to feel. It was too complicated. It still felt too complicated.

. . . . .

JAROD HAD CAST the image of Graeme and Samir taking hands and added his own sense of the situation. He tried to project Samir's concern and Graeme's confusion. He ended up sharing the story about the hurling pitch, because it seemed related in some way Jarod couldn't fully put words to. It was a complex mood to try and model, but he did what he could.

It turned out to be the right thing to do. That night when he saw Mirahe, she ran up to him and threw her arms around him. She began crying and would only say "Bakti." Bakti was her younger brother. One cycle down on Labicittá, he got into a fight with their father and left the island. He had never returned, and Mirahe had never been able to find him on EarthWeb. Jarod just held her. He didn't have to tap in to understand.

The next morning, Clautoon buzzed their door and asked for Ava. As soon as he saw her, he burst into tears and buried his head into her hair, whispering what must have been an apology. Awkwardly, everyone else tried to look away as she stroked his face and repeated, *"E bene. E bene."*

And then that afternoon, Jarod decided to stop in during lunch to visit Graeme. He saw Imogen sitting on the edge of Graeme's bed, stroking the side of his face and speaking to him in soothing tones. "I could have lost you," Jarod heard her say. He slowly backed away from the room and left them alone.

All in all, it was a bit much, particularly happening suddenly like that. At another time in his life, Jarod would have written these events off as coincidence or some happy narcotic in the drinking water. But now that he had been on Station long enough, he had come to believe in StationWeb. He knew that casting into it could be like dropping a coin in a wishing well, only instead of hoping some magic fairy would grant your wish, you would hope that everyone else on the web could grant it.

The mood values made StationWeb different from EarthWeb. Station had a small, wholly interdependent population, so not only was it possible to measure the mood, it was important to do so. Such a system wouldn't work on Earth, since the concept of the mood of billions of people didn't even make sense. But Station never had more than a few hundred people regularly cycled up at any one time. If Station had had regular web contact with the planet, the anomalies introduced into the system would mean that mood would no longer be a meaningful measure of any kind of collective experience. But within StationWeb, mood mattered. Everyone could influence it and be influenced by it.

So Jarod didn't just use StationWeb, he was a part of it. He cast into it what he had to offer and took away from it what he needed. The fight between Graeme and Samir had been a kind of rupture within the field, and it needed to be repaired. The image of the two men taking hands and making amends had spread like salve over all of Station. It was like the broken bone that became even stronger after it healed.

· · · · ·

BY THE TIME Graeme and his family were to leave, people genuinely were sorry to see them go, as Jarod could tell when he tapped in to survey the mood. A sizable crowd had gathered at the space elevator gate to see them off on the morning they left. They buzzed around the departures gate, pacing in different directions to generate energy on the flexible floor, all seemingly talking at the same time.

Graeme sat in the center of the action in a transit chair. He no longer had to wear the bandage on his nose. His face was a little puffy, and he still seemed peaked, but he was smiling when he took hands with Samir and a whole host of friends he had apparently made at the sauna room. It was easy to forget, but Graeme could be a personable bloke.

Ava was a mess. She and Clautoon were pawing each other, foreheads pressed together and tears streaming down her cheeks. Jarod wasn't quite sure how they were going to get her to board the climber. Over the past few days, the two of them had worked nonstop recording music and shooting footage for Ava's school project. It turned out that Shi-Lu, the last of Suha's childhood friends from before the revolution, was Clautoon's great-grandfather, so he arranged another interview for her. Between the sound mixing and the video editing, and whatever else she and Clautoon were doing, Ava had barely come back to the rooms to sleep. Jarod suspected she would be wiped out on the trip back to Australia.

Imogen looked the best she had the whole trip. She was talking and laughing with people, acting like she had known them her whole life. At one point, she even told Mirahe something about wanting to spend more time on solar arrays the next time they visited. Who was this woman?

Jarod and Mirahe stood shoulder to shoulder alongside Graeme and Imogen. As the whirl of action surrounded them, they both pumped handgrips and intervened in whichever conversation was coming their way. So much personal news and gossip was being swapped, one would have thought there was no need for StationWeb. One of Mirahe's nieces had been accepted to university in Jakarta. A cousin would be taking the administrative training sequence down on Labicittá. The astronomers had picked up another pulse from COSMOS-AzTEC3, though there was no agreement as to what the pulse indicated. Samir passed along a bamboo shard card to Graeme with information on biochar heating systems, and Graeme promised he would look into it when he got back to Australia. One of Jarod's coworkers took him aside and told him he should read Alexey's latest missive, so some things hadn't changed at all. Mirahe's uncle's condition had not improved as much as they had hoped, and it looked like he might have to go down the Cord to the hospital on Labicittá. One of Clautoon's friends gave Ava a hand model of a slideboard with a carbon nanotube surface. This caused a round of hugging and more tears.

When the shuttle loading was announced, Graeme, Imogen and Ava came together and said a last round of goodbyes to Jarod and Mirahe.

"Take my hand, brother," Jarod said, bending down toward Graeme and grabbing his wrist.

"Now, what is it I'm supposed to say back?" Graeme asked as he took hold of Jarod's wrist.

"You say 'safe,'" Jarod replied. "Just 'safe.'"

"Then 'safe' it is." Graeme pulled Jarod down into a hug. "It's been a hell of a trip. Now it's your turn to come back to Australia."

"We've got some vacation time coming when we cycle down to Labicittá in about six months. I'll try to make it happen."

After the second boarding call sounded, the family finally made their way through the gates and, after the floor was turned off and stopped registering joules, the crowd slowly drifted back to their daily lives. Jarod wanted to stay to watch the climber descend. It wasn't very dramatic, at least no more interesting than watching an elevator head down a shaft. But the planet below was an incredibly diverse palate of blues, greens and whites, suspended against a speckled black canvas. He hoped he would never fail to appreciate it.

Mirahe must have sensed his mood because she squeezed his arm and brushed her nose against the gauge in his ear.

"Are you going to cast something?" she asked as the climber slowly disconnected from Station. It accelerated as it dropped along the carbon nanotube Cord toward the Earth.

"I will, when I can model what I'm feeling. There's a lot to account for."

"You'll need to complicate your model further. We're going to need to cycle down to Labicittá early this year."

Jarod turned and looked at Mirahe. His first impulse was to worry that something was wrong, but he could see by the flash in her eyes and the upturned corners of her mouth that she was happy.

"I'm pregnant."

Ava

Ava tried to ignore it, but the chat indicator
from Kareela wouldn't leave her alone. It
popped up on her lenses, on her homework screen,
even on the bathroom mirror. Ava never should have
shared the PEPod from Clautoon with her. Now
Kareela wanted a direct feed to all the raw footage
of her time with Clautoon, and Ava didn't want to
give her access.

Which, Ava had to admit, was kind of *strano*.
After all, she and Kareela had been best friends since
pre-pre-Kindergarten, and they had always given
each other full access to each other's footage. And
it wasn't as if Ava was trying to be all *misterioz* or
anything. After all, she had sent Kareela the PEPod
in the first place. It was just that she didn't feel
comfortable for some reason sharing everything.

Which Kareela must have felt was unfair, since
Kareela always shared everything, including all the
footage from when she and Timtayo hooked up.
Which was more than Ava wanted to see, to be
honest. But Ava didn't have a good reason to hold
back, so all she could do was ignore Kareela's puls-
ing green dot even though it felt like it was burning
a hole in her retina.

Besides, Ava had work to do. Her project for
class was due at the end of the week, and it had to

be good enough to justify missing three weeks of school in the middle of the term or she'd be *geschroefd*. Now that she had decided to edit her footage in standardview instead of just compiling for hyperview, the project was taking a lot longer, and sometimes it took on the feel of a boring Pacific history class. It just didn't seem like the editing would ever be finished. In a compilation, you didn't have to make choices. That was the advantage of hyperview. You could just throw in everything and let the viewers' automatic settings do the editing for you. They could decide how long they wanted it to be, they could skip historical background if they wanted, they could default deactivate smell sensors.

But everything was different with standardview. In standardview, you had to make editing choices. Which meant you had to decide why someone would care about something in the first place. That required a whole different way of thinking.

Originally, Ava had planned to just compile for hyperview, so she had just dumped in all the footage, starting from when she first got to Station and was staring out into deep space. Because it was the first time she had ever seen the stars from beyond the atmosphere, she kept every second of footage. In hyperview, that was what you did. But in standardview, that was just really boring. She ended up editing an hour of footage down to just a couple minutes on the most familiar constellations. But you could watch it in real time and fill in the gaps between the edits. It was like Clautoon had said about music, the silences were as important as the sounds. Now she couldn't stop thinking about her footage the same way.

Clautoon. She had to stop thinking about him. At least for tonight. At least until she got this project done. But as soon as he was on her mind, the automatic montage in her head was triggered, and she had to stop and watch the whole thing again. The sequence was synced to one of the songs they had recorded together, and it showed their first meeting when Clautoon was busking and playing his bass and Ava joined in with him. She loved the look of surprise on his face when she first picked up the triple sticks and began jamming. It was the most use she had ever gotten out of two years' worth of otherwise worthless percussion lessons her mum had made her take.

The montage was mostly made up of footage she had taken of Clautoon, a lot of close-ups of his face and his amazing profile, but she had incorporated some images Clautoon's friends had taken of the two of them on the slideboard slopes, with Clautoon helping to make sure she didn't fall as soon as the slideboard slipped down the embankment. And there was even a little bit from her mum that was shot when they all went out to dinner that one night. She only included that because it showed she and Clautoon in front of that giant aquarium of fish.

But the montage wasn't in hyperview, so it didn't include everything. Which was okay. Ava didn't really want to revisit those bad few days when they weren't speaking to each other. Which was all her father's fault anyway. He almost ruined the whole trip because he couldn't control his temper. As a little girl, she'd been scared to death of her father when he got angry, but now it was more an embarrassment than anything else. The most random things would set him off, like an overcooked steak at a restaurant or an autocar driver that he thought went too slowly. Which was completely *dilsiz* because autocar drivers were programmed for the speed limit.

As the montage faded out, Ava realized that she had been thinking about her father instead of paying attention to it. Which was really sad because nothing in her life had been as intense as her time with Clautoon, and what did it mean if she could be distracted from it? It was bad enough that Clautoon couldn't be reached via EarthWeb. Kareela had said it was kind of throwback-romantic that she and Clautoon could only communicate via PEPod, like they were sending each other messages in bottles. But Ava wasn't so sure. Mostly it was just inconvenient.

There was a rap at her door, and the RoBro came in to announce dinner in that stupid computer-generated British accent of his.

"I told you not to come into my room," Ava said, tossing a pillow at the RoBro. It bounced off his helmet head and fell harmlessly to the floor.

"Our mother has requested your appearance at the dinner table in five minutes, Miss Ava," the RoBro repeated.

"She's not your mother. And don't call me 'Miss Ava!'" she shouted as the RoBro rotated on its base and rolled out the door. It left the door to her room open. Which was on purpose and just to annoy her. When the last system upgrade to the RoBro introduced custom accents, it became more aggravating than ever. Ava missed the 1.0 version, when it just rolled around after her and could only squeak and whistle.

Five minutes wasn't enough time to edit, so she closed her file and blinked it into a backup. She would get back to it after dinner. The chat indicator flashed again. Which meant that Kareela couldn't take a hint. So Ava decided to get it over with.

> hey reela girl

>>Where u been? I'm tryin 2 chat u 4evr?

> i got to finish my project for tomorrow

>> I totally want 2 steal Clautoon from u. Sooooo cute.

> not going to happen kareela

>> Let me hyperview ur footage.

> i already sent the PEPod

>> I know, I scanned it 3 times already. Don't hold out.

>*>*> DINNER >*>*> DINNER >*>*> DINNER >*>*> DINNER

> i got to go that's my mum being subtle

>> Send it b4 u eat!!!!

> maybe later bye

Ava left the chat and made her way downstairs. Her mum and dad were already sitting at the table, and they were holding hands. As Ava walked in, her dad leaned over and kissed her mum.

"Ugh, stop please. The RoBro is in my seat," Ava said.

"I am simply preparing the surface for Miss Ava," the RoBro announced, spinning out of her seat and onto the floor.

"Dad, make it stop calling me 'Miss Ava.'"

"RoBro, heel," her dad said, leaning back into his own chair. RoBro rolled over to her dad's chair and went into power reserve mode.

Her dad grabbed a ladle from the table and picked up Ava's plate. "Ava, tonight's dinner is delicious, though it looks a bit like a coral reef. Do you want one or two scoops?"

Ava glanced at the bowl in the center of the table and the oddly shaped blobs it contained. Her mum had started cooking exclusively vegan ever since the truth about Ava's father's heart condition had come out. She was dipping pretty deep into the recipe archive for whatever it was tonight using seitan, kumara and what looked like spinach.

"Just one," she said. "Can I have some bread?"

The bread was sitting right in front of her mum, but her mum didn't answer. She was zoned out again, but a different kind of zoned out. It didn't seem like she was screening anything on her lenses. It was more like she was thinking or something. Her dad took the plate of bread, passing it to Ava. Her mum snapped back to attention.

"You with us again?" her dad asked.

Ava's mum smiled a silly kind of smile, as if she was in on some kind of joke the rest of them didn't get.

"Sorry, I was just remembering that trip we took to the Great Barrier Reef. Do you remember how incredible that was?"

"Strewth, it was," her dad replied. "Beautiful sight, that."

"It's hard to believe that the reef is still there. Everyone had thought it was so fragile, yet it survived the climate change. And here it is now, still with us. Still remarkable."

Ava could see her mum's face redden as her voice rose.

"Sorry, I just think it's something that should be appreciated. It's so easy for us to get wrapped up in our lives and not notice the wonderful things around us. Things are getting better all the time." Her mum started to stand, then thought better of it and changed the subject. "So, Ava, have you heard from Clautoon?"

"No, Mum, I already told you. It takes time to send PEPods down the Cord from Station."

"Well, then tell me about your project for school."

"I've been spending a lot of time working on it. But I don't think it's very good."

"I don't understand why this one is taking so long," her dad interjected. "You usually whip these things off in no time at all."

"Graeme, she's editing," her mum said. "That takes longer."

"Editing." He scoffed. "I don't think I've ever edited anything in my life. I don't see what's suddenly wrong with hyperview."

"It's not the same, Dad," Ava said. "I wouldn't expect you to understand."

Everyone resumed eating. To be honest, there were times over the past week when Ava began to wonder what was suddenly *wrong* with hyperview. When people could default autoedit to their preference settings, they could see the things that intrigued them and someone in Ava's position wouldn't have to guess at what others would find interesting. There were reasons almost everyone liked hyperview better. But Clautoon and his friends hated it. They said it was the death of creativity, and they never used it, even when they cycled down to Labicittá and could get on EarthWeb. And she trusted them more than her dad. She was sticking with standardview. *Begåtts.*

Her mum and dad were holding hands again and smiling at each other like they were lovesick. Or maybe just sick. Ava didn't know what to make of them. It was better without the two of them arguing all the time, but they were way too old to be feeling each other up in public. She swore she would never be like that, and she had actually created an event on her calendar reminding her not to be like her parents. It was scheduled to alert her twenty years from now.

Then there was a flash on her cornea, and Ava shot out of her chair. Her parents were both startled.

"It's the PEPod from Clautoon!" she shouted, running out of the room. "It just got here!"

"You can view it at the table," her mum shouted, but Ava was halfway up the stairs and ignoring her anyway.

She went into her room, closed the door and hopped onto her bed, surrounded by pillows, blankets and the stuffed koala she had had since she was a little girl. She triggered the PEPod from Clautoon and settled in for the experience.

Her bedroom faded from her vision and was replaced by Artsutanov Plaza on Station. The plaza was crowded with people milling back and forth, and the scent of herbs growing in the plant beds was in the air, but it was the vastness of space beyond the view windows that dominated Ava's vision. Ava heard the sound of a stand-up bass behind her and tried to turn around. Of course, she couldn't choose to turn around. This wasn't hyperview. She had to wait until the POV shifted 180 degrees, and then she saw Clautoon, only he was hanging upside down in gravboots and still playing a fairly complicated jazz piece. Ava laughed and called out, "Clautoon, you are too funny." Why did she do that? She knew the image was just a representation of Clautoon. Still, she wanted him to be in the same room with her. When Clautoon finished the song, his gravboots lowered him to the floor, and Clautoon flashed her a big smile. Which Ava thought was sweet.

Then the scene flashed to Clautoon's rooms, and this time Ava saw herself. It was archival footage of her visit to Station. Ava remembered this moment. She had wanted to punch the bass up because it was hard to hear Clautoon unless he was soloing. But Clautoon always wanted the bass low down in the mix, and Ava had gone along. In the end, she wasn't necessarily sure that was the right decision. Even now, watching herself make the same choice, she wasn't sure it was the right one.

There was another flash, and now the scene shifted to one of the bounce rooms on Station. It was covered in graffiti, and music played in the background. Ava looked around to see if she was in the footage, but all she saw was Clautoon and some of his friends floating around in weightlessness. Having grown up on Station, they had spent so much time playing around without gravity that they looked like ballerinas, twisting and leaping gracefully. Weightlessness didn't come as naturally to Ava, and she had always felt like she was about to lose control and slip away somehow. Even now, even knowing she was just streaming footage, she was a little uncomfortable, afraid of that second when she would have to leap into a void and trust that there would not be any gravity to pull her down.

As Clautoon somersaulted into a landing on a side wall, Ava realized that his movements were in sync to the song that was playing. Ava had thought the music was dubbed into the footage, but it was actually playing over the speakers in the bounce room. It was one of the songs she had written with Clautoon. She watched as Clautoon caromed back and forth off walls as each new measure began. When she realized what he was doing, it made her dizzy. It must have taken forever to get the timing down. And then when the chorus of the song kicked in, some of Clautoon's friends floated into the side of the frame and started lip-synching the lyrics.

The last part of the PEPod was just Clautoon talking, staring out at her with a canvas of stars behind him. He told her that he listened to their music a lot. He said to say hello to her family from him. His great-grandfather, Shi-Lu, also wanted him to wish her well. All of Clautoon's friends wanted to see her project when she was finished with it. He said that their time together had stayed with him, and he would always treasure it. And then he said he had one last thing for her. A chord from the Cord: a D minor. The image faded to black as the chord sounded. It was kind of sad. *Triste.* And then it was over. The PEPod seemed so short. In hyperview, it would hardly have even counted as having started. But it meant so much just to hear from Clautoon, even though she felt farther away from him now than ever. She blinked a backup.

She wished she had something to send back to him right away, but she'd been working on this project since she'd gotten back and still hadn't finished it. And she knew why. It was the Shi-Lu interview. It had to be in the final cut. He was someone who had actually known Suha, someone who had actually fought the Marsites during the revolution. But she kept putting off looking at that footage because she wasn't sure how to edit it in with everything else.

Now was as good a time as any though, so Ava brought up the Shi-Lu interview and previewed it. Shi-Lu's image appeared, and she was struck again by how old and frail he was. Which was *hloupý*, of course, since he was practically one hundred years old, so what did she expect? Still, all through the interview, she had worried that he was going to fall out of the transit chair. And she didn't know what to make of his hair. She didn't know human hair could grow that long. She would have thought it would have gotten in the way or even stuck under his transit chair.

It seemed like every movement was a struggle for Shi-Lu, but he still managed a kind smile. And he had tried to answer all of Ava's questions. It helped that Clautoon was next to him the whole time. Clautoon had to serve as a kind of translator for her. Which was not what she expected. Ava had never thought of herself as having an accent, but apparently Shi-Lu had trouble understanding her English.

She started by asking him about how he met Suha, and he talked about the two of them attending the Marsite school on Station. He really went off on the Marsite teachers. She was amazed at how much he still hated the Marsites. Not that she blamed him. But it all had happened so long ago, and he spoke about one of his Marsite teachers like she had just punished him yesterday. Then, during the revolution, all the schools had to go underground, and he attended secret classes in bedrooms and storage areas. He had had to fight to learn, not like now, he said, with a wagged finger in Clautoon's direction.

But Suha had been gone by then. All the time of the revolution had come after her, so Ava tried to get him back to the subject. Shi-Lu talked a little bit about the weightlessness dock with the Dead Zone, though he hated to use that term now, he said. Suha had been the best of them all in weightlessness. She would practice the flips and spins until she was nauseous, but that was her way. She was always the most intense of them all. At the time, being in weightlessness was so exciting. Who could guess that it would be the very thing that would make so many of his generation so sick? When Shi-Lu said that, he gestured down to his legs, which Ava could tell were shriveled and withered even through the thin blanket he wore over them.

When Ava had done her initial research, she found that historians still disputed whether or not the Marsites knew the lockdown would cause the weightlessness disease or whether it was just an unintended consequence. But she could already guess what Shi-Lu thought about that. So instead she asked about Suha's vidiaries and whether Shi-Lu knew she had been making them. He laughed and said no, no one knew about them. Of course, they had all seen her with that ridiculous camera goggle on, making her look like half a robot. It just seemed like she was playing with a toy.

"We were just children," he said. "Everyone forgets that. Even my great-grandson here, who would rather just play his music instead of paying attention in school, he is older now than I was when Suha and I were friends. But he can take so much for granted. Yes, so much and so little."

He flashed a smile at Clautoon, and something caught Ava's attention. She paused and scrolled back. She looked at the old man's smile again, and then she realized what it was. He had the same smile as Clautoon. It was the first time she had noticed the resemblance, and it scared her because this was what Clautoon would look like as an old man. Not with the weightlessness disease, of course. They were really strict on Station about exercise and making everyone cycle part of the year down to Labicittá so that the disease couldn't strike again. And if you ever questioned why, all you had to do was look around at the old people in transit chairs who could never leave Station. It was hard to think of Clautoon ever becoming old. She hated to think of herself that way, though it was hard not to with her mum always there in front of her.

That was the worst thing about being a clone, more or less knowing what you were going to look like when you were old. Well, no, that wasn't quite the worst thing. The worst thing was that her mum was always sure she understood what Ava was feeling just because they had the same DNA. "Genetics is not destiny, Mum," Ava would say. But that didn't stop her mum from thinking she always knew everything about Ava. You would have thought her mum had grown up in the twenty-first century or something.

It was the last part of the interview that was difficult to watch, and she still felt bad about it. She thought she had asked a pretty harmless question: What was the hardest part about living on Station during the occupation? She had thought he would talk about the cramped quarters or the limited food or even just use the chance to trash the Marsites again, but instead he talked about being separated from his family. She knew that the Marsites had intentionally kept families apart during the lockdown as a supposed way of ensuring loyalty. It was supposed to be temporary, but during the lockdown, families had no contact with each other for years.

Shi-Lu talked about his sister and how he hardly knew her as a little girl. His sister and father were forced down to Labicittá, leaving him and his mother alone on Station, living in a room the size of a closet. And down on Labicittá, there was little work back then, and his father was less of a man without his mother. His father was not the kind of person who could care for his sister as she needed. As she grew up, there was trouble. Then Shi-Lu began to cry. Serious *choro*. Ava didn't know what to do.

"But I do not cry for her," Shi-Lu said, tightly twisting one of his long locks of hair around his fingers. "I have shed many tears for her already. I cry now for myself, because I am less of a person for not having been able to help her. Please do not make your project about triumphant heroes inspired by Suha. There is not an aspect of life on Station today that is not a sad echo of all that we have lost. So much and so little."

"Great-grandfather, do you want to stop?" Clautoon had gone over to sit next to him.

But Shi-Lu waved him off and collected himself. He went back to talking about Suha, and even told some funny stories about how they had stolen equipment from the Marsite soldiers, and then he complained about kids today on slideboards clogging up passageways. By the end of the interview, they were all smiling again. Shi-Lu even presented her with an ink-on-bamboo scroll that he had made of the Earth at night as seen from Station. It was beautiful, and she loved how he created the effect of lights on the Earth simply by not coloring the bamboo. She had felt like a real *idiootti* for not bringing anything to give him.

She looked up at the scroll, which was on the wall right next to her bed now. It was gorgeous, but now that she looked at it with the memory of Shi-Lu breaking down still vivid, it seemed kind of sad. Shi-Lu had sketched a planet that his illness would never let him visit again. And now she knew why she couldn't finish her project. She had done exactly what Shi-Lu had told her not to do. She had created a project all about "triumphant heroes inspired by Suha," all about Station as a place where problems had been solved and everyone was happy. But that wasn't true. Station was a mix of good and bad, pleasure and pain, just like everywhere else. Which was pretty obvious, so why didn't her project show that? Why was she reluctant to let people see that?

Ava paused. She knew why. Because then she'd have to open up everything, and that would mean compiling her project in hyperview. But that would also mean sharing her time with Clautoon. She didn't want to do that, not because she was too private, but because part of her didn't know if they would ever see each other again.

She closed the interview and opened up Clautoon's PEPod again. She listened closely to what he said at the end. She replayed it a second time before she realized Clautoon also wasn't sure if they would ever see each other again. It was nothing he said, but she could tell in what he didn't say that this message was a goodbye. Of course, she had known it would be difficult to visit each other. It wasn't easy to get from Australia to Labicittá, never mind to Station. But they could both be going to university in a few years. They could go to the same school, couldn't they? They could keep sending PEPods until then. They could be together, couldn't they?

Or was this just what happened to people? Did people just drift apart unless there was something tying them together? Had they said goodbye for good? Did Clautoon realize this was going to happen all along? She scrolled through his footage until she got to the image of his last message. In his eyes, was there a sadness, a sadness like that in Shi-Lu's eyes?

There was a rap at her door, and her mum asked to come in. Ava realized she was crying. She wiped the tears from her eyes and said,

"Come in." Her mum opened the door and walked into her room, followed by the RoBro.

"Ava, you've been up here a while. Is everything okay?"

"Miss Ava has not finished her dinner. Shall I reheat it for her?"

"RoBro, go recharge, please," her mum said. At that command, the RoBro spun out of the room and left for the recharging platform.

"Everything's fine, Mum. Except…except I think I'm going to have to start my project over. I wasn't doing it right. The narrative is all wrong. I was just showing a little piece of Station, capturing moments when I saw something I had already expected to see. The project needs to be about what I didn't expect, what I didn't know, what I still don't know. It needs to be bigger. It needs to take on more."

"It sounds like it needs to be in hyperview."

Ava looked up at her mother, seeing eyes identical to her own staring back at her.

"You're right, Mum. It does need to be in hyperview. I need to stop trying to control the narrative. It needs to be in hyperview. I guess sometimes you have to see everything in order to appreciate anything."

Ava's mum's eyes started to tear up. She stepped forward and hugged Ava tightly. "Oh, Ava, I wish it hadn't taken me so long to learn that."

"Mum, are you okay?"

Ava's mum let go and stepped back. "Yes, I am. I am now."

She turned to leave, and Ava was surprised she hadn't asked about Clautoon.

"Clautoon said to say *halo*."

Ava's mom turned back. "That's nice. He was a sweet boy. *Un ragazzo dolce.*"

Dead Zone

Suparman

The second half of Suparman's double shift began in fifteen minutes, and he used the brief respite to sit and massage his thighs with penetrating oil. The recent fluctuations in gravity levels on Station had been bad for his legs. He would not be able to rest again for the remainder of the shift, and it had already been a long day.

It was required by the Marsites that he announce his name at each table he waited on in awkward Business English—"Hello, I am Suparman, and I will facilitate your food transaction." His name was pronounced "Su-PAR-man," but his name was very humorous to most Marsites, and he had heard many jokes about the old comic book hero. Apparently, that character with a similar name was still popular on Earth because rarely did an evening pass without at least one of his tables bursting into laughter at his expense. But this was the least of his concerns when dealing with the Marsites.

The Marsites posed many challenges. They took offense easily, and Suparman had seen coworkers reprimanded or replaced for a lack of deference, the nonstandard use of Business English or perceived gestural slights. Fundamentally, the Marsites wished that only Marsites resided on Station, but such a thing was not possible. For all their technical expertise, the Marsites were really only astronauts, and they could not run Station on their own. Even someone like Suparman, who had worked almost exclusively in food services since the occupation, also had training in orbital nutrition and emergency medicine. So the Marsites reluctantly put up with individuals who had spent most of their adult lives mastering the complex systems needed to make Station function.

Nor, now that he considered it, did the Marsites really wish to run Station. Station was merely a stopping point for them, a place from which to launch their grand scheme to colonize and then terraform Mars, turning it into some kind of new Eden. For years now, since the Marsite invasion had given them control of Labicittá and Station, they had put a halt to all astronomical and energy export projects. All but the essential solar arrays were removed, and huge launch bays had been built in their place. The space elevator now was constantly delivering freight shipments from the planet below. All work on Station was dedicated to sending unmanned supply launches to the surface of Mars. By the time the first humans arrived, the Martian surface would be so crowded with equipment that people would want to colonize Jupiter. Or so the joke went.

Of course, such a joke would never be repeated in front of the Marsites. They tended not to find humor, well, humorous.

At the turn of the hour, Suparman stood and straightened his jacket. The rest of the waitstaff was busy serving the enlisted soldiers in a separate and larger room. Suparman, as the senior member of the staff, worked in the officers' dining center, though a central kitchen served both rooms. With a nod from the server he was relieving, Suparman stepped out and surveyed the room. There were a dozen officers clad in space fatigues and unigoggles sitting in pairs and trios. Suparman instinctively cataloged all the visible weaponry. This was one of the disturbing features of the Marsites, their insistence on being armed at all times. He worried that they were always one argument away from a sidearm exchange. Twice, there had been shooting incidents elsewhere on Station that had resulted in section hull breaches. Fortunately, the sections were isolated and the outer core had remained secure or count-less lives could have been lost.

Many of the individuals in the room were unfamiliar to him. There had been so many new arrivals now that the first manned launch to Mars was approaching. Of course, Suparman was to know nothing of the impending launch, but Marsites were not particularly good at keep-ing secrets, especially when they were drinking together.

His first table was a group of three officers he had served many times before. Two of them worked in security, and one was in logis-tics. They all had that top-heavy look he had come to associate with Marsites, a combination of weight lifting, growth hormones and muscle grafts. He thought of this body type as the Marsites' unofficial uniform. The security officers were no trouble. Suparman was not interesting enough to merit their attention. But the logistics officer did not like it if Suparman looked him in the eyes. It may have had something to do with the time Suparman had to help him back to his quarters one night after he had too much to drink.

Nevertheless, Suparman introduced himself with his head hung down, as if the officers were new to Station, showing interest only in their drink orders. Then he returned to the kitchen and squirted differ-ent flavor packets into glasses with water and grain alcohol, which he delivered to the table. He informed the officers of the evening's specials, which were also on the menu they could scroll through on their unigoggles. After taking the officers' dinner orders, he went back into the kitchen and reported them to the cook, who began adding another array of flavor packets to various protein spreads and vitamin supplements.

When Suparman returned to the dining center, another table was occupied, and this one gave him pause. There was a single officer sitting there, one who was slighter in stature than other Marsites. He also wore an elaborate set of braces on his legs, so that it looked like he had a mechanical exoskeleton. It was D'Onforio, a high-ranking officer who posed unique challenges.

Suparman hesitated, but then D'Onforio caught his eye, and the annoyance in the officer's face was impossible to miss. Suparman quickly went to the table.

"Hello, I am Suparman, and I will assist with your—"

"Just bring me a drink, for chrissakes. I've been waiting forever." D'Onforio stretched out his left leg with a wince. He reached around the braces to massage his thigh.

Suparman knew that D'Onforio always had the same drink, a concoction meant to approximate the taste of gin, but he was required to ask for a specific order. To do otherwise was to imply that he knew individual habits of Marsites, and such knowledge was officially forbidden for security purposes. But D'Onforio had turned his attention to his leg, and Suparman thought it best not to disturb him. He returned to the kitchen and quickly made up the officer's drink.

The problem with D'Onforio, Suparman knew, was that he was not really a Marsite. He may have been as committed to the colonization project as much as the others, but he was a generation older than the rest of the men and women looking to cast their lots on Mars. They were veterans of the Resource Wars. To them, the Earth was nothing more than a series of battlefields on top of dwindling gas reserves and sequestered CO_2 deposits. They all believed that the Earth was beyond redemption. But D'Onforio, like Suparman, had come of age in a different era, a more hopeful time when progress still seemed possible, which made things both better and worse for the two of them. Like Suparman, D'Onforio was not motivated by desperation but rather by disappointment.

It was surprising that someone as old as D'Onforio was even allowed to be among the initial group of colonizers, but his presence was undoubtedly a testament to his political connections. He differed from the other Marsites not only in age and size but in personality. He was a playwright, of all things, about as far from a soldier as one could get. His best-known work, *The Conqueress*, became infamous when a series of actresses suffered emotional breakdowns after performing the lead role, which caused some critics to call for a ban on the play. D'Onforio's response had been to say it was not necessary for an actress to have a breakdown after performing in his drama. That would only be the result if the role were played properly.

It had been quite a scandal at the time, but that was many years ago, back when Suparman had been a university student down on Labicittá. D'Onforio could not have been long graduated himself. And now neither of them was young.

Suparman placed the drink in front of D'Onforio and alerted him to the specials that were also on the menu he could scroll through on his unigoggle. D'Onforio flipped up his unigoggle so that he looked directly into Suparman's eyes.

"Forget the menu. Do you have anything made out of real food? I don't think I can eat another tube of flavor gel or whatever the hell it is you serve up here."

Suparman paused. He suspected that D'Onforio felt the same kind of gravity pains in his legs that he did. This made the officer irritable, and Suparman would have to proceed very carefully.

"There are greenhouse tomatoes, though they are not seamlessly integrated with the nutritional entrees. However, with biscuits they would provide value-added eating."

"A tomato! That sounds like heaven. Bring one immediately— what was your name again?"

"Suparman, sir."

"Ah, yes. Well, here we are. Man and Superman. Discoursing over a tomato. Why don't you bring me another drink as well?"

"Right away, sir. I will raise the bar."

Suparman returned to the kitchen, and gave the order to the cook, who took it with a raised eyebrow. The tomatoes were not for general consumption, even among the officers. Suparman told him they were for D'Onforio, and he didn't need to say anything else. D'Onforio was well-known on Station, though less for his writing than for his role in the aerial raid on Labicittá that initially brought the island under Marsite control. Perhaps it would be more accurate to say that he was well-feared.

While the cook went to the pantry for tomatoes, Suparman mixed another drink. He felt a twinge in his leg and wished he had put on more essential oils before his shift. But he was running low, and he would need to ensure that his daughter, Suha, the forgetful child, remembered to pick up more for him at the dispensary. She was a handful, that one, nothing like her little brother, Jati, who was gentle and obedient. Suha would rather run around with her friends than take on the responsibilities she must as long as her mother and baby sister, Rima, were on Labicittá. And Suha would lie right to his face, smiling as she deceived. She was a girl who needed a mother, and he wished for the hundredth—no, for the thousandth—time that they could all be reunited, that the Marsites would end the family separation policy. How ridiculous it was for the Marsites to think such a policy would ensure loyalty. It had only created anger and misery. Already the lockdown had gone on for years longer than anticipated. He doubted that his baby, Rima, who was no longer a baby, had any memory of him at all other than as a face on a screen.

There was hope that after the first manned mission launched, the powers that be would relax the family separation policy. But Suparman knew that after the first manned mission, there would be the second one. And then the third.

It did not take long for the cook to return and prepare the tomatoes and biscuits, and he had taken care to arrange them in an aesthetically pleasing manner. Suparman saw the plate and suggested that the cook sprinkle on some dried herbs. The cook clearly did not appreciate Suparman's recommendation, but he did as he was asked. Suparman took the plate and glass and brought them out to D'Onforio just as the officer was finishing his first drink. He placed the meal in front of D'Onforio and watched as D'Onforio straightened up in his seat.

"Ah, now this is food." The officer picked up his utensils and immediately cut into one of the tomatoes, sending juice squirting onto the table. "You've done well," he said to Suparman.

Suparman gave a nod and retreated from the table. Another pair of officers had been seated in his section, so he quickly approached them and introduced himself. "Hello, I am Suparman, and I will assist with your food transaction."

The officers immediately broke out in laughter. "Well, hell, Superman," one of them said. "I'm Batman and this here is Green Lantern, and we want to get drunk."

Suparman smiled at the officers. "I will strive to maximize the leverage of your order."

It was a busy night, and Suparman was glad just to get through it. Between officers wanting a quick dinner before a shift began and others wanting to drink and relax after work, there was a lot to balance. But Suparman did his job well, and there were no problems. Even the dyspeptic D'Onforio seemed pleased. When Suparman came to clear his table, D'Onforio regaled him with a story of his Mediterranean childhood, how tomatoes and countless other vegetables grew outside his bedroom window and how the cut lawn would send the scent of wild herbs wafting into the air. He even patted Suparman on the shoulder as he struggled to rise from his chair.

At that moment, D'Onforio seemed only like a man who was chasing experiences that could match the intensity of his memories. And it was only because Suparman could identify with that desire that he did something he should have known better than to do. He took from his pocket the vial with the remaining essential oils that he had saved in case the pain in his legs became unbearable. He placed it into D'Onforio's hand.

"If I may, sir, it appears that your legs suffer from the gravity fluctuations, as do mine. Might I recommend this application? I find it brings relief."

D'Onforio took the vial with puzzlement and read the printing on its label. "*Natural remedy. Massage onto legs as needed.* You find this helps?"

"Very much so, sir."

"Well, I will give it a try. Thank you very much, Suparman." D'Onforio pronounced his name correctly. The officer then flipped down his unigoggle and wove though the tables, making his way out of the dining center with an erratic gait, braces clicking with his every step and a gun slapping against his hip.

• • • • •

BY THE TIME Suparman's shift was over and the dining center had been cleaned, it was late. He made his way through the narrow corridors on Station, stopping only once to glance out a viewport hole. He chose a porthole that looked toward deep space. Lately, he had found the view of Earth too discouraging. As a child on Labicittá, he had memorized all eighty-eight constellation names and their locations. Now he found he could remember only the zodiac and a few others. Nevertheless, the view remained spectacular, a speckled canvas onto which dreams and desires could be sketched.

He said a brief prayer, though it was more a plea, for his family to be together once again, and he continued down the polished aluminum-lined hallways. In the silence, he could hear his footsteps echo on the metallic floors. When he got to his residential section, he had to stoop to get through one of the port doors. Because this was one of the oldest sections of Station, the doors were small, even for someone of Suparman's slight stature. Though the cramped quarters had long been a complaint among those who resided on Station, they had become a feature after the Marsite Occupation, as these narrow doorways were practically impossible for the muscle-bound Marsites to fit through. As a result, though the Marsites had taken control of the rest of Station, they had left much of the older residences untouched. The Marsites all resided on the other side of Station, near the launch bays. From what he had heard, the Marsites' residences had bigger doorways but were crowded with bunks to accommodate all the newly arriving soldiers.

Suparman was quiet as he keyed his way into his rooms. It was late enough that Suha should have put Jati to sleep and been in bed herself, though she probably would not be. The space they shared was not designed for three people, but he made the best out of the situation. The common room combined a living and dining area with a kitchen section. It was connected to two small bedrooms (well, one bedroom and one converted closet) and the bathroom. The whole living space did not add up to ten square meters, which proved a challenge considering how children constantly created clutter.

The common room was quiet, and Suparman noted with approval that the dishes in the kitchen section had been washed. He glanced into Suha's room and saw that she was not in her bed. He immediately became angry. Had she left Jati by himself to go out with her friends? What if he woke up alone? He was too young to be unaccompanied. He would be scared. Could Suha not be trusted with basic responsibilities?

He ventured into the room that he and Jati shared to ensure that his son was safe. And there he saw Jati and Suha lying asleep on the bed that Suparman and Jati shared. His children lay side by side, she with her arm underneath her brother's narrow frame. Apparently, Suha had fallen asleep alongside Jati while putting him to bed. Of course, she would not abandon her brother. She could be trusted with responsibilities that were appropriate to her age. He felt bad that he had assumed the worst about his daughter. She deserved more respect than that.

Staring into the serene faces of his sleeping children, he could not help but be captivated by their beauty. Their smooth skin and fine hair were perfect, and he was again amazed that a flawed person such as himself could be their father. Of course, they were children with the problems children had, be it Jati's constant desire for attention or Suha's rebellious nature, but in their essences, they distilled his and his wife's best qualities. Jati's features still had a baby's softness, and Suha, despite having cut her hair as short as a boy's, was becoming, like her mother, a beautiful woman. In moments like these, his separation from Aanjay, his bride and love, was a physical pain in the pit of his stomach. It was difficult to bear not being able to share experiences like these with her and to have no similar experiences of his baby girl, Rima. What had been lost could never be fully recovered. He would never forgive the Marsites for having separated him and his family.

It had been a long day. Quietly, Suparman changed for bed, fed the fish in the aquarium, and performed ablution. He went out to the main room and took out his prayer rug from underneath the seating unit. He told himself, as he did every time, that this could be his last prayer, so he should perform it as best as he could. He missed attending the Station mosque and being among his brothers, but since the Station Iman had acquiesced to the demands of the Marsites—worse, the Imam seemed to genuinely respect the Marsites—he found he could no longer set foot inside that once-holy place. He hoped Allah would forgive him.

• • • • •

WHATEVER NAÏVE FEELINGS Suparman had had the night before about his perfect children did not survive the next morning's breakfast. Jati was his finicky self, refusing the very food he had relished the day before and whining in that tone of voice that immediately caused a dull throb behind Suparman's temples. Suha was difficult to wake up, and it took her an eternity to get dressed, even though she looked like a beggar by the time she was done. She, too, was reluctant to eat and petulant when he asked her to stop at the dispensary after school to pick up more essential oils for him.

"Why didn't you ask me that yesterday?" Suha complained. "I was over by the dispensary all afternoon yesterday."

Suparman forced a smile, ignoring the twinge in his legs. "Should I tell you again that as a boy I walked—"

"No, not again. I know. Kilometer after kilometer through the hills of Labicittá to school and then to the market in town. And growing up on Station, I have no sense of distance. I think I can give myself that lecture."

"Then please do that small errand for me after school. After you finish your homework, the rest of your time is your own."

Suha said nothing, but her displeasure was obvious as she quickly ate and then stormed out of the rooms without even saying goodbye. At times like this, Suparman was left speechless by her rudeness and at a loss as to how to discipline her. Grounding her only turned their living space into a constant site of hostility. Perhaps this is what came when a girl's only apparent friends were boys, and, worse yet, some of them sons of Marsite administrators. If only Aanjay were here with him. A mother would not have such problems with a daughter.

While Suparman was getting Jati ready to go to the care center, he heard the buzz of an incoming message. He wondered what had gone wrong at work that they would need to contact him this early in the day, but when he looked at the console he saw that the message was not from work. It was from D'Onforio, who had called Suparman to his quarters "at his convenience," which Suparman understood meant "immediately." He shouted at Jati to put on his shoes, then he stopped to take a breath. There was no reason to panic. If something truly bad had happened, security would have come for him. Could he have somehow offended the Marsite officer last night? Could something have gone wrong with the essential oils? How could that be? D'Onforio wouldn't have tried to drink them, would he? But there was so little left in the vial that even if he had drunk the oils, he would get nothing more than a mild stomachache. He cursed himself for being so stupid as to interact voluntarily with a Marsite. Had he learned nothing after all these years of being trapped on Station? Had waiting tables for so long caused him to think of himself as a servant?

He gripped Jati's hand as they left their rooms for the care center. His impulse was to walk as quickly as possible, but what if this were the last walk he ever took with his son? What if he were to be thrown into confinement? He forced himself to slow his pace, to speak with Jati about the day ahead. Jati told him that he hoped to be assigned to the blocks section today or maybe to drawing. They stopped at an Earth-facing port, and he held Jati up so that Jati could look down to the planet below. There was a great deal of cloud cover today.

Jati said, "Look, that one is coffee foam." He pointed toward the surface.

Indeed, there was a large squall cluster visible through the port. Cloud formations folded in on themselves, looking like the foamed soy milk Jati described. There would be rain in Australia today.

"Perhaps a giant cup of coffee lies below it," he said, smiling at Jati as he lowered his son to the ground.

"That cup would be as big as all of Station," Jati replied, extending his arms to illustrate his point.

"Oh, much bigger than that. Someday, we will return to Earth, and you will be amazed at how much room there is on the planet."

"When we go down, will Mother and Rima come up to Station?"

"No, then we will all be together. I can't say when that will be or if it will be on Earth or on Station, but I want you to know we will all be together again." Suparman could feel his voice start to tremble, but Jati did not seem to notice.

"Okay," Jati said, and he started walking again. He was unaffected by Suparman's words, and Suparman wasn't sure whether to admire his son's adaptability or lament his lack of attachment to the Earth and to the rest of his family.

After he dropped Jati off at the care center, lingering longer than usual to say goodbye, Suparman quickly made his way toward the Marsite residences. To get there, he had to pass through the chaos of the transfer section. An enormous stream of materials for the Mars colonization was being sent up the Cord on a seemingly constant schedule. Marsites unloaded materials and placed them on small slideboards that could maneuver through the narrow passageways of Station. Then the materials were reloaded onto the Mars-bound ships in the launch bays.

Of course, robots could have done most of this labor, but antipathy to robots was a founding principle of the Marsites. They refused to use robots or to even allow any onto Station. "By our own hands or not at all," as the slogan went. As a result, there was an unending wave of piled-high boxes and metal containers passing through the hallways, pushed by Marsites with those three-part collapsible sticks. It reminded Suparman of the pictures he had seen in a history text of the men who moved boats of freight down water-filled canals.

After waiting for a gap in the slideboard loads in front of him, Suparman was able to pass through to the Marsite residential sections. D'Onforio resided in the larger of the two areas, where the men were quartered. The smaller number of female Marsites lived in an adjacent but separate location. He showed his pass to a guard, who checked him in on a console and gave him instructions on how to find D'Onforio's room. Suparman nodded and aimed to appear grateful before making his way down the wide hallways. He was surprised by how loud it was here. The voices of men shouting, or perhaps arguing, echoed throughout the chamber. At one point, he took a glance into one of the rooms and was shocked to see that it was lined wall-to-wall and floor-to-ceiling with bunk beds. He couldn't imagine how the Marsites were able to live in such tight quarters. That, perhaps, might explain the occasional gunplay.

D'Onforio's residence was located at the end of a long corridor. As Suparman approached it, he felt himself becoming nervous. He had to remain in control. He could not show that he was afraid. Marsites only had contempt for fear. Taking a deep breath, he swept his hand across the indicator. After a brief pause, the door slid open and Suparman found himself staring into the most sumptuous residence he had ever seen on Station. It was arranged as a large great room, with a bedroom, dining area and kitchen all seemingly blended together as if a designer had organized it. And the furnishings were the most luxurious he had seen outside of a vidocumentary from when he lived on Earth. There were plush sofas, wall hangings made from expensive fabrics and decorative sculptures. The astonishing array of colors shocked him, as he had become accustomed to far more spartan styles borne out of deprivation. And guns were everywhere, mounted on the walls, strewn on the table. One even lay near the entrance at his feet.

"Well, don't just stand there. Come in," D'Onforio's voice called from the far side of the room.

Suparman stepped inside and tried not to stare as the door slid closed behind him. D'Onforio approached, and for a second, Suparman feared the officer was going to punch him, but instead he reached out and eagerly grabbed Suparman's wrist.

"Welcome. Or what is it you say up here? 'Take my hand, brother.'"

"Safe," Suparman replied, though he felt anything but safe at this moment.

D'Onforio relaxed his grip and led Suparman over to one of the sofas, gesturing for Suparman to sit next to an overstuffed pillow. Then the officer grabbed a screen from an end table and took a seat on a chair across from him.

"Well, I suppose you're wondering why I asked you here?"

"Yes, sir. But I am very client-centered, and I understand the needs of today's highly competitive marketplace."

"I'm sure. Well, Suparman, last night I had one of the best night's sleep I have had since arriving on Station. That oil you gave me worked miracles. My legs haven't felt better since I was on Earth."

So that was why he had been called here! He couldn't help but breathe a sigh of relief. "It is quite an impactful formulation."

"That it is. That it is." D'Onforio began scrolling through the screen in his lap. "But I have a question as to how it is that after living here on Station for years now, in more or less constant pain, I finally am given relief, not by any of the Station physicians, but by a waiter. Hm?" D'Onforio looked up into Suparman's eyes.

"I…I seek to maximize customer satisfaction," Suparman replied, looking down.

"Stop talking like you're an idiot. I expect that an individual with, what does it say here…?" D'Onforio swiped at the screen again. "…a certificate degree in Anglophone poetry, yes? Such an individual can probably do better than babble in Business English."

Suparman wished he could see what information D'Onforio was looking at. His personnel records were probably available to any Marsite officer.

"We are required to use certain language in my position."

"Well, you're not at work now. Talk like a person. Tell me what was in that medicine you gave me."

Suparman paused briefly, then described the essential oils. Though he did not know a great deal about their chemical makeup, he knew something of their origins within varieties of tropical plants. They were originally brought up to Station for their aromatic qualities. It was only by accident that their usefulness in mitigating the effects of full-gravity deprivation was discovered.

"But there is no published scientific research on their use in orbit," Suparman explained. "That is why the Station physicians do not know of them."

"Well, why didn't you tell them about it?"

"One in my position does not…tell…physicians what to do."

"It's ridiculous," D'Onforio said, jabbing at the screen in front of him. "Here you are with one, two, three different degrees…"

Suparman actually had four degrees, but he stayed silent.

"…and you're serving glorified dog food every night of the week. Meanwhile, every day they send more muscle-bound dolts up the Cord, even though this place is worse than a fraternity house during a rush week. That's not the way it is supposed to be. Mars needs the best and the brightest individuals if it is going to succeed. Instead, we've got room after room of the most obnoxious risk-takers I've ever seen."

D'Onforio paused, and Suparman sensed that silence was not what was required.

"It is…your project… That is, it is the next step for humanity. You do us all a great service." The words almost gagged him as he said them, though he had heard similar statements often enough in required training sessions and various public announcements.

"Is that what you think? Is that what you really think?"

Suparman nodded. He felt the sweat as it began to form on his brow.

D'Onforio continued. "Well, if that is so, then I have a proposition for you. Would you be interested in joining the colonization project? I'm not saying this just because you helped my legs, though I am grateful. And I can't promise that my word alone would be enough to get you accepted, but I do carry some weight with the authorities. It would be good for the project to have more people like you with some actual experience living in orbit. And, ironically, your time waiting tables has probably given you some good training in putting up with all the mushbrains who now get to lay claim to being Marsites. Now, I know that in the past some of our leadership has been, let's say, insensitive in their dealings with your people. But as we head into such an important per—well, we need better relations. Your involvement would be good from many angles."

He paused, and the silence between them was thick. D'Onforio leaned closer to him and continued.

"I don't have to tell you that your efforts would be historic. It's not just a rhetorical flourish in speeches; the colonization of Mars *is* the future. This will be your chance to shape history, to write humanity's next act."

"I… It is a great honor, what you are saying. But…I have a family."

"Ah, a family. I should have known." D'Onforio tossed the screen aside, and it automatically rolled up into a tube. He stood up from the seat and began pacing in front of Superman.

"I will make one last appeal, so listen carefully. Earth is finished. Do you follow the news from the planet? Collapsed ice shelves, uncontrollable climate change, famines that cease even to be notable anymore. It is only going to get worse. Mars isn't simply humanity's next step. It is our only step. So if your concern is really about your family, you won't want to join them down on a dying planet; you will want them to join you on Mars. Once we establish a beachhead and show that Mars can be made habitable, the real battle will be to keep the masses on Earth from joining us. Mars will be for those of us who are not afraid to do great things. Superman, this is your chance to also be a superman."

D'Onforio had paced while speaking, gesturing broadly, before stopping at the crescendo of his monologue at the center of the room where the overhead light shone down on him like a spotlight. Superman could not help but think that he was imitating one of the actors that had performed in his plays.

"I thank you…" He had to choose his words carefully. "And I am honored by your consideration, but I fear you greatly overestimate my skills. My training is all in orbital medicine and nutrition. The skills required for your heroic colonization of Mars far exceed my abilities. I have learned to serve on Station. My knowledge is bound to this place no less than Station itself is tethered to the planet. There are others far more deserving of your attention."

He paused and looked directly into D'Onforio's eyes. The officer stared back at him, and it was all Superman could do not to begin shaking.

"Why don't you sleep on it?" D'Onforio suggested slowly. "I'm still not sure I'd be able to get around the bureaucratic hoops to make a staffing change at this point. But this offer won't be made twice. I suspect you undersell yourself, Suparman. Be careful or you'll be waiting tables the rest of your days."

Suparman nodded in what he hoped was a thoughtful and considered way.

"I don't have to tell you," D'Onforio said, picking up the screen and unrolling it, "that our conversation has been strictly private. Your discretion is required."

"Of course, sir." Suparman waited for what D'Onforio might say next, but the officer's attention had already been drawn to something on the screen. "Is there anything else, sir?"

"No, that is all. You're dismissed. But if you could try to secure more of those tomatoes for me for tonight, I would appreciate it."

"Of course, sir. I will make sure of it."

He bowed his head slightly as he rose and backed toward the door, waiting to see if D'Onforio might have an additional request. When D'Onforio turned his back on him to rise from the couch, Suparman moved quickly, reaching down to the ground then straightening up. D'Onforio did not turn back toward him, so Suparman stepped out into the hallway.

When the doors slid shut behind him, he was alone, and his body began shaking so much he had to lean against a wall to support himself. When he had stopped shaking visibly, he went back to the checkpoint and showed his pass again to the guard, sweat building on his brow. He could not relax until he passed through the gauntlet of the transfer section and back through a narrow doorway into his own residential section. He wouldn't have time before work to go back to his rooms, but he just wanted a momentary interlude from the Marsites and all that they represented.

He found a nook where he could sit on the floor and contemplate what had happened. In his mind, he had envisioned so many worse outcomes (being thrown in confinement, losing his position, having his children taken away from him) that it was hard to believe he was okay. With a little space, he could even appreciate the irony of the whole situation. As a young man, he had actually been very interested in Mars. This was long before the Marsites, long before Mars was seen as an escape from Earth. Back then, Mars was simply one interesting option for ways in which Station could be used. He had spent many an evening sipping coffee with fellow university students in Labicittá and debating the merits of solar energy vs. astronomy vs. planetary exploration. At the time, he had been quite a proponent of colonizing Mars. After the first successful Mars landings, a permanent settlement seemed the logical next step. Such an endeavor was much more feasible now that ships could be launched from Station without the expense and environmental damage of launching rockets through the Earth's atmosphere.

Now, he looked back on those arguments with the same sense of embarrassment with which he viewed his wardrobe from that period. He was so naïve then, so eager to prove himself, so driven to get up the Cord to Station. It was his mother's wish for him and her mother's before that. They had done so much to ensure that those who had made Labicittá their home would have an opportunity on Station. Suparman's success was to be as much a vindication of their efforts as his own. Of course, that was all before he had met Aanjay and before they had had a family. Such things change a man, give him new responsibilities and a greater capacity for appreciation.

Though all the excuses he offered D'Onforio had merit, even if there were no impediments to his joining the colonization of Mars, he would never pursue such a fool's errand now. To live out one's days on a remote planet outpost with strangers would be a life not worth living. What would he not do to be with his whole family, simply walking along a beach or sitting down to a meal together? Mars could hold no greater pleasure.

In his head, he began composing a message rejecting D'Onforio's offer. "While honored by your consideration, I regret that I would not prove worthy of your confidence."

. . . . .

IT WAS A busy shift at work. Marsite officers streamed in throughout the afternoon and evening with barely a respite. Most days, Suparman had been able to use his own dinner break to pick up Jati at the care center, but today was so busy that he had to message Suha to pick up her brother and bring him home. He didn't even get to eat dinner himself as he tried to stay ahead of the steady, hungry wave that threatened to sweep over the dining center. His legs pulsed with pain.

At one point, he served D'Onforio, who was eating with one of the few female Marsite officers. Neither man gave any indication of their conversation earlier in the day. Suparman served the tomato dish that D'Onforio had requested, and the officer accepted it without comment. He seemed very engaged with his dining companion, a short though notably muscular woman whose hair was shaved off half her head in what was apparently a new style on Earth. The shaved side revealed a large scar running the length of the woman's scalp. She also appeared to be Chinese, which was unusual since China was not part of the original consortium of countries that had created Station. China's own attempts to create a space elevator had thus far failed to come to fruition. There was only a handful of Chinese nationals among the range of peoples on Station.

Suparman resisted the urge to stare, though he tried to eavesdrop on their conversation. He could tell that D'Onforio and this new officer—he heard D'Onforio refer to her as Jia Chiang—knew each other well. He could also tell that she was a cautious person. Any time Suparman glanced in her direction, her eyes met his, and her end of the conversation trailed off whenever he approached the table. D'Onforio was less discrete. A couple of times he spoke heatedly about an "announcement" and the "trouble it was bound to cause," as if anyone left on Station wasn't aware of the upcoming manned launch. D'Onforio and his companion ate and then departed without incident.

Finally, after a mountain of meals had been served, the dining center closed, though it still took hours to clean up and prepare for the next day. By the end, even the younger men and women on the staff were exhausted. It was all Suparman could do to stay on his feet. His legs throbbed as if he could feel the blood coursing through his veins. Slowly, he made his way back to his rooms. It was late, and the hallways were deserted. He realized that he hadn't informed Suha he would be gone so long. He had been too busy even to think about the children.

When he arrived at his rooms, he had no idea what to expect. He found Suha asleep at the dining table, propped up in front of the wall screen, a chessboard as her pillow. He looked into his bedroom and saw that Jati was also asleep. The kitchen area was clean, and the evening's dishes had been washed. He walked to the table and stood over Suha. She had been doing her astronomy homework, though she had also been screening a show and doodling in a sketchbook at the same time. And then, on the counter next to the table, he saw a vial of essential oils. He was so grateful that Suha had remembered to pick it up that he could have broken into tears.

He went into his bedroom and quickly began to undress for bed. As he dropped his clothes to the floor, there was a loud clatter that made him jump in panic. But silence followed, and the children did not stir. How could he be so stupid? Suparman gingerly picked up his clothing and pulled out from his pants pocket the gun he had taken from D'Onforio's room earlier and could only hope that D'Onforio would not miss. The whole day he had worried that someone would notice the bulge in his side pocket, but he was so tired that he had briefly forgotten about it.

If he were to take such risks, he would have to be more careful, regardless of how busy or tired he was. The Resistance was in such an embryonic stage that one foolish mistake could end it all. But there was important work to be done, and he would no longer stand to one side and watch the Marsites take away all to which he had devoted himself. His family deserved better. They all did.

Suparman placed the gun in a drawer of clothing. Tomorrow he would need to take it out of his rooms and add it to the steadily growing cache that the Resistance was accumulating in hopes of one day throwing off the yoke of the Marsites. The Resistance was small, but it was growing stronger and better equipped. This would be one contribution he could make, and he was prepared to make more.

Quietly, he finished undressing and applied the oils. Almost instantly, there was a soothing sensation. It was the first physical relief he had felt all day. He stared into the next room at his daughter for a minute before he would have to wake her and walk her over to her bed. She had the profile of her mother, but he had to admit, her personality took after his. He, too, could be stubborn, though he had learned over the years to wear a mask of acquiescence. But then, in other ways, Suha was her own person, as much a mystery to him as a distant galaxy.

He and Aanjay had thought they were providing their children with such opportunity when they had first come to Station. It had been a time of great anticipation and excitement, a time when Station was at the forefront of scientific advances, rather than a transfer station to Mars. But now, with a planet in crisis and Station under occupation, he feared for his children's future.

When Suparman finished applying the oils, he fed the fish and watched them snap at the flakes on the surface of the water. He took pleasure in his aquarium, though it now felt like a luxury he did not think he deserved. Still, when he looked through the glass, he was reminded of the fish he saw as a child while he swam in the coves along the coast of Labicittá. As a boy, he found the fish an annoyance when they tickled his feet as he swam. But now he appreciated them in ways that a child could not. He watched them glide through the tank, seeming to take pleasure in the fluidity of their movements. For all he knew, they were as content here as they would have been in the ocean water below. Perhaps they couldn't tell the difference. But he could.

He was tired and needed to sleep. He gently woke Suha from the table and guided his daughter to her bed. Though she walked under her own power, it didn't seem as if she ever woke up. Then he went to his own room and nudged his son over before resting a grateful body next to him. As he descended into sleep, he was briefly aware that he had forgotten to pray.

Suha

At first, Suha thought she had nailed it. Her launch from the ledge was solid, and she caromed off the view window right into the first backflip. But midway through the second flip, she lost momentum, and she could feel the pull of the dead zone. She tried to dolphin kick back into the no-grav, even though she knew it wouldn't help. Once gravity had you, you were just so much meat. Now she was dead zoned, floating and staring up at the boys on the ledge who had told her she couldn't do the trick.

"Suha, you stupid grommet," Darian shouted at her. "I told you the second flip was too much."

"I'll get it next time," she said, trying to sound like it didn't matter. "Just throw me the cord."

The boys ignored her. Darian pushed off the ledge and sunk into the low-grav over by the loading bay. Uxío and Shi-Lu followed, dropping out of view. She wanted to complain, but she knew the rules. If you dead zoned, you had to wait until the end of the run to get pulled out. She guessed they already had been floating for about fifteen minutes. It would be at least another ten before they started feeling sick from the gravity changes and would have to leave. If they stopped to get her now, no one would get a good run in, so she couldn't blame them for ignoring her. She would have done the same.

There was nothing for her to do but hover and stare at the abandoned dock, or even worse, gaze back at the awful Earth through the view window. Suha still couldn't figure out why the dock worked the way it did. Except for the no-grav rubber room at the rec center that the Marsites had closed down, all of Station was set up to simulate Earth gravity. This dock had been abandoned as long as Suha could remember, and it shouldn't even have been sucking up atmosphere. But the whole thing was crocked up, full-grav on the ledge, no-grav in a couple sections, low-grav in others, and a dead zone that pulled you in if you got too close and kept you floating like one of those tomatoes growing in a jar of water.

Suha's stomach churned at the thought of food. She tried to lie still to fight off the nausea and reran the trick in her head to see if she could figure out where she had gone wrong. She hardly noticed that time had passed. When she looked back at the boys, she saw Shi-Lu take a swan dive off the ledge. He started falling in full-grav, and it looked like he was going to smash his skull on the floor below. But then he hit the low-grav, and it slowed him down. His momentum kept him moving through the no-grav and he flipped before he hit the floor so that he was able to get his feet under him, then he pushed up against the surface, traveling through the different gravity levels until he got close enough to the ledge to grab the underside. It was a pretty sick trick, but Suha had already done it days ago.

Still, she shouted Shi-Lu's name and gave him a fist-up.

"Shi-Lu," she yelled. "That was diamondz."

Darian was standing on the ledge, and he put a hand down to haul Shi-Lu up. Uxío sat next to them with his head between his legs.

"Ready to puke yet?" Darian called over to her.

"I'm light," Suha lied. "I could sleep here."

"Right," Uxío scoffed. "I'm about to launch my lunch."

Darian turned away from her, like the pussbrain he could be. Suha couldn't understand why so many girls in her class thought he was cute.

Actually, she couldn't understand why girls thought any boys were cute. They were pretty gross, even if they were her friends. Finally, after delaying as long as he could, Darian took the polypro cord that was attached to the ledge and reeled it out to the center of the dead zone so that Suha could grab it.

"Let me try one more time before we leave," Suha said as she was pulled back in. When she shifted out of the dead zone into the low-grav, she felt her body lurch.

"You missed Shi-Lu's body-grind up against the glass," Darian said as he tugged on the cord. "It was gnar enough."

Suha glanced over at Shi-Lu, but he looked down, trying not to smile. The body-grind wasn't an easy trick. When Suha approached the deck, she could feel the shift to full-grav. Her body got heavy, and her stomach sank. Darian grabbed her arm and yanked her up.

"Let's go already." Uxío didn't even bother to lift up his head.

"One more time and then *bisa pulang*." Suha didn't care about the nausea. She knew she could do the trick if she started to twist into the flip sooner.

"Speak English." Darian scoffed. "You're just going to complain all day if we don't let you, aren't you?"

Suha said nothing, and then Darian answered his own question. "You are. Okay, one chance."

Darian picked up the cord and wound it up as he stood back next to Shi-Lu. Suha nudged Uxío with her foot, and he slid toward the wall. Then she took a breath and looked down at the dock. It was just metal and view windows like the rest of Station. She had to see past what was there to keep her mind on the gravity currents. It had taken them weeks to map it out, to remember where low-grav shifted into no-grav, to know how to let the dead zone tug you where you wanted to go without getting trapped by it. When a trick worked, you flew like you were out of your body, like you were part of space and not just staring out at it like a fish in a bowl.

Suha spread her arms and launched off the far side of the ledge, bracing for the break out of full-grav. She pushed off hard with her legs, bursting through the bubble into no-grav and soaring across the bay straight toward the viewport. Then she went into a tuck and threw her arms back to spin her legs forward. Her legs came up just in time for her feet to connect with the glass. She pushed up hard and thrust her arms down, twisting her body up into the low-grav. The low-grav would pull her down toward the dead zone, so she had to hope she had enough momentum. If she had positioned herself right, the pull of the dead zone would send her back toward the ledge. She closed her eyes and tucked into the first flip, feeling nothing but spin. She flipped again, only opening her eyes when she felt the turn end, and she found herself staring up at the boys on the ledge. Shi-Lu whistled. Darian clapped. Even Uxío looked up.

"Suha, you're a flipping girl." Darian smiled and leaned down to grab her arm. He pulled hard and jerked her up onto the ledge.

"Can we go now? She can be the flipping queen if she wants." Uxío stood and started walking toward the port door.

Suha wanted to smile, but the nausea was getting stronger. She leaned against the wall for balance and followed Uxío. She felt the room spinning, but she knew it would pass after they left the dock and rehydrated with some ginger water. But the feeling of flying, that would be with her all day long.

. . . . .

SUHA WAS STILL in a great mood when she got back to her rooms. But when she walked in and heard the voice of her father cut through the silence, she realized it was time for prayers. She saw her father on his rug. He hated to be disturbed then, so she slipped into her room and put in her buds.

A double! She was still amazed that she had done it. Just a little while ago, it was *sem medo* just to do a single flip; now she had a double to her name. No wonder the boys didn't have much to say. She didn't think they'd be able to touch that.

She had schoolwork to finish for tomorrow, but it could wait. Shi-Lu had upped a new song for her to listen to. Well, not "new" exactly. Who knew what was new anymore? Now that the lockdown was measured in years instead of months, Earth might as well be in another solar system. By the time the latest song made it up the Cord, it wasn't the latest song anymore. She had no idea what music people were actually listening to down on the planet. If she were to go down to Labicittá again, she wouldn't even feel like part of her own generation anymore. Although since the announcement, it didn't look like she had to worry about that problem.

It took forever to down the song from Shi-Lu, and then when she plugged into the wall console and listened to it, it sucked, like she thought it would. Why did Shi-Lu keep asking her to listen to music she hated? She couldn't remember the last time she had heard a good song from Earth. Or maybe it was a good song. Shi-Lu liked it, so probably everyone else in her class did too. Why couldn't she be like everyone else and be interested in the things they thought were important? She didn't care about music from Earth or which boys the girls in her class thought looked like movie stars from Earth.

Suha took the buds out of her ears and flopped down in her bed, wishing for the millionth time that she had a porthole in her ceiling so she could see out into space. Darian said the commander had one in his bathroom, but she didn't think she'd ever get a chance to see where the commander went to shit, so she'd probably never know. Of course, Darian was probably making the whole thing up. He lied a lot. Suha wasn't sure she even liked hanging out with him. Her father would have liked it if she just hung out with a bunch of quiet girls who wore head-scarves. But Suha didn't really belong anywhere, and she knew it.

There was a tapping on her door, and she told her father to come in (it had to be her father, since Jati never knocked before bursting into her room).

"Ah, you are here. Jati said you had arrived, but you were so quiet I didn't notice."

"I didn't want to bother you. You know I hate it when people bother other people. Did you want something?"

Her father paused. Suha thought the lines around his eyes were getting deeper. "I need to ask you to watch Jati tonight. I was called into work unexpectedly, for a meeting."

"On your only day off?"

"Such things happen." Her father walked over and leaned over her. "I would appreciate it, *putri saya.*" He gave her a hug and a kiss on the forehead. Ever since the announcement, her father felt that she and Jati needed lots of hugs and reassurance.

"Va bene," she said. "But tomorrow I really need to go over to Info Tech and get someone to diag our console. It's taking so long to down the Earth feed, it would be faster to just Jack-and-the-beanstalk it down the Cord."

"Yes, that's fine. I... Yes, it is as if we are dealing with an ogre who would grind our bones..."

Her father trailed off and started getting choked up. Shit. She didn't mean to set him off, but almost everything upset him since the announcement. The day it happened was the first time she had ever seen him cry. Now he teared up practically every time he took a deep breath. He hugged her again, and it was all she could do not to tell him that the announcement didn't really matter. Sure, like everyone else, she had been shocked at first to hear she would likely never be able to leave Station. Of course, there had been all kinds of rumors that something was wrong once some people who went down the Cord started dying, but Suha wouldn't have guessed that the problem was spending too much time in space. But despite the plates throughout Station that made it feel like Earth gravity, bodies weren't completely fooled. Bodies reacted as if they had all been in zero gravity during the lockdown years. The weightlessness disease was affecting people, according to the doctors who had spoken during the announcement, and the lockdown was like a giant experiment to see how long people could spend in space. Apparently, not as long as they had.

But now that Suha had gotten over the announcement, she realized that it didn't really matter to her. So what if she could never go down to Earth again? She hated Earth. But telling her father that would only upset him more. Now that it looked like they would never see Labicittá again, it was the only thing he thought about.

"*Ayah*, it's okay," she said when her father stood and wiped his eyes.

"It's not okay," her father said, straightening himself up and inhaling deeply. "But it will be. I swear it to you."

· · · · ·

INFO TECH TURNED out to be a timeburn. She had hoped she would get bumped up the queue if she went and griped in person, but it was just a headbang. They said, "Crucial operations have led to restrictions in recreational bandwidth," which meant the Marsites were hogging the processors and screw you. According to her father, before the Marsites arrived, everyone had rollout screens like down on Labicittá, and Station wasn't dependent on ancient built-in wall screens. But the rollouts were one of the first things the Marsites restricted, along with open meetings, travel up and down the Cord and basically anything else that might be fun. What was next, oxygen?

Suha didn't have to be back to her rooms until later, so she decided to go over to the loading bays. There was usually something interesting to see there, and with all the freight being moved around, you never knew what might fall off a container. She had scored a cool torque inducer that way once. But Marsites didn't like it when you just hung around, so when she got to the bays, she had to make it look like she had a purpose.

The bays were packed, as usual. Slideboards were backed up near the entrance to the Cord, and the hallways were jammed with shipments waiting to squeeze through. There was a big bottleneck because someone had packed a slideboard too high and it wouldn't clear the low ceilings. Now it had to be unpacked by hand while everyone else waited. One Marsite was up near the top of the stack, hacking away at the fastener ropes with a huge blade. Away from the action, a group of musclehead haulers were leaning against their container boxes, tapping their power sticks against the metal boxes in rhythm. They didn't sound too bad, and one of them had even broken his stick down into three parts to triple the effect. Now, that was *érdekes*! It sounded amazing.

Suddenly, there was a crash, and everyone looked over to see that the shipment causing the jam had toppled over. One of the Marsites screamed that he was trapped. All the haulers flipped down their unigoggles and ran toward the accident. Suha had to jump out of the way to not get trampled. She tried to figure out what had happened, but she couldn't see where the boxes had fallen. All she could hear was shouting. When she heard someone scream "get back, motherfuckers," she knew it wasn't a good time to be hanging around the Marsites.

As Suha slipped down the hallway, she saw one of the power sticks that a hauler had left on the ground. She quickly glanced around to see if anyone was paying attention. No one was, so she broke the stick down into its three parts and shoved it into her pant leg. It fit, but she couldn't quite bend her knee, so she had to shuffle down the hallway awkwardly. She hoped she wouldn't bump into anyone.

But as soon as she rounded the corner, a whole crowd of Marsites came running with flashing-red unigoggles beaming in front of their faces. She pressed herself up against the wall and thought she had better seem useful.

"That way! That way!" she said, gesturing. "I think someone is trapped!"

The Marsites ignored her as they passed by, which was all she wanted anyway. She moved away from the accident, looking like she was limping with the power stick jabbing into her ribs. There was no way she'd be able to get back to her rooms like this. She needed to find a way to hide the stick, or she would have to ditch it.

The boys would be amazed to see her with a power stick. She had heard one of these things could push five hundred kilos. She wondered if Darian would be able to get a slideboard, since he lived in the Marsite section. If they had both, they could move just about anything. Not that they really had anything to move, but it would be *unglaublich*.

Suha darted into a side hallway and saw a maintenance room. She twisted the port door and lucked out. It was unlocked. She flipped on the light, peeked around to make sure it was empty, and stepped inside, closing the door behind her. Then she took the power stick out, just to try and push some things around with it. When she got it in her hands and turned it on, she could feel it pulsate. That must be why it sounded so distinct when the Marsites were tapping it. It wasn't just metal on metal, it was as if the stick vibrated whatever surface it hit. There was a rack of pipes stacked up against the wall of the room. Suha stepped over to it and started tapping on the metal. The stick thumped and pulsed, and the pipes echoed back. She broke the stick down and tried to play the rhythm she had heard the Marsite play before, but she couldn't move all three sections at once the way he did. But she could bang out a beat at least.

"That the best you can do?" a voice sounded from behind her.

Suha dropped the stick and spun around. She peered into the corner of the room where the sound had come from and saw a Marsite sitting on the floor behind a crate. Where did he come from? He had his unigoggle flipped up and a bottle of something next to him on the floor.

Suha turned to run, but she heard another group of Marsites outside in the hallway. She was trapped.

"I've heard better rhythm in a busted hydraulic drill ass-deep in bedrock," the Marsite said. "And that sounds like a recycling chute at an aluminum factory." The Marsite raised his bottle to his lips. Suha tried to figure out where his accent was from, but she could never tell people from Earth apart. He was just another big guy with a buzz cut.

"Girl, what are you doing here?"

"There was an accident outside. One of the containers fell over. I think someone might be hurt."

"Well, that explains why you aren't out there, but why are you in here?"

"Well, why are you in here?" she said without thinking.

The Marsite laughed. He took another sip. "Fair enough. Fair enough. There ain't too many places to hide out on this Habitrail. Here, check this out." The Marsite stood up awkwardly. Suha backed toward the door.

"Relax," he said. "I'm just going to show you how it's done."

The Marsite picked up the power stick and took off his unigoggle. He started pounding away on the pipes with all three sections of the stick, varying the patterns until it sounded like a whole percussion section was at work. Each time the stick struck a pipe, the metal seemed to shimmer. It was something to hear and see, and for a minute, Suha forgot to be scared.

"Wow!" she said when the Marsite stopped.

He smiled then stumbled. "Maybe I'll front the first band on Mars, or maybe the only band on Mars." He offered the stick to her. "But that's me. You're going to need to practice."

She didn't take the stick, and she wasn't sure what to do. She could tell the Marsite was drunk, but he didn't seem like a threat. But how could she know what he would do?

"I'm not a musician," she said, keeping her hands at her sides.

"Neither am I. Not anymore at least. Who knows what I am?" He put the stick on the ground and went back to the bottle. He took a sip and stared back at Suha.

"I'm sorry for you, for all of you. The announcement, I mean. You know, no one knew, nobody thought..."

"Whatever," Suha said. "I hate the Earth. I don't care."

"Yeah, I guess I hate it, too. But, still, you can't ever go back now. At least that's what the doctors are saying what with all the years you all spent in artificial gravity. That don't bother you?"

"Shit, no. Gravity is overrated. And it's not like you're ever going back either. I mean, once you get to Mars and all."

"That's right. That's right. It won't be long now. Won't be long." He took another draw from the bottle, and then he reached down and pulled something out of a box. "Here, take this. Consider it a consolation prize."

Suha saw that it was one of the new VRCams. She took it in her hands and turned it over. It was top-of-the-line. She'd read about them, but she'd never seen one. It was as light as a pair of glasses. She couldn't even figure out where the works were. But she'd read the specs. Twen-

ty-four hours of recording on a single charge, on-the-fly intuitive editing with brain wave sync. It was seriously *doux*, and she wanted it.

She looked at the Marsite. Now was the part where he asked her
to come over and thank him. She knew what to expect. They'd all been
warned by their parents. Don't let them get you alone. Don't let them
touch you. She'd already messed up just being here. She wondered if
she could just grab the glasses and run. Would he be able to catch her?

"Just take them," he said. "Just go."

She didn't have to be told twice. She turned to leave, but he
grabbed her arm. She froze.

"Put it in a box. And take the power stick, too. Just learn how
to play the damn thing." He placed the VRCam and the stick in a
container and put it in her arms. She looked at him, trying to figure out
why he was doing this.

"Just go." He turned away from her, and she said a quick thanks
before opening the door and exiting into the hallway. She could still
hear a lot of commotion down where the accident had been, so she
quickly walked in the other direction, cradling the box and wondering
what the hell had just happened.

· · · · ·

IT HALF KILLED her to have to wait to use the VRCam until
after her father left for his meeting. She knew he would be all worried
if he saw her with it, and then she would have to explain about the
encounter with the Marsite, which would make him completely *gila*. So
she told Jati to go feed the fish and leave her alone.

But of course the fish tank got boring fast, and Jati soon burst into
her room without knocking.

"What's that?" Jati pointed at the glasses.

She knew she would have to let Jati in on the secret, and the only
way to keep him quiet was a bribe, so she told him how the glasses
worked and gave him the power stick to play with.

It turned out that he got how to use the stick right away. For a
little kid, he had a great sense of rhythm, and he figured out how to use
the three sections at once without even having to have it explained to

him. He just started tapping away on the floor, walls, his shoes, playing with the different resonances while the stick buzzed in his hands. Suha strapped on the VRCam and recorded him banging on their table, then testing the stick on all the kitchen utensils. He started to bang on the aquarium, which made the fish freak out and dart in all directions. Suha made him stop. Their father would be all *sinting* if anything happened to his fish.

The VRCam looked a little like a unigoggle, though it covered both eyes and the lenses were larger than what the Marsites wore. But all she had to do was think a command and the glasses did it. Think zoom, they zoomed. Think slo-mo, it all slowed down. She still couldn't figure out how the intuitive editing worked. All she had to do was think of two clips together and they would get spliced. She could even edit while filming, which was amazing though it made her head hurt after a while.

She shot footage of Jati drumming away from every imaginable angle and distance, and the whole sequence blended together, almost seeming to edit itself. By the time Jati got tired of the sticks, it was way past his bedtime. Suha swore him to secrecy and got him to lie down. She stayed in her bed playing with lighting features of the VRCam, shooting her hand in X-ray, translucent and ultraviolet. But eventually she got tired, too, so she tipped her bed away from the wall and opened up her secret hiding place, a section of the wallboard that she had carefully loosened so that she could get to the panel opening behind it. It was where she had kept her old paper diary and toys she didn't want to share with Jati. Now she placed the VRCam and the collapsed power stick into it and repositioned the bed. She had just settled down to sleep when she heard her father get back. He came into her room to check on her, and she pretended to be asleep. He kissed her cheek, and she could feel tears on his face.

· · · · ·

DARIEN LAUGHED WHEN he saw her wearing the VRCam. "What are you? A cyborg or a console?"

The VRCam was a little big, she supposed. But she wasn't wearing it for fashion. She shouldn't have been surprised that Darian didn't get it. He wasn't into anything that wasn't his idea first.

Suha had thought twice about bringing the glasses to the dock with the dead zone. After all, she wasn't sure what would happen if people knew she had the VRCam. It was a gift and all, but it wasn't like she could prove that. She didn't even know the name of the Marsite who had given it to her. She didn't even know if he was supposed to have it. Now that she thought about it, he had probably stolen it off a shipment.

But what good was having this amazing technology if she didn't use it, and what place would be better to record than this dock? That meant she had to let the boys in on her find. She had thought they would all want to use it, and she was surprised that they weren't really interested. That was fine with her. They all wanted to master the double flip now that she had been able to do it, and they left her alone to float in the no-grav section and record. She could tell the raw footage was amazing even as she was shooting it. The automatic stabilizers made all the flips and turns seem smooth, and somehow, though Suha wasn't quite sure how, the footage even captured the feeling of weightlessness. When she pushed off the ledge toward the viewport, it looked and felt like she was launching herself into deep space. She shot Shi-Lu as he sprang up from full-grav to low-grav, and the cam automatically pulled back, like it had known what to expect.

"Hey, Suha," shouted Uxío, "get this."

Uxío was standing at the edge of the ledge. When Suha turned so that the glasses were pointing at him, he collapsed as if he had been shot by a gun and fell from the ledge, fast at first until he reached the no-grav and started bobbing in the air. Suha caught his descent and zoomed in when he opened his eyes and had a stupid grin on his face.

"How was that?" he asked.

"Cheeseball," she said with a scoff. Uxío had no coordination, so he needed to be funny to do anything meme worthy. She pushed off toward a viewport and glided over to it. She had already taken a lot of footage of deep space, but she felt herself drawn to it again. Looking out into space through the VRCam, she felt more free, less bound to her body. She didn't care if she was flat where she should be fat and fat where she should be flat. It didn't matter. She looked out in the direction of Mars, and she got the appeal. She was tired of feeling tethered to the Earth. The Cord choked her, made it seem like the only things that mattered happened on the planet, particularly since the announcement. All of a sudden she was supposed to feel all nostalgic for the planet she barely remembered being on. Now that they couldn't leave, all anyone wanted was to get off Station.

But not her. What did Earth have for her? Her main memories were having her mother always worried about her. Worried she played too rough, worried she would get hurt. She remembered one time being at the beach and her mother rushing into the water all the way up to her hijab because she thought Suha had gone too far from shore. It's not that she didn't miss her mother or her little sister. She did. It was her mother, after all, who taught her to read and helped her build her first circuit, but Suha needed space. Not physical space so much as psychic space. Her mother was always trying to get into her head. With her father, as long as she kept her room clean, her head was her own.

And it wasn't like she'd never see her mother again. They could come up the Cord if the Marsites let them, as long as they didn't stay long enough for the weightlessness disease to affect their muscles. But Suha didn't care that she'd been in the artificial weightlessness so long that she could never adapt to the planet again. It looked like all of them who had been on Station since the lockdown would always be here. For her father, who had made getting up to Station his life's goal, life on Labicittá was now the only thing he seemed to care about. To be honest, she had more memories of her mother lecturing her on a console about how to behave than she did of being with her mother on Earth.

If this was where she was going to spend her life, so be it. She didn't care about Earth. She had the whole universe here. What wouldn't most people on Earth give to be where she was now, messing around in semi-weightlessness with this amazing cam?

She turned back toward the boys and recorded them fumbling as they tried to master her routine. Shi-Lu wound up stranded in the dead zone, grasping for the cord to get pulled out.

She could have stayed here all day if the nausea would have let her. But it was coming on, so she kicked off the wall and drifted back toward the ledge. No one else had been able to land the double, though Shi-Lu had been close, and he said he would get it tomorrow. Suha filmed him saying it to keep him honest.

But they came back the next day and the day after that, and he still couldn't land it. Finally, Shi-Lu made Suha do the double again. This time she did it wearing the VRCam, which threw off her balance a little bit, but she still landed the routine. Shi-Lu must have learned something from it because he went next and hit it solid. Suha had filmed him and got some decent shots. She had ideas for some other sequences. She wondered if two of them could do the routine in tandem. Maybe she and Shi-Lu could, if Darian would record it.

But the four of them were never together in the dock again.

· · · · ·

WHAT WOULD YOU call it when lockdown got worse? Really-lockdown? Double-lockdown? According to her father, now that the manned Mars launch was imminent, the Marsites were all on edge, excitable and nervous. Suha didn't get it. They had been planning to send people to Mars the whole time she'd been on Station. After all, that was the whole reason the Marsites took over Labicittá and Station. They'd been flinging unmanned droneships to Mars for as long as she could remember. What was the big deal now that a manned flight was going? It would just mean fewer Marsites on Station, which was fine by her. But now there were guards everywhere, and you needed passes to move around, so a trip to the dock was definitely out, and it was hard to communicate via console with the insane new bandwidth restrictions as well.

With nothing but time to kill, Suha worked a lot on her footage. She was really starting to master the intuitive editing features on the VRCam. She had put together a few pieces, though she didn't really know what to call them. They were mostly just her thoughts accompanied by footage she had shot, mostly in the dock but also elsewhere on Station when she could use the VRCam discretely. They were kind of like things she had written in her old diary, but the footage also had background music courtesy of Jati with the power stick and some old audio. Vidiaries maybe?

She had created one entry that was all about Marsites moving cargo through the hallways, focusing on what assholes they were to each other and especially to non-Marsites. Another was all about Jati and how good he had gotten with the power sticks. The piece she liked the best was shot entirely out of viewports. It showed nothing but stars, and she had added a voice-over about why she didn't care if she could never go down to the planet again. Earth was just a ball cut off from the universe by atmosphere. Up here, things could be seen clearly.

· · · · ·

THE DAY OF the manned launch, all the schools and even the eating halls were closed. It was like an equinox holiday, except that everyone who wasn't "essential" was expected to be in the gathering hall. Suha didn't want to go, but her father insisted they all be there. As she feared, there was just a lot of standing around and listening to Marsite speeches. The hall was packed with people standing in front of the viewports, which was *bodoh* since all the ports in the hall pointed toward Earth and the launch bay was on the other side of Station. She asked her father if she could go look for her friends, but he gave her that "no, and why would you even ask?" look.

Standing in the crowd made her realize how many people smelled weird, but at least a couple of the Marsites made speeches that were unintentionally funny. There was this one old guy with leg braces who jumped around the stage a lot, talking about the "future of humanity" but looking like he could collapse any second. He'd be lucky if he made it to the future of tomorrow. Darian's father also made a little speech about how the Mars mission brought together the smartest people across generations, which didn't quite fit with Darian's inability to solve quadratic equations, but whatever.

But then the microphone was handed to a female Marsite Suha had never seen before, and the universe stopped. At least Suha's universe. The woman was in uniform, and she was really ripped. She had a fierce look with half her head shaved and some serious battle scars on her scalp. And for the first time, Suha realized what the phrase "chiseled features" meant. Suha stared at this half-beautiful and half-terrifying woman, trying to decide which half was which.

"Who's that?" Suha asked her father.

"A colonel. I believe her name is Jia Chiang."

Suha forced herself to not just stare but pay attention to what the woman was saying. Jia Chiang spoke with a clear voice and careful enunciation about the opportunity to start over and how it applied not just to the colonization of Mars but to those who would continue to stay on Station. Is that what they were doing? Starting over? She hadn't thought of it that way before, but the announcement marked a beginning as much as an end. The woman said that even when it seemed like so much had been determined for us, we could choose the meaning of our actions. We could choose what we felt was important. Every one of us. When the woman stopped speaking, she was given the loudest applause of all. But then again, she was the only speaker who even acknowledged that anyone besides Marsites were on Station. Suha stared at her until the woman disappeared off the edge of the stage. Suha had never seen anyone like her before.

Finally, after everyone who could possibly give speeches had given one, they flipped on a screen behind the podium and a view of the launch bay exterior appeared. Suha realized this was all going to be anticlimactic. It was just going to be a ship going to Mars. There must have been a dozen of those a year since she could remember. It wasn't going to look any different just because there were people inside. But a countdown was a countdown, and she joined in with everyone else, shouting her way down to zero and cheering when the ship detached from the station and began to float away.

It wasn't as dramatic as videos she had seen of old-style rockets blasting off from Earth, but that was the point. Taking off from

Station was easier and cheaper, and it did less environmental damage. The exterior lights followed the Mars-bound ship as it drifted further away from Station. It looked like it was moving slowly, but she knew from her astrophysics class that the slingshot release out of Earth's orbit would send the ship flying toward Mars. As it receded into the distance, people started gathering up their things and getting ready to head out. Jati looked like he could use a nap, and he was resting now in their father's arms.

Then the ship exploded.

Suha was looking at the screen when it happened, and she gasped when the bright blast of blue-white light appeared. There was no sound, and the crowd was hushed. Everyone stared at the image, which glowed for an instant, then disappeared. Suddenly, the floor shook. Suha's father grabbed her hand.

"It's just a shock wave," he said. "Don't worry."

Around them, people started screaming. A Marsite officer came up to the microphone, but it had been turned off, and he began shouting at the crowd, saying something Suha couldn't make out. Her father kept hold of her hand and quickly pulled her toward the exit. Then there was a banging sound, and someone near them fell to the ground. People shouted and rushed to get out of the gathering hall.

"Stay with me!" her father yelled. He jerked her arm, pulling her into the mass of people trying to jam their way to the narrow exits. They squeezed into a hallway, leaving behind the screaming and more banging sounds, which she now realized were gunshots. As they ran back through Station, Jati kept asking what happened, but her father said nothing, and neither did Suha. When they reached their rooms, Suha's father shut the door behind him and engaged the dead bolt.

• • • • •

THE THREE OF them huddled in their rooms. At first, they could hear others scurrying for relative safety. But it wasn't like there was any place to hide on Station.

Suha tried to get on the console, but it was just flashing a message to "return to quarters and await notice," which is where they were and what they were awaiting. Suha's father paced around the room. Neither of them wanted to say anything while Jati was with them. He just played with his metal blocks like it was another afternoon. When it seemed clear that nothing was going to happen fast, their father prepared some protein paste and crackers and they all sat around the table, chewing and staring at each other. After two games of chess with her father, both of which Suha won, even that became boring.

"Well, what should we do to occupy ourselves?" her father asked as they finished eating.

"Tell me a story," Jati asked.

"Not a story!" Suha complained.

"Jati, that is an excellent idea," Suha's father said, ignoring her. "Let me tell you a story about when I was a boy."

Suha groaned as her father became nostalgic and began to tell all the old stories about Labicittá. They heard all about growing up near the base of the Cord and about the ocean. Her father got all emo and said how sorry he was that he had never been able to take them fishing. He swore that when they had children, he would find a way to take his grandchildren fishing, like his own grandfather had fished with him. Suha said she wasn't planning on having children and she was a vegan, so she didn't want the children she wouldn't have to kill fish.

Her father ignored her again, and Jati asked to hear about the robot pilot. It was his favorite story, so Suha had no choice but to listen.

"My grandfather had been trained as an engineer, and he repaired old robots during Moore's interregnum. He had also designed a very special automaton. You have never seen such a machine because the Marsites are so opposed to them. My father said he created his robot so he would have company on fishing trips. The robot was designed to be a pilot, but it had also been programmed with an array of ancillary knowledge. It told stories about long ago, and jokes too, though I was too young to understand most of them. When we went out fishing, the pilot would talk the entire time, telling stories that made my father laugh. And the robot was smart. One time my father was telling me about a large skipjack tuna he had caught and the robot cut him off, saying, 'Do not tell fish stories where the people know you; but particularly, don't tell them where they know the fish.' I laughed, and my father cursed and muted the robot."

"Did the robot catch fish?" Jati asked.

"I do not believe so. The robot only ever piloted. But I remember what it said: 'Verily, all is vanity and little worth—save piloting.' That, and the robot did not have legs, so I think fishing would have been difficult for—"

Suha interrupted. "You never told me the robot didn't have legs, and I've heard this story a hundred times."

Her father smiled. "Well, sometimes a story must be told a hundred and one times. No, the robot had a sphere at its base, which allowed it to move well on flat surfaces, but my grandfather always had to lift the robot into his boat."

"But what about that story you told me about the time the robot trapped a burglar? How could it do that without legs?"

"It didn't trap the burglar exactly. It was just following an old instruction that hadn't been updated. This is still a problem with robots today. In fact, it is why my grandmother never allowed the robot—"

Suddenly, a loud siren sounded and the lights in the room went out. Dim emergency bulbs snapped on, and the cabinet with the oxygen tanks automatically sprung open.

"What's happening?" Jati screamed.

Suha's father moved quickly. He grabbed a tank and a mask and brought it over to Jati.

"Jati, listen to me. There is an emergency, and the oxygen supply has been interrupted. I do not know what it is, but you must put on this mask."

"Is it a drill? We have drills at the center."

"I do not know, but let us say yes. This is a drill, but a very serious drill."

Her father slipped the mask over Jati's mouth and adjusted the oxygen flow, then put the tank into a sling that fit around Jati's shoulders.

Suha had already put her tank on, and she waved her father away when he tried to help her with it.

"*Jangan repot-repot!* Do your own."

Her father hesitated briefly but then retreated to the cabinet and arranged his own tank. Suha went over to the console and tried to punch in for information, but the screen was locked up now. The atmospherics had never failed before, at least not since she had been on Station. Had the explosion on the ship done something to Station?

Suha knew they weren't even supposed to leave their rooms in a case like this, but she wondered if their neighbors knew what was going on. She was scared. When she moved toward the door, her father stepped in her way, giving her the "no" headshake but not saying anything. Her father went into his room and came back with a small device Suha had never seen before. He plugged a small cable into the fish tank and started cranking a lever.

"What's that?" she asked, her voice muffled by the mask.

"It's a hand-powered dynamo. The fish tank will not receive emergency power, so I need to make sure I can power the oxygen bubbler."

As her father spun the lever around, the lights in the fish tank rose again and the familiar bubbles appeared on one side of the aquarium. After a few minutes, her father stopped, shaking out his hand.

"We'll need to do this until the power is restored."

Jati wanted to try the dynamo, and her father let him, with the standard injunction against breaking it.

While Jati was occupied turning the crank, Suha asked her father what he thought had happened.

"I do not know. But if there had been some kind of explosion or a meteor impact on Station, we would have felt it. Let's just wait."

So they waited. With the lights barely illuminating the room, there was little for them to do but stand around the common area table staring at one another. Suha laughed.

"We look like, what are they called, cusba divers?"

"Scuba," her father replied. "It stands for self-contained underwater breathing apparatus. They were an early influence on space suit design."

"*Ayah*, really? Can the lesson wait until later?"

Jati went over and leaned next to his father, who put an arm around Jati.

"Do not worry. We will know what to do soon."

But they didn't know anything for hours. They were left in their rooms, worrying about how much oxygen was in the tanks and wondering how long the heat that was stored up within Station would continue to warm them. Eventually, her father tired of stories, and Jati fell asleep on the floor. Finally, with a flicker, the lights engaged and the oxygen alert deactivated. As Suha and her father removed their masks and took off the tanks, a new message appeared on the console, one that seemed to have been hastily prepared.

ATTENTION

TODAY, A GREAT TRAGEDY BEFELL HUMANITY, AND REST ASSURED THAT VENGEANCE WILL REST WITH THE STRONG! OUR BROTHERS' LIVES WILL NOT HAVE BEEN LOST IN VEIN, AND THE PERPETRATORS OF THIS AWFUL CRIME WILL FEEL JUSTICE! STATION WILL BE SEARCHED FROM ONE END TO THE OTHER. DO NOT LEAVE QUARTERS UNTIL FURTHER NOTICE!

Suha read the message twice, with her father looking over her shoulders.

"What does this mean?" she asked.

"I'm not sure," her father said, "but it appears they think the destruction of the ship was intentional."

"Was it?"

"It—why would you ask me? I can't imagine it could be. No, we would know if it was. But then again…I really don't know anything."

"Well, what are they searching for?"

"At this point, anything they can find, it appears. Don't be fooled by the bravado. Whoever wrote this message is scared."

"And also needs to go easy on the caps lock. Well, what do you think happened?"

"I don't know. A spaceship is a complicated machine. Any number of things could have gone wrong. But the Marsites will need someone to blame. We must all be careful, particularly—"

Her father stopped midsentence and quickly turned into his bedroom. He came out a few seconds later with a package in his hand and headed toward the door. This time, it was Suha who held out a blocking hand.

"Wait, you can't go out there. It's not safe. Who knows what the Marsites will do?"

"I can't wait. They will likely be searching rooms."

"What's in the bag?" Suha asked.

"I can't tell you."

Suha and her dad stared at each other.

"I can help you hide it," she said, maintaining eye contact.

Her father's eyes narrowed and then blinked. "Very well. How?"

Suha stepped over Jati and led her father to her room. She tipped back the bed and opened up her hiding place. Her father looked in at the VRCam and power stick. He stared back at her and started to say something before pausing.

Suha spoke. "The panel is heavy, and it's lead-lined, so it will be hard for a scan to pick up anything back here."

"Yes, this will do." He opened up his package and took out a gun. Suha stared at him.

"I don't want you to think I use this," her father said. "Nor do I hope to use it. And I am counting on you not to touch it or let Jati know that it is here. I will remove it from our rooms when I can. I must be able to trust you."

Suha nodded. "I know. I'm not a child."

"You are a child," her father said. "I'm sorry to involve you, but there is no choice. There are some of us organizing to oppose the Marsites. We are gaining in numbers, but our cells are isolated. I cannot imagine blowing up a ship. No, something mechanical must have gone wrong. Still, you must tell no one, not even your closest friends, especially not your Marsite friend. One misspoken word and lives could be lost."

"*Ayah*, I understand."

"You must."

He placed the gun into the hiding place and secured the panel. They both moved Suha's bed back into place, and then they went into the common room and watched Jati, who was sleeping peacefully on the floor.

"It is time for me to pray," her father said. He moved Jati into the bedroom. Suha went to her room to give him some privacy. She briefly thought about joining him, which would be wrong. Instead, she lay on her bed and tried to wrap her head around all that had happened.

When the day began, she was glad just to be out of school, but then she saw that incredible woman, and the Marsite ship blew up, and now her father was hiding guns. It was like everything was flipped upside down. She should have felt awful, but she couldn't help but find it all exciting.

• • • • •

IT WAS NOT long before the Marsites came and forced them out of the room for the search, although a word like "ransacking" would have been more accurate. They weren't even really searching. They just wanted to break shit. Suha and her family stood out in a hallway with other families from their section while Marsites went from room to room hollering and swearing. It was like one of Jati's temper tantrums when he was a toddler, only these tantrums involved huge men with guns.

Everyone was scared, and nobody had to be told to keep quiet. They all huddled together until the Marsites had broken everything that looked smash worthy. Then they had to listen to an incoherent rant with lines like "you have unleashed a fury you do not comprehend" and "Mars will rise from the ashes," none of which made sense unless you realized what her father had said: the Marsites were scared, and Suha knew that being angry was an easier way to be scared.

Suha had been watching the Marsites and didn't realize that Jati had drifted away from her. Suddenly, one of the Marsites started raving, and she saw that he had picked Jati up by his collar. Jati cried out, and

Suha didn't even think. She ran full tilt toward the Marsite and jumped on his back. The Marsite grabbed her and whipped her around, and then the three of them fell to the floor. There was screaming everywhere. The crowd, the Marsite, Jati, even Suha, but then a voice broke through the din, a voice Suha immediately recognized.

"Sergeant!" the voice said.

They all stopped and turned to see Colonel Jia Chiang. She was approaching at a mean clip, and her face was flushed.

The Marsite dropped Suha and Jati. He saluted. Suha was ready to put her hand up as well.

The sergeant started to say something, but the colonel spoke first. "Sergeant, I cannot have my finest soldiers dealing with children. Report on the search here."

The sergeant cleared his throat, then spoke. "We haven't found anything, ma'am, but I can't say we've gotten much cooperation here."

"Understood." She turned to the other soldiers. "Excellent work, all around. I need you in Sigma sector. I want all of you to go to Sigma. I need you on frontline duty."

"Yes, ma'am," the men said in unison. They saluted and marched out of the area without looking back. It all seemed pretty orderly, but Suha could tell that the colonel had just slapped down the sergeant in a way that made it possible for him not to lose face. That must be what it took to be one of the Marsite leaders.

Suha and Jati hadn't moved from the floor. The colonel kneeled down and inspected them. Jati jumped to his feet.

"I wasn't scared!" Jati insisted.

A small smile appeared at the corners of the woman's mouth. "No, indeed. It was you who was doing the scaring."

The woman placed her hand on Suha's cheek, and Suha felt the blood rush to her face. She instinctively grabbed the woman's hand, and then the fire raced throughout her body.

"You must take care of your brother," the woman said as Suha looked directly into her eyes. "These are dangerous times."

Suha couldn't say anything. She let the woman help her to her feet, and Suha didn't want to let go of her hand. The woman gave her a quizzical look before turning to the crowd and informing everyone they would now be allowed back into their rooms, and then she just disappeared as quickly as she had arrived.

Suha didn't know what to think. She realized immediately that she had never been attracted to someone like she was now drawn to this colonel. She'd never seen someone so impressive. She needed time to think about what this all meant. Everything was upside down. And that was before they even got into the rooms, where things were even more confusing. Furniture was smashed, clothes were scattered on the floor and food had been knocked out of the cupboards. Worst of all, they had smashed her father's aquarium, and fish lay dead on the floor. When Jati saw that, he started crying, and their father choked up too. Suha was just mad. Her father put the dead fish out of sight, and Suha saw that one of the fish had found a spot at the bottom of the broken aquarium where there was still a puddle of water. She shouted to her dad to come over. He saw the fish with barely moving gills, and he immediately filled up a water pitcher and moved the fish into it. He ran into his bedroom and found the dynamo. He hooked it up to the oxygenator, which fortunately hadn't broken when the tank was smashed, and balanced it on the top of the pitcher. He pumped away at the dynamo until the sound of bubbles could be heard in the pitcher.

"Come, Jati. I need you to help." He handed the dynamo to Jati, which didn't seem necessary to Suha, but it got Jati to stop crying. She got the point. They were all in this together.

The fish survived, and her father made a new tank for it out of one of those containers they grew tomatoes in over in the dining center. So that was a happy story. But it was one of the few. Half a dozen people had been killed in the gathering hall in the chaos after the explosion, and four more died when the oxygen was cut off and their tanks malfunctioned. One of the teachers in her school was among those who had been shot. People on Station were scared, and the Marsites were scared even worse. Suha should have been scared, too, but she couldn't stop thinking about the colonel, the touch of her hand, the warmth of her eyes, the power of her command.

Later that day, the gravity all of a sudden went out on Station. Just as people had gotten their rooms cleaned up, everything that wasn't fastened down just started floating. It was crazy. One second she was cleaning up dishes after a meal, and then next second her feet just kicked out from under her and she started bobbing in the air. Then, just as quickly, the gravity came back, and she fell to the floor along with some shattering dishes. Suha had been able to get out of her rooms and check in with the neighborhood grapevine. The rumor was that the Marsites were doing all of this on purpose, just to scare people. Suha also heard that the Marsites had cut the oxygen after the ship exploded for the same reason. Suha believed the rumor, but her father said the Marsites were trying to operate Station with as few non-Marsites as possible, and they weren't quite up to the task.

Then the next day, the Marsites discovered a weapons cache, and they really lost it. All the schools were closed, and extra guards were placed in all the residential sections. Non-Marsites were supposed to be confined to their rooms, but that only lasted for a few days. Her father was right about one thing. The Marsites couldn't run Station themselves. They tried to keep things tight, but pretty soon passes were being handed out like candy just so life on Station could go on. Suha had three she could use, and two of them were legit.

But the schools were closed, officially at least. Uxío's mom started running classes out of her bedroom, and one of her dad's coworkers ran another in the pantry of the dining area. These classes were kind of intense, especially when any issue, like space nutrition, touched upon life on Station. Tomato seeds were passed out, and suddenly finding the best hydroponic methods for growing them became an urgent political action. The other thing that changed was that suddenly parents were all into kids stealing things. Anything you could lift from a Marsite was part of the struggle now. This was great. Suha could roam the halls casing different sections of Station and do it with her father's permission.

Suha had had to adjust her sense of her father to allow him to be someone who even knew what a weapons cache was. But after that day of the explosion, her father wanted to act like nothing had changed. He still rode her about getting her homework done, and when the cell her father was in had a meeting in their rooms, he made her stay in her bedroom. But she had rigged up an audio link so that she was able to listen to what they were whispering about. That's how she found out that hardly any shipments had come up the Cord since the ship exploded. The food stores were getting depleted, and the docks were practically empty. It seemed like the Marsites had suspended plans for another manned launch until they figured out what had happened to the first one.

Without regular school to attend, Suha had a lot more time to herself, and she spent a lot of it on the VRCam. She'd put together almost a dozen pieces by now, mostly just about her life or about sections of Station. She could spend hours shooting and reshooting, then editing and reediting. Her friends were bored out of their minds, but Suha was eager for the time. She had never seen the Marsite that gave her the VRCam again. At some point, she realized that he must have been on the ship that exploded, which made her feel sorry for him. He didn't seem like he even wanted to go to Mars.

Some of the vidiaries Suha made were personal, though others were about all that was happening on Station now. Anywhere she could sneak the VRCam, she shot footage. The secret schools, the theft runs. When she wasn't editing, she was thinking about the colonel, Jia Chiang. Suha wished there had been someone she could talk to about the colonel, about how drawn she was to this Marsite leader. But who would understand? Some things had to be kept to herself.

Suha found reasons to go over to the docks, hoping she would catch sight of the colonel again. One day she and Shi-Lu were walking around with passes that allowed them to go to the dispensary to get medicine. No one needed medicine, but it gave them a chance to sneak back into the dock and float around for the first time since the explosion. She had brought the VRCam and the power stick, and she'd put them in a big refrigerated medicine case she'd stolen. Since her pass was for the dispensary, nothing was going to look out of the ordinary.

They got to the dock without a problem, and it was great to be free to float again. Suha walked right up to the edge of the platform and did a backflip into empty space, falling through the full-grav and slowly decelerating as she approached the floor. She landed on her hands and pushed off, but she lost her balance and seriously *geschraapt* her palms on a jagged piece of metal. That threw off her concentration, and she mobbed the whole trick. She had to paddle back to the wall so she could pull herself back up to the ledge.

"Out of practice, huh?" Shi-Lu said. He took a swan dive off the other section of the ledge and half flipped to push off a port window. He glided back up to a kinked rail in the no-grav and used his momentum to cartwheel it. It was sick.

"What tricktionary did you pull that out of?" Suha asked as she took the last few meters to the ledge hand over hand.

"It's Darian's. He and Uxío have been coming here almost every day."

"I hope he didn't show the dock to anyone in his Marsite class. If too many people find out, it'll get closed down."

"He won't. He's the one who came up with the rules. No one comes alone. No one talks about it."

Suha wasn't sure she entirely trusted Darian, but she wasn't going to waste the time before she got nauseous thinking about him. She strapped the VRCam on her head.

"Slip the works again on the cartwheel trick. I want to shoot it."

Until the nausea started to come on, they were hard-core, flipping trick after trick like it was a circus. Shi-Lu didn't miss a move, and at one point he even spun around while playing some kind of white flute made out of a PVC pipe. It was the stupidest thing Suha had ever seen, and Suha wasn't surprised a bit when Shi-Lu said that this was Uxío's trick. Suha's hands stung a little, but she ignored them and shot enough footage to keep her busy editing for days. By the time they had both had enough, they were bobbing under the ledge and panting for breath.

"Let's go," Suha said. "I'm going to puke in the no-grav."

"Chóng gāo de," Shi-Lu replied. "I don't want to float through that."

They had just started pulling themselves up toward the ledge when Suha heard the door open. She hadn't expected Darian and Uxío, and she was just about to shout up to them when she heard an unfamiliar male voice with one of the accents she associated with the Marsites. She pressed herself to the wall underneath the ledge, and Shi-Lu fell into place beside her.

As Suha listened, she heard that there was more than one man above her. They were grunting and giving instructions to one another. "Over here." "No, here." Suha wished she could see what was going on, but if she could see them, they would be able to see her.

"What are we going to do?" the deeper of the two voices said.

"Just dump it here for now. We can figure out how to get rid of it later."

There was more grunting, and then suddenly something dropped down right in front of Suha and Shi-Lu. It fell quickly through the full-grav, slowly through the low-grav, and lost momentum in the no-grav before it hit the bottom and bobbed back up. As the shape turned, Suha saw the half-shaved and scarred head of Colonel Jia Chiang. She was dead.

Suha wanted to scream, but she was too scared.

"What the—" said a voice from above.

"What?" asked the other voice.

"Look, something's wrong with the gravity here. It's floating."

"Christ. Just leave it. We don't have time. We can come back later and fish it out. Nothing works the way it's supposed to up here."

Suha looked over at Shi-Lu. He was pressed flat against the wall beside her. Suha turned back toward the dead colonel. She turned her glasses on and started filming the body as it slowly rotated in the no-grav, drifting inescapably into the dead zone.

They stayed pressed against the wall for a long time until Shi-Lu tugged Suha's sleeve. She looked over to see that his face was pale, and she didn't feel too well either. They had been in the dock too long, and they had to get out or they would both pass out. With a nod, Suha pulled herself onto the ledge. She glanced around and up at the control booth that looked onto the dock. Everything was still. She helped Shi-Lu onto the ledge, then took off the VRCam and put it in the medicine case that the Marsites fortunately hadn't noticed. They quietly exited the dock.

The hallways were empty. She pulled Shi-Lu into an alcove that was sheltered from view where they could recover. Shi-Lu threw up in the corner. Suha didn't have the strength to complain. They sat quietly for a minute while their bodies adjusted.

"You know," Suha said eventually, "it's a good thing we have these dispensary passes. I think we're going to need some meds."

Shi-Lu nodded. The color was coming back to his face.

"We have to tell Uxío and Darian," Shi-Lu said, stumbling to his feet. "They have to know so they won't try to go to the dock."

"But don't tell anyone else. This has got nothing to do with us. It's just Marsites vs. Marsites."

"I don't know," Shi-Lu said. "I don't know. I'll see Uxío tonight, and maybe I can get over to Darian's tomorrow."

"Let's wait until they know. Then we can figure out what to do."

Shi-Lu nodded. Then he stepped over and threw his arms around Suha. She stiffened and pushed back.

"You just puked! Don't touch me."

Shi-Lu looked embarrassed, and Suha was sorry she had snapped at him, but what was he thinking?

"Sorry," he said. "It's just—be careful."

"Don't worry. This has nothing to do with us," Suha said. But she felt it had everything to do with her, like much of her life had just been sent drifting into space.

• • • • •

THAT NIGHT THE oxygen went out again, and then so did the lights and heat. Fortunately, her father had gotten more hand-cranked dynamos out of scavenged (or stolen) scrap. Apparently, everyone was making them now. The three of them sat huddled in the common room wearing oxygen tanks and blankets, breathing through masks and spinning the handles of the dynamos that were hooked up to a heating coil. It was still cold, but they would be okay. Her father told them it reminded him of fishing trips with his grandfather when they would sleep on the beach around a campfire.

Except for oxygen tanks, Suha thought. And the masks. And the Marsites.

Suha didn't say much. Her thoughts kept returning to the colonel's body.

Midway through the night, everything came on again. Bright lights woke them up, and even the console popped on as if everything was normal. Her father moved Jati to his bed and went back to sleep himself, but Suha was wide awake.

She reviewed her footage of the colonel floating in the dock. Suha still thought she was beautiful, even now that she was dead. Suha remembered the speech that the colonel had given the day of the launch and the feel of her touch when the colonel had saved her. Suha couldn't imagine what could have happened to her. The colonel had seemed so in control, so powerful. Suha would have liked to tell her father about what had happened, but how could he possibly understand what she was feeling? She didn't understand it herself.

She watched the footage again, and without even realizing she was doing it, Suha started adding commentary, which was intuitively edited in. She just wanted to figure out what was going on, and maybe making a vidiary entry was the way she did that. What had happened to this woman? Why would she have been killed? Why was Suha so drawn to her? Was this why she was never interested in any of the boys around her? But how could she have been attracted to a Marsite?

Suha zoomed and cropped at the end of her piece to show the face of Colonel Chiang. It was a gruesome shot, but it was the footage she had to work with, and Suha wasn't going to turn away from anything now. The colonel had a beautiful face, but it was the scar on one side of her head that Suha couldn't stop looking at. How had that gotten there?

That's when she saw something she hadn't expected. There was a cut on the colonel's neck, right on the jugular. That must be how she had been killed. But it didn't look like blood around the cut.

Suha closed the footage. She took off the VRCam and put it in a bag. The only way to know if what she saw meant what she thought was to go back to the dock. She grabbed one of her passes and quietly put on her shoes. Then she thought for a second and pushed her bed out from the wall so she could get to the hiding place. The gun her father had put there had not been touched since the day of the explosion, but she took it now, sliding it into the bag. She had to be prepared for anything.

Station was quiet and seemed deserted. The Marsites made lousy guards, she knew. They all found routine work beneath them, and as long as you could figure out where different sentries would meet to talk to one another and stay away from that, you could avoid most of the pass checks. Still, being out this time of night would be hard to explain, so Suha took back hallways and a few shortcuts through service passages. She made it to the dock without running into anyone.

Inside the dock, the lights cast a dull glow on the body of the colonel in the dead zone, where she floated silently. Suha slipped down the ledge, tied her bag to one of the support beams and grabbed the cord that was already tied up. She double-checked the connection and slung the loop of polypro over her shoulder, tying the end to one of her ankles. Then she dropped off the ledge and fell straight down to the floor, quickly at first, then slowing. When she hit the bottom, she pushed off with her feet and reeled out the wire behind her, drifting toward where the body floated.

She kept a tight grip on the end of the cord, since it was the only thing that would get her out of the dead zone. As it turned out, getting into the dead zone on purpose was pretty easy. All she had to do was push toward it and let gravity kick in. She felt the tug and soon found herself bouncing and dipping next to the body of the colonel. She told herself that she was here to answer a question, that she shouldn't think of the colonel as having been alive. But as soon as she saw the body's open eyes, she froze. Jia Chiang was her name, Suha remembered. The eyes were beautiful. Suha made herself look away from them. She grabbed Chiang's hair on the side of the head that had hair and pulled it toward her back. This gave Suha a view of the cut on her neck, and as she pulled back further, the cut opened up, revealing what Suha thought she would see.

Instead of blood and gore, the colonel's neck was an array of circuits and chips. There was still biology involved, some muscle tissue was interwoven with the circuitry, but this was mostly machine. Chiang was transhuman. Or at least she had been.

Suha could see how that would get her killed. Marsites hated transhumans almost as much as they hated robots. But how did a transhuman become a Marsite colonel in the first place? Wouldn't medical checks have revealed her circuitry? And why would a transhuman want anything to do with Marsites? Finding an answer just created more questions.

Suha started recording, holding Chiang's hair back tightly to show the cut in the neck and the combination of muscle and machine that was revealed beneath it. She dubbed in audio with some thoughts as to why Chiang might have been killed and wondered out loud about how she could have gotten onto Station in the first place. When she had said all she had to say, Suha closed Chiang's eyes with her fingertips. She softly took the woman's now cold hand.

"Take my hand, sister," she whispered, squeezing gently, then letting go.

She started reeling herself in along the cord. There was the sound of the dock doors opening. She heard voices.

Suha knew she was in trouble. Quickly, she yanked at the cord, jerking her body back toward the dock. As Suha bounced ahead, she realized she was still recording through the VRCam. While she kept moving hand over hand, she looked up toward the ledge. There was a pair of Marsites at the entrance, fortunately with their backs toward her. As she heard the sound of the door closing, Suha finished pulling herself in under the ledge.

She breathed quietly and deeply, trying to settle her head and stomach. She could hear the men above her shuffling across the deck.

Then one of the men said, "One, two, three—"

She heard the sound of heaving, and something plunged right in front of her, falling quickly through full-grav before slowing and bouncing inevitably toward the dead zone to join Colonel Chiang. It was the body of another Marsite, judging by the uniform. She had seen him before, the day the ship exploded. He had given one of the speeches before the launch. He stood out because he wore leg braces and he was so much older than the rest of the Marsites. He looked even older than her father.

"So," said one of the voices from above. It was a voice she recognized from before. "What are we going to do with them? We can't just let him and his toy float around in there."

"I've got it figured out," another voice responded. "Don't worry about it. Let's get rid of all this gear."

Suha heard the two men move to the far side of the ledge, and then boxes and machinery dropped down into the dock. From that far spot, they missed the gravity changes altogether, and all the stuff fell in a heap onto the floor below. Suha couldn't figure out what all the equipment was for. She hung the cord on one of the ledge supports and pressed herself up against the wall so that she could shimmy up to the bottom of the ledge. When she reached the bottom of it, she took the VRCam off and slowly raised it above the floor level so that it could record.

She wasn't exactly sure where the Marsites were or what they were doing, so as soon as there was a pause in the boxes plunging to the floor beneath her, she took the VRCam down and put it back on. She stared down at the mess of equipment, clothing and actual paper books that lay below.

"I hope that's all of it," she heard from above.

"I think so. I sure as hell hope so. Chiang was the only one D'Onforio waved through clearance. The idiot. What could he have been thinking?"

"Who knows? It's hard to believe. I remember when the battle for Labicittá happened. He was a true hero then."

"And a true corpse now. For all we know, it was his robot that sabotaged the ship. And if it wasn't, it still—hey, grab that slideboard. Let's head up top."

Suha heard the Marsites leave. She spun back her footage and blinked it into review mode. It showed two Marsites, big buzz-cut guys she didn't recognize, in front of a loaded slideboard. There wasn't much to see. They picked up boxes and threw them over the ledge. She switched back to record mode and zoomed in on the bodies and then on the pile of equipment. Some of it looked like it could have circuitry for a transhuman, but most of it was just regular junk, clothing and blankets, even a few fancy-looking pillows. Why would the Marsites want to get rid of that? Suha needed to examine what was in the pile. She tied the end of the cord around her ankle. She figured that even if the Marsites returned, she could pull herself back under the ledge before they saw her. She had at least ten minutes before the nausea got to be too much.

Suddenly, there was the sound of a motor starting up, and Suha felt the whole room shudder. She lurched forward instinctively and took a deep breath. At the far end of the dock, she saw the ancient bay doors start to open. A burst of compressed air sent the two bodies tumbling out the bay doors and into space. Suha scrambled over to the bottom of the ledge. She strained to pull herself up. Another burst of compression knocked her backward. She held onto the ledge support. Behind her, she saw the equipment being catapulted out into space. She had to get out now. She fought the urge to breathe and pulled as hard as she could to get onto the ledge. She got to her feet and ran toward—

Shi-Lu

You can take the new passage along the outer perimeter of Station, but the shortest route to Uxío's office is through the gathering hall, and there is no reason you shouldn't walk through it like everyone else. Because you are like everyone else. So you join the post-shift crowd that is congregating at the cafés and along the walkways and forge through, refusing to see anything in the gathering hall that isn't there.

But then the lights come up and everyone applauds, as they now do at the official twilight time every evening. And that's when you hear the gunfire. You immediately crouch down behind one of the benches to take cover and reach for your weapon, but you can't find it. Damn it, you're exposed! You have to hope the Marsites don't have a bead on you. Where is your gun? You glance over quickly to the other side of the hall, where the Marsites have their barricade.

Only the Marsites aren't there. They haven't been there for over a decade. You know that. You know you know that. A polished metal floor now gleams where the barricade once stood. Of course, you don't have a gun.

You step out from behind the bench and sit down on it. Your heart is racing, so you take deep breaths, as you've been told to do whenever you have a flashback episode. No one seems to have taken any notice of you, and you can't decide if that makes you feel better or worse.

You had been in the gathering hall on that day, many years ago now, when the lights came up and signaled the Marsites' defeat. Everyone had applauded then. The lights seemed so strong at first that you thought the Marsites had some new kind of laser weapon. But those around you knew better. It meant that the Resistance had taken control of the inner core of Station from the Marsites. Your fellow fighters rose to their feet, some with tears streaming down their faces while they clapped and shouted. You should have joined in, but you had gotten so used to living under emergency lighting that normal light seemed too bright. You covered your eyes while others hugged and celebrated.

The Marsites had known what the coming of the lights meant as well, and it didn't take long for the holdouts in the gathering hall to surrender. When they gave themselves up, you were shocked to see them. They no longer seemed enormous and intimidating. Instead, they were gaunt and emaciated, out of food and living in their own filth. They had piled their weapons in a nearby corner of the hall and cowered silently. That corner was still there. It was right in front of you. Of course, now it was a garden with miniature roses and mustard greens. Even the smell of death had been erased. People around you now simply passed through the hall, moving busily from one side of Station to the next. These people from Labicittá who had come up the Cord, full of energy and with plans for the reconstruction. Sometimes you wanted to make them stop and remember what had happened here. But, of course, it was not something they could remember. They had all been on Earth during the Marsite Occupation. There was so much all these new people had missed. So much and so little.

You have a rollup screen crumpled into a ball in your pocket. It pings to let you know that you are late to meet Uxío. You get to your feet, but you are tired and your legs hurt. You feel like an old man. Maybe you are one. You don't have the energy all these fresh-up-the-Cord people do. And you will never get used to carrying one of these rollup screens around. They've said it is just temporary until a better mobile system can be established on Station, and since the Marsites had stockpiled so many of these screens for the trips to Mars that never happened, it makes sense to use them for the time being. Besides, you're not sure you want to get implant tattoos or whatever it is they use down on Earth to communicate. The revolution was successful without much communication technology at all. But whenever you make a point like that, people from Labicittá shake their heads or simply refuse to argue with you. It's like you are a generation older than everyone your age on Earth. Maybe more than a generation.

The screen in your pocket pings again. You will be late to meet with Uxío, but this will not be a surprise to him. Being disappointed by you is something Uxío must be used to by now.

You wind your way out of the hall and through a corridor that leads into one of the newer sections of Station. It is unbelievable how much construction has been done in the last few years. If it doesn't slow down soon, rings of additions will encircle all the parts of Station that you grew up in. But this expansion will have to come to an end soon. After all, there is only so much work to be done in space. And you should know. You have held and lost just about every job there is to be had. The only thing you have a harder time hanging onto is a girlfriend.

Uxío's office is in the new administrative complex, a maze of aero-gel viewports and sleek, polished corridors. There is hardly an edge left on Station, what with all the malleable building materials that have been invented in the last few years. You make your way down the tube-like passages without corners, kicking the edge of your shoe along the wall just to scuff the pristine surface.

You wish Uxío had just stopped by your rooms instead of making you come to the office. There is no joy in being over here and having Uxío's success rubbed in your face. Not that you blame Uxío. You would rather have Uxío in the leadership than another bureaucrat from Labicittá. Uxío had been through the revolution at least, and he has the scars to prove it.

Still, it is hard to forget that Uxío had been the most immature of all of you back during the occupation. He was a boy who could make a joke but barely do a flip in weightlessness. Who would have guessed that he would become an important figure on Station, the youngest person in the leadership and a married man with a little daughter? The revolution changed so much. So much and so little.

Even though it is twilight, things are still busy in the administrative section. These new people seem to work all the time, and they stride down corridors quickly, swiping at their screens while carrying on conversations. It makes you tired just to watch.

There is no one at the reception desk, so you make your way down to Uxío's office. The office is ridiculously large, as big as the rooms you and your mother share. You can see Uxío through the open doorway, wearing a formal administration uniform, and he has the bearing of someone in authority. Still, it is hard not to see some part of the little kid Uxío had been. Uxío stands next to his desk, stepping up and down in place. He has a rollup screen mounted in front of him, and he is swiping at it dramatically with both hands.

"One time," you say, interrupting Uxío, "I screened a history packet from the planet. It showed this old sport called American football, and during the rest session, musicians replaced the athletes and marched around the field playing instruments. The leader of the musicians wore a large feathered hat and used his arms to perform some kind of ritual. That's what you look like right now."

Uxío laughs and taps his screen so that it rolls up into a tube. He steps over to you. "Good one, Shi-Lu. Take my hand, brother."

"Safe," you reply, gripping Uxío's wrist tightly.

"Come look at this." Uxío flexes and releases his grip. Then he leads you to the side of his desk. A square panel is slightly raised off the floor. Uxío steps onto it and begins walking in place again. He picks up his screen and rolls it open before handing it to you.

"This new material captures the energy emitted each time I step on it and then stores it. See the indicator window on the screen? It lets me know how many joules I'm generating. They can produce these things incredibly cheaply now. We could install special floors like this throughout Station, and they would pay for themselves in captured energy in just a few years."

You poke at the panel with your foot. "And so we would just bounce through the halls instead of walking?"

"You'd get used to it pretty quickly. I've had this floor panel in my office for the past week, and I hardly do any work sitting down anymore."

"Then don't forget to calculate in the extra savings on chairs."

"You can joke now, but this is the wave of the future."

"'Wave?' What kind of word is that for those of us who will never see an ocean?"

Uxío pauses. You do not mean to bring the conversation to a dead stop, but you have a way of doing that. You can't help but puncture the plans of those who want to change everything on Station. Puncture. That is another word that doesn't quite mean the same thing for people who are surrounded by the vacuum of space, always one mishap away from catastrophe.

"Well, *apa pun*," Uxío continues. "Thanks for coming to see me tonight. Or is 'night' also an irrelevant term since we live in space?"

"No, I think 'night' still makes sense. Just don't tell me that I need to be more grounded."

Uxío smiles. "I'm concerned, my friend, that you need to be more grounded."

You offer a mock sigh.

"But, really," Uxío continues, "you were not at the dedication ceremony for Suha's memorial. You were missed."

So this is why Uxío wanted to meet with you. He has called you here to make you feel guilty, as if you don't already feel guilty enough. You turn away and walk back toward the entrance to the room.

"I couldn't do it," you mumble. You can barely hear yourself.

"It was a very nice event. You wouldn't have found it sad. It was really a celebration. All these people coming up the Cord from Labicittá, they all know Suha's story. Most of what they know about us, they know because of her, because of those vidiaries she made."

You have only watched a couple of the video pieces Suha created, but you regularly deal with people who act as if they know you because you appear in a number of the vidiaries. *Tell us about Suha. Can you still do those tricks in weightlessness? What do you really think happened to her?* They bother you when you are trying to eat or when you are just sitting on a bench wanting to be left alone. Perhaps you can talk about Suha to Uxío or to others who were on Station during the occupation, but you want nothing to do with these people from Labicittá who always want "just a short interview" about Suha before they go back down to the planet you will never see again. "Cycle down," they call it, like it was a natural order of life.

"Shi-Lu, did you hear me?"

Uxío must have said something, but you have gotten lost inside your own head. This happens more and more lately. It is one of the reasons you don't like to leave your rooms. At least your mother knows not to ask you questions.

"Yes, I heard you."

"Well, are you going to visit the memorial? I really think you should. It would be good for you."

You turn and move back toward the doorway.

"I don't need to see a memorial. I can see Suha whenever I close my eyes. Floating in space. I'll never forget."

"You're not the only one who misses her."

"I didn't say that. I just don't need you to tell me how to mourn." You feel your voice rise, and you see that you are gesturing toward Uxío with your finger.

Uxío raises his hands. "Fine. Besides, it's not like I ever have much luck getting you to do what I want."

You run a hand through your hair. It is surprising how long your hair has gotten. Maybe you should cut it. It probably makes you stand out more than you want. But when the fashion on Labicittá became those stubble cuts, you decided to let your hair grow as long as it could.

You look back at Uxío, the oldest friend you have, maybe your only friend now. After Suha's death and the battles that followed it, the two of you had fought shoulder to shoulder in the hallways and slept side by side in oxygen masks when the Marsites cut off life support. He was there to help you wash the blood off your hands after a battle with the Marsites, and he would wake you when the nightmares of those battles caused you to scream out in the middle of the night. And it is not as if Uxío has suffered any less than you. Uxío's mother died in Marsite confinement after she was caught teaching an illegal school.

And then there is Uxío's face. You have gotten used to it, but the scars around his left eye where the bullet shrapnel hit him will never fully heal. The doctors said it was safer to keep the bullet in his head than to try and remove a piece that close to the brain. So Uxío always carries a piece of the revolution with him as well.

You look up at your friend and into the new digital adaptive eye that has given him a sort of sight. Uxío had said that he can see different spectrums now—infrared and X-ray—but images do not appear quite as crisp in the new eye. When seeing really matters, he says he closes the digital eye. You can understand that.

"I'm sorry, my friend," you say. "I wish I could have been there to see the memorial. Maybe some other time."

You start to make your way out of the office.

"Wait," Uxío says. "That's not why I asked you to come in. Can you close the door? This will only take a couple minutes."

You step back into the room and gently slide the door closed. You stand facing your friend, who now looks a little nervous.

"After the ceremony at the memorial, I went to the dock, to the dead zone. It was my first time back there, and it was hard to see. I…I just wanted you to know that. I haven't forgotten. I want you to know that because we just got…an unusual visa application. Take a look."

Uxío rolls his screen into your hands. You see a standard short-term visa form. You processed plenty of these during the months you worked in the embassy wing. That was one of many jobs Uxío has gotten for you that you lost. The application is from someone named

"Kebangkitan," who looks to be some kind of missionary, though the Technological & Metaphysical Institute is a denomination you have not heard of before. If it had been up to you, you would have kept all the missionaries down on the planet where they belong, but Station policy is to admit a limited number of them from a range of faiths. They do not make many converts up here, but they always pay the full freight price for passage up the Cord.

"So why are you showing me this? If his credit's good, overcharge him and smile." You hold the screen up to Uxío, but he doesn't take it from you.

"Read the personal statement."

You scroll through to the personal statement section at the end of the form. This is where people beg and plead for a visa, either by dropping names of anyone in a position of power on Station or by offering up some melodramatic account of looking up at the stars as a child and wishing one day to be there. The missionaries' applications tended to use more quotations from various holy books, but the model still held.

But there is something different about this one. Though it speaks of redemption as the path to serenity, this applicant, Kebangkitan, seems to already know a lot about Station, too much in fact. His statement isn't about saving people on Station but about how people on Station saved him. He speaks of Suha as if he had known her. *The only time in my life when I was grounded,* the statement says, *was when I floated high above the world, nauseous and at peace.* And then you understand. The applicant, this "Kebangkitan," is Darian, your childhood Marsite friend.

You glance up at Uxío in disbelief. Uxío nods to your unasked question.

"How the... Is he serious?"

"He is. I had people on Labicittá check him out. He's been a monk in this Metawhatever Institute for about five years. That's when he changed his name. Prior to that, he served time for drug possession and dealing, but he talks about all that at the end of the statement. You know, when Darian was deported with the rest of the Marsites, I didn't give any thought to what he would do next."

In an instant, you try to orient your memories of floating in the dock alongside Darian with the voice in the statement. They don't fit together.

"The Marsites shot out your eye! They killed our friends! Are you trying to tell me you've forgotten?"

"*Jangan konyol!* I have not forgotten, but hear me out. It's been more than ten years now. Things have changed. We have changed. I think it would be good for us—for me and you—to make peace with Darian. Read the rest of his statement."

You toss the screen onto Uxío's desk. It bounces and rolls up into a tube. "I don't need to read it. How can you even think of letting a Marsite back onto Station?"

"He's not a Marsite anymore. And face it, he never really was one. His father was the Marsite. Darian was just trapped on their side."

"He could have crossed over and fought beside us. He chose not to."

"Yes, that's true. He also could have taken up arms against us, but he didn't do that either. And besides, do you remember how young we all were? We were children!"

"We were not children!" you shout. Then you pause. That's not what you mean. Of course, you were children. You're not sure what you mean.

Uxío sits on the edge of his desk. Then he speaks again, more quietly. "Darian was once our friend, and he's suffered as well. His father died in confinement on Labicittá after the revolution. Darian was in and out of jail before becoming a monk. His life hasn't been pleasant."

"He can choose to stay on Earth. You and I don't have that choice."

"And how can you blame that on Darian? You know if he had been on Station long enough for the weightlessness disease to take effect, he'd have been trapped here just like us. Look, I forwarded a copy of his statement to you. I want you to read it. I won't approve his application if you're against it. But I think it's the right thing to do."

You turn toward the door and walk out without saying another word, then storm out of the administrative section, forcing bureaucrats to the side of the corridors as you pass them. But that only makes you feel like a bully, which only reminds you of the punishment you doled out to captured Marsites so long ago. You push that thought from your mind and stop at one of the aerogel viewports. The aerogel is only semi-translucent, and the Earth below appears as if it is covered in mist. Still, the planet looms massive below, its horizons falling away against the backdrop of space. You have heard that on Earth the ground appears flat, that one cannot see far enough to where the Earth begins to curve. That is hard to believe. There is nothing but curves as far as your eye can see.

Darian.

You would like to say that you never give him a thought, but that is not true. You think of Darian often. How can you not? So many memories of Suha involve Darian and Uxío. How many afternoons had you all spent floating in the dock together, performing tricks for one another in the weightlessness and semiweightlessness? How many times had you gone as a pack to comb the launch bays for cast-off equipment? So much laughter. So much energy. They are the memories that made your life bearable.

Which might be how Darian feels as well. But Darian is a fool to think he can reclaim his past on Station. Everything changes, and those changes leave you behind. But let Darian come up to Station and find that out for himself. You won't stand in his way, but you know he will not like what he finds. There is no serenity here. Maybe none anywhere.

You wander through the corridors again until you stand at the entrance to the gathering hall. You hesitate, not wanting to provoke another flashback, but you don't think it will happen this time. How can it with the noise and laughter of a group of children using slide-boards up against a newly reconfigured wall in the gathering hall? You smile. The architects from Labicittá who know so much had not consid-ered that all these smooth, curved surfaces were ideal for kids on slide-boards. You watch as a child with one of those Labicittá stubble cuts races toward a wall, throwing himself and his board onto the floor. The slideboard automatically conforms to the curve of the wall and continues up practically to the ceiling before the board's built-in accelerometer kicks in, causing the board to pivot and bring the rider back to the floor in a heap.

An older kid is next, a lanky girl who seems to be wrapped in fabric rather than wearing clothes. This is one of the new fashions that has come up the Cord. The girl races toward the wall and throws herself and her board to the floor. But instead of collapsing onto the board, she lands in a handstand. The board rides up the wall and onto the ceiling until the girl looks like she is standing in the air. Then, just before the accelerometer kicks in, she turns the board off. Girl and slideboard fall to the ground. She lands on her feet, holding the slideboard over her head.

"Atlas!" the girl shouts.

It is a great trick, and you are impressed. The girl's friends whistle at her and bang their boards against the floor.

"Who's going to top that?" the girl asks. For an instant, you expect Suha to take up the challenge. You start laughing at yourself, but you must be laughing too loudly, because the kids turn to look at you. Now you feel ridiculous, so you leave the corridor and walk into the gathering hall, past the kids with the slideboards and into the section of the hall where the last battles took place.

You remember how hungry you had been then. The Marsites hadn't been the only ones running out of food and ammunition. Whole sectors of Station were uninhabitable, and it had been weeks, maybe months, since the last supply shipment up the Cord. It was only after the surrender that you learned that the people on Labicittá had seized control of the bottom of the Cord from the Marsites. You would likely be dead now if it hadn't been for that. But during the revolution, you hardly gave Labicittá a thought. You assumed you would have to fight the Marsites alone for everything. You never considered that you might have allies.

You have to admit that it was Labicittá that made the revolution successful, and without them, there never would have been a reconstruction. Without Labicittá, Station could never have supported itself. It still can't. Of course, looking back, how could you not have realized that the anger toward the Marsites would have been as great on Labicittá as on Station? They too had had to live with an occupying force that cared little for anything but Mars. Your own family on Labicittá had suffered. When your sister and father came up the Cord to reunite with you and your mother, they were like strangers.

You stop at the gathering hall exit, realizing that you have walked entirely through it without a flashback. But you haven't ignored the hall either. You were thinking about what had happened the entire time, but it was just a memory. You turn and glance back at the slideboard kids at the far end and the strolling couples along the garden pathways. It is just a hall for gathering now. Perhaps you can live with that.

Though your mother will have dinner waiting for you, you now know what you must do, and you now feel like you can do it. You turn down a passageway that leads toward the launch bays and the dock. You have heard that this whole area is slated for a renovation now that flights to Mars are a thing of the past.

These hallways are familiar to you, though they seem out of place now. The rectangular design might have been good for moving freight on slideboards, but there is something cold and unwelcoming about them. Maybe there is something to be said for the new curved walls.

You might have gone to the dedication ceremony if the Suha memorial was in a different location, but you had been offended that they would put it right where she died. What kind of tribute was that? But, of course, that was just an excuse you had made up. You haven't gone back near the dock since Suha's death. You aren't entirely sure you want to now.

As you near the location, you take a deep breath and step around one of the angular corners. To your surprise, you see Suha's father, Suparman, sitting in a transit chair. Fortunately, Suparman is facing away from you and can't see the look of surprise on your face. Suparman is staring out toward the memorial where it is suspended in space just outside the viewport.

You consider leaving. You hadn't expected anyone else to be here. But Suparman turns and catches sight of you. A big smile appears on the old man's face, and he waves. As you shuffle over, Suparman takes a screen from his lap and points it toward the floor. A floor tile sinks down, rotates, and reappears with a chair. Suparman rolls up the screen and gestures to the chair.

You sink down into the chair. Suparman extends one of his bony arms.

"Take my hand, brother," the old man says in a raspy voice.

"Safe," you reply, gingerly and briefly gripping Suparman's wrist.

"I think she would be pleased with this," Suparman says, gesturing toward the memorial. "It is what she would have wanted, don't you think?"

"Yes, I do," you say, but you don't think Suha would have liked it. Or at least she would rather be alive than memorialized.

"I find it comforting here. It is a place where I have come to feel closer to Suha. Do you feel that?"

"Yes, I do." You wonder if you sound as unpersuasive as you feel.

"I come here often now at the end of the day before evening prayers. Just to sit and think."

Suparman turns back toward the memorial and says nothing. You understand that you are being invited to do the same. You have seen images of the memorial on your screen, so you are not surprised by its appearance, but it is different seeing it in person.

The memorial is a mobile of sorts that floats in space just outside the view window. At its center is a bust of Suha, though not in the way you remember her. The bust wears a VRCam, making it look like Suha has old-fashioned glasses. But otherwise the sculpture is a fair representation. The bust is surrounded by an array of salvaged metal and space junk captured by Station's protection field. It looks a little cluttered, but it is an interesting repurposing of satellite parts and pieces of abandoned spaceships. Suha would have appreciated that. The part of the sculpture you don't like is the cord that keeps the memorial tethered to Station. Maybe it is meant as homage, but it seems morbid to you. Why celebrate the moment of Suha's death? Her death says nothing about her life.

But there is no way of separating the two now. Suha is as well-known for her death as for her life. You are among the few who still has vivid memories of both. You have often pushed away thoughts of that day, but you open yourself up to them now, and the memories strike at you in rapid bursts.

It is the morning after you and Suha discovered the body at the dock. Your mother has made a spicy paste dip for breakfast. Your left shoulder hurts, maybe from all the flips and presses you did in the dock the day before. You leave right after breakfast because you have to find Darian before school to warn him to stay away from the dock. But as soon as you get out of your rooms, you can tell something is wrong. People are quickly moving through the corridors, whispering, and some are crying. You don't talk to anyone, but you follow the crowd that is forming on the space side, near the viewports.

You know something is wrong. The crowds in the halls line the viewports, silent. You force your way in front of a port, and what you see seems unreal and impossible.

It is Suha. She is wearing that ridiculous VRCam she so adores. Her body hovers next to Station with limbs extended, and the long polypro cord that you use to pull one another out of the dead zone is tied around one of her ankles. That is the only thing that keeps her lifeless body from floating out into space. How has she gotten out there? You can't imagine. But she is dead. There is no doubt about that.

What happens next? Your memories are not as clear after that. But the silence of the crowd is eventually replaced by tears and anger. It seems to take the Marsites hours to retrieve Suha's body as she floats out in front of everyone. And then the Marsites will not turn her body over to Suparman for a funeral ceremony. Nor will the Marsites release the footage from the VRCam. The Marsites claim her death was an accident, but no one believes them.

It is the beginning of the revolution. It is the moment when they realized that the Marsites were willing to sacrifice them all, and the fighting begins almost immediately.

But now your thoughts stray away from the battles of the revolution, which your mind usually cannot avoid. You think instead of Suha and of your time playing together as children, and of falling in love with her, or falling in love as much as an innocent boy can. Images of Suha flash into your head, leaving you feeling exhausted and wasted.

All of a sudden, you feel a nudge on your shoulder. You turn. Suparman is extending his arm with a tissue. You realize that tears are running down your face, and you take the tissue.

"Thank you."

"Have you heard recently from your family on Labicittá?" Suparman speaks while continuing to stare out toward the memorial. "There's quite an interesting election campaign happening down there."

"No, I don't really follow politics on Earth." You dab your face.

"I have tried to keep up with it more lately. Jati, my son, is involved in politics now. It is important that we try to understand life on the planet, that we stay a part of those conversations."

Jati is one of the few who had lived on Station during the occupation and been spared the weightlessness disease. He had been young enough and strong enough that it hadn't impacted him fully, and he had been able to leave for the planet, traveling back and forth up the Cord at will. The last time you saw Jati was at the Station departure gate. At the time, your father and sister were going back down after another disastrous visit when your family did nothing but argue and get in each other's way. It made for quite a contrast with Suparman and Jati. Jati had a marriage contract, and he had been there with his wife and baby son. Suparman had been in his transit chair, bouncing the boy in his lap and laughing.

"Shi-Lu, I asked is your sister still in university?"

"I'm sorry. I—I don't know. I haven't heard from Labicittá since they went back down."

You see a frown pass over Suparman's face. What does the old man expect from you?

Suparman reaches into the pouch of his chair and pulls something out of it. He holds it out to you with an open palm.

"Take this. Do you know what it is?"

It is a shard of some material. It is hard but not metallic. You don't recognize it.

"It's bamboo. When I was a child, this lined the floors I walked on. There are now plans to begin growing it here, on Station. Isn't that remarkable?"

"I suppose it is." You turn the bamboo in your hand and press your fingernail into its surface.

"I must be getting back, but I have a favor to ask you. I am going to be interviewed tomorrow by a historian from Labicittá about the occupation. I am afraid my memory is not what it once was, and I fear I will forget some important details. Would you accompany me and help me with information? I would consider this a personal favor."

You hate being interviewed. You probably turn down one or two requests a month from people wanting to speak with "a friend of Suha's." But you cannot say no to Suparman. You nod and mumble your consent.

Suparman rolls out a screen and begins swiping at it. "I have forwarded the arrangements to you. I thank you."

"I—I'm sorry. I wish I could do more, that I had done more."

Suparman's lips curl. He places his hand on yours.

"I thank you for all you have done and all that you will do. Keep that bamboo. See what you can make of it. I hope we will need to find many uses for it in the future."

Suparman presses a button on his transit chair, and it lurches forward to the viewport. Suparman reaches out and puts his hand on the surface between him and the memorial to his daughter. He holds it there for a moment, then turns the chair back to you.

"I will see you tomorrow."

"Yes, you will."

Suparman's transit chair slides out of the corridor, leaving you sitting alone, staring out at the memorial, out at the face of Suha. You are glad you have come to see it finally. You should have come sooner. Uxío was right, as he usually is.

There is much you need to prepare for if Darian is truly to travel up to Station. You realize that there is much that is new here with which you are unfamiliar. You will need to learn about those things, at least so that you can show them to Darian when he arrives. This is what Uxío intends, you now see, for you to be a kind of guide to Darian, and, in assisting him, to guide yourself.

BOOK

I

Mnemonic Device

Palik

Palik looked up from the workbench when he heard the birdcall. He had customized the buzzer on the front door of his shop with facial recognition software and a *Birds of the World* audio feature. Now, when customers came in, he could tell what to expect by the type of call.

If a customer looked generally content, such as when bringing in a robot for an upgrade packet, the opening door would trigger the *skreer* of a Micronesian kingfisher followed by a loud *kewp-kewp-kewp-kewp*. But if a customer's face bore a glare of annoyance because an obstacle-avoidance work-around patch didn't take, then the incredibly irritating *ka-wow ka-wow* of the common koel would sound. Then again, if someone came in because Palik had fixed a robot so well that it now operated better than it had out of the box—if that person's eyes were lit up with the kind of joy and appreciation that a retina scan could recognize—well, then the melodic whistles and tweets of a song thrush would fill the repair shop. He hadn't often gotten to hear the song thrush.

In fact, the call that sounded now was the maddening bleat of a channel-billed cuckoo, and without even turning from his workbench, Palik knew that meant that Hamdani had entered the shop.

Hamdani had been his father's oldest friend from his home village, the man whom his father credited with saving his life and helping the family settle here on Labicittá. "All we have we owe to this man," his father had said about Hamdani, though usually only after a few drinks. Before his father passed, he had made Palik promise that he would continue to repay this debt. Palik, of course, would do all that he could to solve Hamdani's problem.

But Hamdani's unsolvable problem was that he was the least intelligent person on the island of Labicittá. He was a man who found on-off buttons too confusing and who didn't understand why solar panels needed to be pointed toward the sun. Palik had once tried to show him how to replace fuel cell batteries himself rather than having to bring his autocar to a dealer. Hamdani responded, "No, do not show me how to replace them. If I learn, my wife will expect me to do this myself."

Slowly, grudgingly, Palik turned to see Hamdani standing in the open doorway, letting the cool air escape the shop and using one hand to mop his forehead with what looked to be a child's diaper. In his other hand, Hamdani held a cord that dragged a small domestic robot behind him. The robot looked a little like Hamdani. They both achieved balance through a low center of gravity.

Hamdani gave the cord a tug and pulled the robot over the threshold, allowing the automatic door to close and the sound of the cuckoo to fade away. Palik stepped away from his workbench and wound through the trench created by crates of machine parts and circuit boards until he had reached the old man.

"Take my hand, brother," Palik said, putting his arm forward.

Hamdani reached out with the hand holding the diaper. Palik instinctively pulled back.

Hamdani laughed. "Do not worry, Palik. This is my new invention. I have found that my grandchildren's diapers are more absorbent than a handkerchief for the sweat of my brow, and they give me a baby-powder-fresh scent. Sniff my head."

Palik pulled back further.

"Palik! Only one time have I mistakenly grabbed a used diaper. I believe this may be the invention that makes my fortune."

"I do not doubt it, Hamdani," Palik said. Palik not only doubted it, he was sure using a diaper as a sweat rag did not qualify as an invention.

Palik turned sideways to maneuver past Hamdani in the narrow passageway between the reconditioned robots and consoles in the front of his shop. One of these days, he would have to reorganize this place. He crouched down beside the domestic robot and scanned the idiot panel. There were no indications of anything out of order.

"So, Hamdani, what seems to be the problem here?"

"Peh, this bot! It hates me. Yesterday, it purposely hit me. It's been nothing but trouble since you convinced me to buy it."

Palik bit his lip. He had told Hamdani to never buy this brand of robot. The reason it cost half as much as the standard model was because it was half as reliable.

"It turns on, but it won't take commands," Hamdani continued. "I may have a hernia after pulling it all the way over to your shop."

"Ah, you should have let me check it remotely." Palik picked up the robot and carried it back toward his workbench.

"Perhaps, perhaps," Hamdani said, following Palik through the winding pathway to the back of the shop. "But you know I prefer a personal touch. I am not a man of the cloud like you."

Palik tipped the robot onto the workbench so that he could examine its underside. It had a standard 360-degree sphere propulsion mechanism, though this one was made with the cheapest parts available. It was designed to be used on microfiber carpets, not the bamboo floors that were typical on Labicittá, and it should never have been dragged through the downtown streets to a repair shop. Palik could see that the sphere had become pitted and would need to be replaced soon, but it spun freely for now.

"Do I have your permission to activate the voice history?" The law required customer consent before checking voice records, after one too many family secrets had been given a public airing back in the early days of these machines.

"I have nothing to hide," Hamdani said, spreading his arms wide as if to indicate openness.

Palik reached over to the circuit board and triggered the voice activator. There was a pop, and then a computerized voice with an upper-class British woman's accent could be heard.

"I despise you, you disgusting man! Why don't you clean up after yourself for once, you pig—"

Palik muted the sound.

"See, what did I tell you! This robot hates me."

Palik went back to the idiot panel and called up a menu.

"Hamdani, I think I see the problem. The customized settings are in masochism mode. That might explain the hostility."

"Well, I am *machismo*, am I not? I want a robot that gives me respect."

"Let me see what I can do here." Palik scrolled through the settings menu, settling on "docile" and activating the child safety features. That would at least keep the robot from hitting Hamdani again, not that he didn't deserve it. "I'm going to put the robot on a transit cart for you. Take it home and let it fully reboot and recharge overnight. It should be okay in the morning. This one is on me."

"I knew I could count on you. You are too good to me, Palik. You know that?"

"The thought had crossed my mind."

Hamdani laughed and patted Palik on the shoulder as they walked toward the door. "Perhaps you would like to invest in my invention."

"I'm just a poor Labicittá repair shop owner. If you need investors, you should go over to the Cord where the money is."

"Perhaps, perhaps. But I'm not sure those with their eyes on the stars can see what is in front of—"

Hamdani stopped when he walked into the doorjamb. He readjusted himself and continued.

"Well, please think about my offer. I've left you a diaper on the workbench."

Palik could not muster even a fake gesture of gratitude, but Hamdani went on, suggesting to Palik that he should stop by for a drink sometime, perhaps when his nieces were visiting. They all could have a drink together. Hamdani recommended Palik bring rum, if that was what he preferred drinking.

Palik offered assurances that he would stop by. It would be wrong to say his assurances meant next to nothing because they truly meant absolutely nothing.

But Palik had work to do, so he allowed Hamdani to depart in peace with the robot on the transit cart. He had built in an automatic return protocol in the cart; otherwise he was sure never to see it again. Why had his father put up with this man as a friend? What could he have possibly done to have earned his father's lasting gratitude?

He watched out the side window of the shop as Hamdani paused at the corner and pushed the robot to the side of the transit cart. Then Hamdani sat next to the robot and reengaged the cart. The cart lurched forward, sending Hamdani toppling to the ground. He quickly got to his feet and ran off after the cart, which somehow seemed to stay a few strides ahead of him until they were out of sight.

"Idiot," Palik mumbled to himself.

Then a voice from the workbench spoke up. "In the first place, God made idiots. That was for practice. Then he made school boards."

Palik smiled. He stepped over to the workbench and looked down at the robot torso that perched there, placing his hands on the robot's metallic cranium and closing the shutter covering the motherboard.

"Yes," Palik said. "The problem with my business is that it relies upon customers."

"For business reasons, I must preserve the outward signs of sanity," the robot said.

That one didn't really make sense, at least not within the context of the conversation. The algorithm wasn't quite right yet, but it was coming along. Palik turned off the vocalizer, then replaced the skullcap and face of the robot. The face looked particularly good, he thought, and the money he had paid to purchase an actual mustache had been well spent. He hoped the trader who had let Palik shave it off his face in exchange for a couple rounds of drinks found the deal worthwhile the next morning. Actually, he hoped the trader remembered nothing of the transaction the next day, which was likely.

Most of the work on his docket this morning was remote, so he put on his helmet screen, crouched down over the air vent next to his workbench and tripped the switch on the SimulGrav. A rush of air swept him off his feet as the desktop on the screen appeared before his eyes. It was disorienting for a few seconds—it always was—but his body quickly adjusted to the feeling of weightlessness and the sight of an unimpeded virtual starscape before his eyes. If it wasn't for the hum of the air compressor, maybe, just maybe, he would be able to let himself believe he was floating in space. It was a simulation, but it was probably as close as he'd ever get to leaving the planet. Besides, it was better for his back than sitting in a chair.

He had hopes that if he worked through lunch, he might be able to leave early to do some fishing. Initially, he was optimistic, as the first couple items on the docket involved little more than correcting hard-wired anomalies caused by off-the-shelf system upgrades. Two robots, two fixes, all taken care of as he hovered and rotated a couple meters off the ground.

But then his hopes for a short day were cast asunder like circuit boards ripped from a robot by the jaws of an Australian cattle dog. Actually, there was nothing "like" about it. That was exactly what had happened. There was a lot of trouble between domestic robots and Australian cattle dogs. The dogs always tried to herd the robots, for which they could not be blamed. They had been bred to herd livestock, not to live in city apartments. But the robots tended to interpret the dogs' movements as hostile, which triggered the evasive/avoidance sequence, and that just got the dogs excited, and the whole thing could spiral out of control until either a dog was cowering and whimpering under a bed or a robot was found out of commission, lying prone like a turtle on its shell.

Palik messaged the apartment for house call permission and high-balled a cost estimate, knowing that the automatic negotiator program would argue him down. But to his surprise, his estimate was accepted as is, and he was given an encrypted passcode. Maybe this would be easier than he thought. He eased off the SimulGrav and removed his helmet when his feet settled back on the ground. Then he turned on the "back in an hour" screen in the front window, put his diagnostic equipment in the back of the autovan and detached the van from its charger. He took the robot torso off the workbench and synced it into the van's steering column. If he was going to be stuck in traffic, he might as well have something to talk to, and the more time he spent in conversation with the robot, the better it would perform.

The autovan pulled out onto the roadway and joined a line of vehicles crawling through downtown. The traffic had become unbearable lately. Ever since the expansion of Station, the island had been overrun by people either trying to get up the Cord into space or make money off people trying to get up the Cord into space. Palik realized, with no small irony, that his business involved making money from people who were making money from people who were trying to get up the Cord into space. He himself was no closer to actually getting passage onto the space elevator than the robot piloting his autovan was to the actual Mark Twain.

"Sometimes, it all seems like a big lie," Palik said to the robot.

The robot turned toward him, and Palik found himself staring into a pretty good approximation of the face of Mark Twain, bushy mustache and all.

"If you tell the truth, you don't have to remember anything."

"Hey, that was pretty good. You made a conceptual connection rather than a literal one. Let's try this: when I was a boy, Labicittá was a simpler place."

There was a slight hesitation from the robot, but then it spoke.

"When I was a boy, there was but one permanent ambition among my comrades in our village on the west bank of the Mississippi River. That was, to be a steamboatman."

"Well, do you think you can use your steamboatman skills to pilot around this traffic?"

"Give a man a tolerably fair memory to start with, and piloting will develop it into a very colossus of capability. But *only in the matters it is daily drilled in.*"

The autovan abruptly lurched out of the flow of traffic and down an alleyway that didn't look wide enough to Palik for them to fit through.

"Stop!" Palik shouted. The autovan halted. "I don't think that's going to work. It's too close."

"It was a close place," the robot said, its voice shifting into a higher register that Palik recognized as Huckleberry Finn. "I was a-trembling, because I'd got to decide, forever, betwixt two things, and I knowed it. I studied a minute, sort of holding my breath, and then says to myself: 'All right, then, I'll go to hell.'"

Suddenly the autovan accelerated into the alley. Palik instinctively closed his eyes and heard the robot give out a whoop that sounded like it might have once been used to call pigs. When Palik opened his eyes, the autovan was zooming through the alley, clearing the walls on either side by centimeters. Palik stayed silent, afraid anything he said could trigger the robot to swerve into the wall.

But the autovan pulled out of the alley intact and swung onto a clear bypass road that led out past the blimpport to where Palik's appointment was. The traffic immediately lessened, and Palik felt it was safe to glance over at the robot who had one hand on the steering wheel. The robot's other hand held an intake valve that Palik had made in the form of a cigar.

"A pilot must have a memory," the robot said in its regular Mark Twain voice, "but there are two higher qualities which he must also have. He must have good and quick judgment and decision, and a cool, calm courage that no peril can shake."

Palik reached over and deactivated the robot, which automatically turned on the van's autopilot. Training this robot was going to be more complicated than anticipated. But, then again, most everything was.

The area over by the blimpport had all been pepper and copra farms when he was a kid. But recently, a lot of those farms had been bought up and turned into housing. They couldn't build these complexes fast enough it seemed. Everyone wanted to come to Labicittá to get close to the Cord, where one's fortune was just a space elevator ride away. Or so the story went.

He tried not to be too cynical about it. At one time, that had been his dream, too. He had hoped his robotic engineering degree would get him a ride up the Cord. But so had thousands of others, many of whom had enrolled in university on Labicittá, hoping that the proximity would make the difference.

It rarely did, he had come to realize. The countries that invested in the space elevator wanted to send their best and brightest to Station. To them, Labicittá was just Lobby City, a necessary pass-through on the way up the Cord. The only use the investor countries had for people on Labicittá was employing them to deliver food, or to care for children, or to fix personal robots. But that didn't stop people from coming to the island with all kinds of get-rich-quick schemes, filling up these new apartments that smelled of freshly cut bamboo and desperate ambition.

With an emphasis on the "desperate." Ever since Moore's Law had been demoted to Moore's Tendency (which meant it probably was really Moore's Exception), the worldwide economy had slowed to a crawl. It had become harder and harder to envision what the future would bring or how it would be brought about. A repair shop suddenly seemed cutting edge.

The autovan pulled up to the apartment complex, one in a ring of identical buildings centered around an empty swimming pool that seemed much too small for the number of units in the complex. The passcode got the van through the gate, and then the complex's autoguide took over the steering and parked the van near an entryway. Palik loaded up a portable transit cart with all his equipment and synced the cart to the complex. Then he followed it through a series of doors, each of which required a retina scan for him to pass. And then there were hovercams that followed him down the hallways. This place was seriously wired for security. He wondered if the hovercams followed people into the bathroom.

In the service lift, Palik looked back over the customer account on his console. Joshua Martin. The name wasn't familiar. But if the customer was living in this complex, he was probably new to the island. After only two more retina scans and one manual passcode entry, Palik was finally able to get into the apartment.

The place was a mess. It looked like it hadn't been cleaned in weeks, with clothes on the floor and takeaway food cartons piling up next to the disposal unit, but that wasn't Palik's initial concern. His initial concern was that he had forgotten about the Australian cattle dog. He was reminded of the dog as soon as the transit cart slid ahead of him into the apartment and the dog ran over to attack it. It was just blind luck that this particular cart was made out of salvaged parts from an old postal delivery servbot. The HypnoMace spray immediately squirted at the dog, leaving him semi-sedated and licking his genitals happily in a corner of the living room.

With that problem taken care of, Palik made his way over to the robot, gathering up the various components that had been ripped away and scattered around the room, where they were intermixed with an array of digivices that looked to have been tossed on the floor as well. When he had collected up the pieces, he saw that it was mostly cleaning attachments that had been ripped off the robot, and though the power pack also had been stripped away, it didn't seem like anything essential had been damaged. This robot was a high-end version of a standard domestic brand, so Palik had plenty of replacement parts on hand.

The repairs didn't take long. He had to microweld a few pieces in place and 3D print some new instamolds for the robot's scarred surface, but once he did that and got a new power pack installed, the robot ran through the diagnostic sequence without a problem. He programmed in a quick cleaning cycle, ostensibly to test the robot's features but really because this apartment was disgusting. The robot spun into action, activating one attachment after another to pick up, steam clean and vacuum. In a few minutes, the common area looked habitable again with clothes off the ground, cushions straightened, the ridiculous number of digivices organized near the projection screen and the carpet sanitized.

The robot moved down the hall toward the master bedroom, where it placed clothes inside a hamper in a closet and began making the bed. Palik had thought that the living room seemed kind of sterile, but the bedroom had even less character. It was a room without any decoration, not a painting or even a digiframe. There was a huge wall-sized projection screen, but the only sign of actual human habitation was a large collection of notably ugly ties. Who was this Joshua Martin? Palik normally wasn't much interested in the lives of his customers, but he couldn't help but be intrigued by the inscrutability of this one.

After making short order of the bedroom, the robot wheeled out of the room past a closed door and put itself on its charging unit. Palik wasn't sure why it had ignored the room with the closed door. He had run a whole-apartment cleaning cycle. He went back to the robot's idiot screen and saw that there was, in fact, a master command override that removed that room from the robot's consideration. That was odd. He was curious, so he tried the handle of the door. It was locked. What was the point of having a domestic robot if you still had to clean part of your space manually? Palik couldn't figure out this customer's contradictory combination of carelessness and caution. Of course, this was nothing for him to worry about, but Palik often found himself concerned about things that were none of his concern.

The door had an old pin tumbler lock. The extension key on his digiwallet was able to pick that in less than a minute. Slowly, he pushed the door open, not sure what he expected to find.

What he saw shocked him. Lying on the bed was a young girl, around seven or eight. He thought she was dead because she was lying there with her eyes wide open and a big gash in the side of her head. But then he saw that the gash was actually just an access panel opening that revealed a mass of circuitry. He was relieved to see that it was just a robot, but it was not a model he recognized.

Someone had put some serious money into customizing this robot. It had a full head of dark hair on the side of its head without the access panel and eyes that he knew had been designed to convey warmth and innocence. Knowing that didn't make the eyes any less effective.

The facial structure looked like it might be of Chinese origin, but he could tell right away from the exposed casing in the head that its component parts were American. Still, the skin graft on the face was amazing, better than anything he could do with his equipment. And the attention to detail was incredible, right down to a random freckle on the robot's right arm. He poked at the freckle and felt the arm give in a way that made him uncomfortable. Then he pinched the robot's upper arm through the kids' pajamas it was wearing. He got very uncomfortable.

He felt the robot's legs and its torso. It all seemed to be biological. This was wrong. The biological percentage was way too high, particularly for a robot built with US-origin circuits. US courts had ruled that any robot with double-digit percentages of biological components violated the Fourteenth Amendment, essentially making them legally human, and most other countries had equally tight controls with serious sentences for possession or manufacturing.

But the biologicals on this robot were way into double digits. It was contraband.

And then he saw blood on the pillowcase. Something told him to take a closer look at the circuitry in the head. Gingerly, he pulled the circuit board back. It was attached to the gray matter of a brain.

Palik pulled back, stunned and horrified. This was no robot. It wasn't even a cyborg. This was a transhuman. This was a girl.

He wasn't sure what to do, but he couldn't leave her there with her brain exposed, so he closed the access panel.

The girl's eyelids immediately began to flutter. She turned toward him and visibly winced.

"Help me," the girl said. "It hurts." She raised an arm toward the incision on her head, but then her arm fell down to the bed. She started to cry.

Palik hesitated for a moment, then reopened the access panel. The crying stopped. A small trail of blood appeared on the girl's skull, and her eyes stared vacantly up at the ceiling again, as if she had fallen into some kind of sleep mode. She wasn't conscious, and she wasn't in visible pain either. He realized instantly why she had been left with the access panel open, or should he say with her brain exposed. Something was wrong with her and someone didn't know how to fix her.

He grabbed his diag equipment from the other room and ran a quick scan. Along with circuits in the head and neck, there was a strand of poxy-silicon that seemed to run parallel to the spinal cord and must have been synced to the nervous system. At least that was what he guessed. There was no way to know for sure without opening her up, and he was a repairman, not a surgeon. He started combing the room, hoping to find some tools that might help him figure out what to do. But if this guy, Joshua Martin, didn't know how to fix his domestic robot, what chance was there that he would know what to do with a transhuman?

He checked the closet, looked under the bed and even tried to hack into the apartment system unsuccessfully. But there was nothing, no repair equipment and not even a manual. What was this guy doing with a transhuman girl?

Of course, he could answer his own question. It was the same reason the guy had an Australian cattle dog in a small apartment and every possible digivice one could imagine. He liked toys. He just didn't want to take care of them.

Palik knew he should report the girl to the police, but he also knew what would happen if he did. If word got out that someone had snuck a transhuman in past customs, there would be hell to pay. This Joshua Martin must have bribed someone to get her onto the island. Customs and the police were under the same ministry, and no one would want a scandal. They could just declare her a robot, which meant that she could just be decommissioned. But she wasn't a robot. Palik knew that.

He could just close the door and walk away. He could pretend he hadn't seen anything. He shouldn't have been in that room anyway.

But he had heard the girl. He had seen her eyes. He could see them now.

Palik's hands shook. He had to make a choice, and neither option was good.

"All right, then, I'll go to hell," he said out loud.

He signaled for the transit cart to come over. It wheeled in, followed by the dog, who was nuzzling up to it, hoping for another blast of the HypnoMace. He opened up the enclosed storage shelf and took out all the equipment. Then he loaded the top of the cart with silicon chips, electric screwdrivers, the holodrive projector and the rest of the tools he used to make a living. He carefully picked up the girl and gently slid her onto the shelf, making sure to rest her head on her pillow. She was small enough that she fit without even having to bend her legs.

Palik closed the door to the shelf, and the cart slowly wheeled toward the door of the apartment. He stopped it momentarily to give the dog another squirt of HypnoMace. The dog panted and lay down, curling around the domestic robot like it was a puppy. Palik gave the dog a quick scratch on the top of the head.

Then he opened the door to the apartment, and the cart passed out into the hallway. The hovercams immediately appeared over his head. He tried to ignore them. Palik quietly accompanied the cart out of the complex and into the parking lot. He heard the sound of a bird.

Ka-wow ka-wow

He recognized the call of the common koel, which immediately made him look for the face of an annoyed customer. He grabbed the largest CPU cracker on the cart and whipped his head around, expecting to see Joshua Martin wanting the transhuman girl back. But all he saw was a real bird in one of the trees.

Ka-wow ka-wow

He needed to get out of here. He was starting to lose it. He carefully guided the cart into the back of the autovan, then detached his robot from the steering column and moved it into the passenger seat.

"There's been a change of plans. I'm going to need to pilot," Palik said, strapping the robot's torso in place.

"Your true pilot cares nothing about anything on Earth but the river," the robot replied, "and his pride in his occupation surpasses the pride of kings."

Palik climbed into the driver's seat and engaged the manual drive. "It's going to be a slow ride home. And I'm going to need you to be quiet so I can think."

"It is better to keep your mouth closed and let people think you are a fool than to open it and remove all doubt."

"Wait a second! I don't think that quotation was actually by Mark Twain."

"It is my belief that nearly any invented quotation, played with confidence, stands a good chance to deceive."

Palik wasn't sure how to respond to that, but he also had more important things to worry about right now. He slowly pulled out of the parking lot, wondering what he was going to do with a stolen transhuman. Actually, kidnapped was the more appropriate term. Either way, he was heading for trouble.

· · · · ·

ANY EXCUSE TO go fishing was a good excuse. The doctor had told him to leave the girl with her for the afternoon. That meant this excuse was better than most, which made the fishing even more enjoyable.

He was at his favorite fishing spot, on the far side of Labicittá, where there were hardly any fish. Most everyone else went to the buffer where the catch was plentiful. Ever since the waters had been closed on the other side of the island as part of the security zone around the Cord, that whole area had become a virtual sanctuary for sea creatures. It was as if some collective fish brain said to come gather in the waters off Labicittá and multiply. Schools of snappers, shoals of sturgeon, whatever you called a bunch of tuna, they all prospered in these waters. But the collective fish brain wasn't too sharp when it came to staying within the boundary of the security zone, and plenty of fish wandered into the open waters of the buffer where many an eager angler waited.

Palik had once been among their number, bringing in huge hauls of fish that were more than he could eat or even afford to freeze. The stink of rotting fish and the guilt he felt over depleting an already over-burdened ocean led him to give up fishing for a while. But he missed the waters, and he longed for the peacefulness of sitting with a line in the water, free from expectations until there was a strike.

This was why he now fished on the far side of the island, where he could be at peace with only the rare fish on his line to distract him and the occasional interruption of a fellow angler, who would tip a cap or sign with a laser guide upon passing, wondering why Palik was fishing on the wrong side of the island. The breeze was comfortable, he had a cool drink beside him and the robot was synced into the boat's steering system. Piloting the boat triggered his robot to share stories about nineteenth-century ocean voyages.

"It was breezy and pleasant, but the sea was still very rough. One could not promenade without risking his neck; at one moment the bowsprit was taking a deadly aim at the sun in midheaven, and at the next it was trying to harpoon a shark in the bottom of the ocean."

Palik was glad he hadn't gone with his first impulse, which had been to create a Ralph Waldo Emerson robot. Long sermons or essays would not have made for a good companion. He was much better off with a robot based on a humorist with a gift for aphorisms like Mark Twain.

Palik cast into waters, but his line landed too close to the boat. What kind of amateur cast was that? He was still distracted. He was still worried about the girl. But he had done all he could. He was right to bring her to the clinic. She needed a doctor, not a repairman.

He cast again, mentally trying to place all his concerns onto his line as his wrist flicked the rod. This time, the line whirred quickly, traveling far from the boat before the lure settled in the waves. Palik eased back into his chair, took a sip of his drink and listened to the robot.

"What a weird sensation it is to feel the stem of a ship sinking swiftly from under you and see the bow climbing high away among the clouds! One's safest course that day was to clasp a railing and hang on; walking was too precarious a pastime."

Palik interrupted the robot. "When my father arrived in Labicittá, it was during a typhoon. Your experience reminds me of the tales he told of washing up on the shores here."

The robot hesitated before continuing in a child's voice. "I don't like this thing of being stripped naked & washed. I *like* to be stripped & warmed at the stove—that is real bully—but I do despise this washing business. I believe it to be a gratuitous & unnecessary piece of meanness. I never see them wash the cat."

Palik paused the robot's audio output. What was that nonsense? The robot tapped its intake valve on the ship's wheel, removing an imagined ash. The training wasn't going so well, as moments like this made clear. The robot could never quite engage in conversation on a human level. But then again, perhaps few humans could either.

"Let's switch topics. Tell me more about the Mississippi River. There is still much I do not know of those waters. I'll just be quiet and listen." Palik reactivated the audio, leaned back in his chair and put his feet up on the rail. The rod felt steady in his hands.

The robot spoke again. "Along the Upper Mississippi every hour brings something new. There are crowds of odd islands, bluffs, prairies, hills, woods and villages—everything one could desire to amuse the children."

Palik still wasn't sure he was doing the right thing for the girl. He had run a full diagnostic when he first got her back to his shop, and all the non-biologicals checked out. But when he switched her on, she was still in pain, and now she was confused as to where she was. He had gotten her to eat some bread, but he couldn't bear to watch her chew and cry at the same time. He had had to turn her off again. It was the pain. What did he know about pain? He fixed robots. Pain was biological.

This was why he had brought her to the clinic, even though it was a huge risk. There was nothing to stop the doctor there from reporting him to the police, except for the fact that most of her patients were illegally on the island anyway. But he had done some work for her in the past fixing an fMRIbot, and he had to hope she would look the other way.

He had been careful. He had brought the girl to the service entrance so no one saw her, and he had pretended he had a delivery that only the doctor could sign for. But when he tried to explain the situation, the doctor had gone through the roof. "How could you bring her here? Why do you even have her? Bloody hell!"

Now that Palik thought about it, she really didn't have good people skills for a doctor. But after he explained the girl's situation and how she was suffering, the doctor softened. That is, if by "softened" one meant that she threw him out of the clinic, telling him not to come back until nightfall. "Get the hell out of here. I'll give it a fair go."

It was just like one of these clinic doctors from Australia to think she was the only person who could cure someone. How many times had he seen these doctors arrive on the island convinced that they were going to solve everyone's problems only to give up and return home within a year? This new doctor was no different. Palik had noted her UV-vulnerable fair skin and the fact that she was sweating even in the climate-controlled clinic, and he gave her no more than six months before she was on a blimp, leaving Labicittá to fare for itself yet again.

The doctor who hadn't been able to save Palik's mother was hardly different. That one was tall, confident and, in the end, utterly useless. To this day, Palik still didn't understand why his mother's body had shut down, only that it had happened while he stood helplessly by the side of her bed, holding her hand but unable to help at all as his father sat behind him in a chair, openly weeping.

A tug on his line snapped him out of his thoughts. For a second, he feared he had made a strike, but it was just the wind shifting directions. The robot adjusted the rudder and kept speaking.

"Since those days, I have pitied doctors from my heart. What does the lovely flush in a beauty's cheek mean to a doctor but a 'break' that ripples above some deadly disease. Are not all her visible charms sown thick with what are to him the signs and symbols of hidden decay? Does he ever see her beauty at all, or doesn't he simply view her professionally and comment upon her unwholesome condition all to himself? And doesn't he sometimes wonder whether he has gained most or lost most by learning his trade?"

"Stop," Palik ordered. "You are supposed to be talking about the Mississippi River, and here you are going off about doctors. A conversation only works if you stay on the same subject!"

He slapped at the robot's intake valve, knocking the cigar-shaped tube onto the deck of the boat.

The robot slowly pivoted toward him.

"He always maundered off, interminably, from one thing to another, till his whisky got the best of him and he fell asleep. What the thing was that happened to him and his grandfather's old ram is a dark mystery to this day, for nobody has ever—"

Palik reached over and deactivated the robot. He reeled in his line and picked the intake valve up off the deck. He gave it a quick look-over to see if it was damaged, then placed it carefully back into the robot's hand. Then he dumped the rest of his drink off the side of the boat into the water. The sun was starting to set. It was time to get back. He had an appointment with the doctor.

· · · · ·

THE SETTING SUN illuminated everything around him in a soft orange light. It would have been a beautiful sight if he hadn't been at the clinic, which was to ugly what Swedish herring were to fish. That is to say, it was small, oily and smelled bad.

The clinic was located in an old industrial area that had never been fully reclaimed. Part of the clinic building was a warehouse/shack that had once stored decorative bricks, and before that it had been part of the equipment staging area when the Cord was built. Palik supposed that gave the building historical significance, but that status alone wouldn't keep the structure standing much longer. A section of the roof had been ripped off during a typhoon, and whoever did the repairs combined bamboo with tin so that the roof looked like a hockey player's teeth after a brawl. A waiting room for the clinic had been added on, and, shockingly, it was even shabbier than the main building. It had been built with donated materials and by available laborers who were rightfully unemployed. The whole structure was off-kilter and flimsy, and a decent exhale could blow it over.

But it was the only clinic that served people without proper ID, which was illegal, but it was allowed to operate so that people wouldn't be dying on the streets of Labicittá. Well, at least so that people wouldn't die on the streets in excessive numbers. From dawn to dusk, there was a line out the door of people who needed much more than the clinic could provide but who were grateful for whatever they got.

For a long time, the clinic had been run by nurses and some volunteers with no medical training at all. But for the last few years, the clinic had had a doctor from off-island. As hordes of people were drawn to the island because of the Cord, seemingly the only technological bright spot in a worldwide depression, the authorities must have realized that they needed help even if they couldn't officially acknowledge it.

But the government still threatened to close the whole operation every time there was some public incident, which was probably the reason why this doctor gave Palik such a hard time for bringing the girl to the clinic. The other reason was that she was just an angry and unpleasant person. She clearly would trigger the common koel's *ka-wow ka-wow* chirp if she ever walked through the doors of his shop. So he took a deep breath before he knocked on the service door, not sure what to expect.

Well, even being unsure of what to expect didn't cause him to anticipate that the doctor would fling open the door and begin punching him in the face. He was so surprised that he didn't even put up his hands to fend her off. His initial impulse was to think that there must be someone behind him that she actually meant to be swinging at. He turned around to look for the person that wasn't there, and then he felt a cut on his cheek.

"You bastard! How could you do such a thing? To a child?"

The doctor's face was bright red with anger. She continued screaming at him as Palik grabbed her wrists and told her to calm down. She didn't, at least at first, and tried to wrench free of his grasp. Palik couldn't think of anything more intelligent to say than, "What? What?"

Finally, the doctor stopped struggling, and Palik released his grip on her hands. For this, he was rewarded with a slap on the cheek.

"Stop!" he shouted, putting his hand to his cheek and coming away with blood. "I'm bleeding."

That, it turned out, was the right thing to say. At least it caused the doctor to respond more like a doctor and less like an assassin. She looked down at her hands. Palik could see that they were shaking.

"Get inside before someone sees you," the doctor ordered.

"Good idea after you scream and attack me," Palik mumbled.

They went into the clinic, and the doctor closed the door. Palik immediately saw that the girl had been placed on a storage shelf that had been adapted into an examination table. The access panel on her head was closed, and she wasn't crying. That seemed good to Palik. The girl turned her head slowly and looked in his direction, but it didn't seem like she was seeing him.

"I have her sedated for now," the doctor said. "It's not a long-term solution, but I'm not going to leave her with her brain exposed, for chrissake."

The doctor grabbed Palik's chin, and he flinched, expecting her to take another swing at him. But she had a swab in her other hand, and she was just cleaning the cut on his face.

"Sorry about that," she said. "Not that you didn't deserve it. I forgot about my ring."

Palik felt the sting of alcohol against his cheek. The doctor let go of his chin and cleaned the blood off an engagement ring. It was quite a rock, a large, glistening diamond. The diamond was nothing like the tiny one he had scraped together money for when he and his ex-fiancé had their short, unhappy engagement.

"You've got me all wrong, Doctor. I'm just trying to help her." He gestured over toward the girl. Her eyes were open, but he could see that she wasn't focusing on anything and probably wasn't aware of anything they were saying.

Palik explained the whole situation again, from seeing the girl during the house call and thinking she was just a robot to deciding to try and fix her. He knew right away something was wrong, but he worried that if he reported her, she would be declared a robot and deactivated.

The doctor was unimpressed. "So your defense is that you're just a kidnapper? Fine, let me tell you what you've gotten yourself into."

She took a deep breath and gave him the full medical rundown. Basically, the problem was that she was a girl and she was growing. As she grew, her body tore against the circuits that had been melded to her. But the circuits were everywhere. It would be impossible to remove them without ruining her spine, never mind her brain.

"And whoever did this to her had to know that would happen. That's the worst part."

Palik nodded slowly. "He thinks she's a toy. At best, a pet."

"Who?"

"Joshua Martin, her owner. Not her owner, her…"

"Her slaveholder. That's all he is."

Palik looked at the girl. Her head was turned so that the gash on her skull was not visible. He turned back to the doctor, who looked tired. There was redness around her eyes. She handed Palik a vial of pills.

"I can try to help, but I can't keep her here. If she were discovered, they'd close the clinic. You can give her these pills for the pain for now, but that's not an answer. There's not a medical solution. The problem is in the circuits."

"I fix circuits. That's what I do. I'll find a way."

The doctor sighed. Palik's assurances didn't seem to go far with her.

"Bring her back if you can't help. There are stronger meds, but they're not for children. Don't let her suffer."

Palik nodded, but at that moment his assurances didn't go far with himself either.

· · · · ·

"FOREIGNERS CANNOT ENJOY our food, I suppose, any more than we can enjoy theirs. It is not strange; for tastes are made, not born. I might glorify my bill of fare until I was tired; but after all, the Scotchman would shake his head, and say, 'Where's your haggis?' and the Fijan would sigh and say, 'Where's your missionary?'"

The robot couldn't eat, of course, but when Palik attached it to the sphere drive, it could roll over to the table, where there was room for it and an ashtray where it would rest its access valve. And because it didn't eat, it tended to dominate the conversation. And Jia—that was the girl's name—liked it when the robot told stories. She found him funny, and she would laugh when the pain wasn't too bad. She didn't laugh enough, so Palik encouraged the robot to go on.

"The principal difference between a cat and a lie is that a cat has only nine lives."

Jia laughed again, and noodles fell from her mouth. Palik told himself to appreciate the moment, the three of them sitting here sharing a meal together. From where he sat, the girl looked like any other child, struggling with chopsticks, her legs swinging under a chair that was too tall for her feet to touch the ground. At moments like this, he could forget that there didn't seem to be anything he could do for her.

For the first couple days after he had taken her, Jia had hardly spoken to him. She had asked immediately where Mr. Martin was. Palik made up a story about Joshua being called off-island and about how he had sent her here so Palik could cure her. It sounded like a lame excuse to him, but Jia accepted it. Over time, she became more comfortable and shared some details of her life with Joshua Martin. Though she was just a child, she worked as his cook and housekeeper and had ever since she could remember. She said nothing negative about him other than that he hadn't been able to make her pain go away, but she didn't seem to have warm feelings about him either. Her attitude was less like a child's than an adult employee's. She seemed to have no expectation of any other kind of life. When he had asked if she had ever been to school, she said no and looked at him as if he were ridiculous even to ask the question. Jia treated him like a nosy neighbor, but she seemed to genuinely care for the Twain robot. She spent every spare moment speaking with it and getting it to tell her stories. It was only then that she truly seemed like a child.

"Jia," Palik said, "thank you for this dinner, but you do not have to cook for me."

"I cook," Jia insisted. "It is what I do. It is my training."

"Training is everything," the robot interjected. "The peach was once a bitter almond; cauliflower is nothing but cabbage with a college education."

Palik smiled. "Well, it was delicious. Thank you, Jia."

"New Orleans food is as delicious as the less criminal forms of sin. I also thank you, Jia."

Palik dropped his chopsticks and stared at the robot, but it was silent, looking straight ahead with its electronic eyes under white, bushy eyebrows.

"Did it just say your name?" Palik asked.

"Yes, I taught him to. He kept calling me Susy, so I fixed him."

"How the—I mean, that's amazing. Did you access the programming input or did you just—"

Palik paused. Jia had raised her hands to her head, and she was massaging her temples. He knew what that meant.

"Jia, why don't you lie down? I can give you some medicine."

"The kitchen must be cleaned."

"It doesn't have to be cleaned by you. I can take care of it. Please."

Jia wanted to argue, he could tell, but when the headaches came on, they came on suddenly. She wasn't even able to walk on her own to the bedroom. Palik had to carry her out of the room and put the pill in her mouth. Fortunately, it took effect quickly, leaving Jia in a daze that at least wasn't painful.

Palik returned to the kitchen. The robot's sensors picked up his approach.

"Many public-school children seem to know only two dates— 1492 and 4th of July; and as a rule they don't know what—"

Palik put the robot on pause and started to clean up the dishes. He wasn't in the mood to laugh. What he wanted was to just go to sleep, but he had a long night ahead of him. Over the last week, he had been spending every spare moment trying to figure out some fix for Jia. There wasn't as much literature on transhumans as he would have thought. At least, there wasn't much publicly available. He was sure there was plenty of research on some of the early military transhuman projects, but all that information was classified, and from everything he could discover, every military that started developing transhumans abandoned the project anyway.

Not that there hadn't been plenty of human modifications. After all, Palik himself had a robotic thumb, courtesy of a boating accident he had had as a teenager. But it hadn't been implanted until after he was fully grown, and he expected to have to get a new one in about twenty-five years. But he had gotten so used to his RoboThumb that he hardly gave it a second thought. Still, he could survive without his RoboThumb. The same couldn't be said for Jia. Her biologicals were only about 60 percent. Her internal organs were intact, but her muscular structure was almost entirely circuit-based, and much of her nervous system had been augmented as well. It was such incredible work that at first he couldn't figure out why they hadn't replaced the bones, which were starting to pull away from the nerves and muscles. That could have been foreseen. Then he realized that that was the point. Jia had a built-in obsolescence. Whatever monster had augmented her had known exactly what would happen.

When Palik had been a teenager, he had had growing pains, his shins aching after a day working in the copra fields. He had felt like his bones were stretching out of his skin, and that's what would happen to Jia. He had to figure something out soon. He had told the doctor he would.

When he finished the dishes, he went down to his shop, put on the web helmet and tripped the SimulGrav by the workbench. He told himself to focus on the problem at hand and let the SenseSearch intuit what he needed. That was the easiest way to find anything nowadays. A collage of sites appeared in front of him. Most he could blink away instantly, and others with the black ribbon reading "Classified" flickered and disappeared on their own. He was left with a handful of articles and instructional videos, most of which involved animal experiments that were, or should have been, illegal.

He removed the helmet and turned off the air, letting himself stand next to the bench. Why was he even bothering with more research? He had looked for information already and knew there was nothing to find. There weren't even records of contraband transhumans, never mind their repair specifications. He crouched down to examine the vat he had set up on the workbench. There were a dozen petri dishes with graphed pig muscle that he had attached to strands of carbon nanotube. They were sitting in a solution of growth hormone. Even in a few short days, they had already begun to expand, binding and enveloping the nanotube. He knew that as they continued to grow, they would stretch and eventually tear from the nanotube. Unless, of course, he could find some substance that allowed for separation.

His initial research had turned up a handful of potential chemicals, though most of them were toxic. He had selected a few others based on nonbinding properties, but he had no idea if they could even be introduced into a biological system. He examined each dish closely, looking for any signs of change, but there were none to be seen. Each dish looked like it had a little bacon appetizer on a round, transparent tray. He smiled, and he was glad he could still do that. He put the helmet back on and triggered the SimulGrav. He would keep searching.

• • • • •

WHEN THE ALARM sounded, Palik suddenly awoke and couldn't get to his feet. He found himself swimming in the air, and for a second he thought maybe he was drowning. But then he realized he was still in the SimulGrav. He was disoriented and hadn't remembered falling asleep at the workbench. But more importantly, he didn't know why the alarm was going off. He blinked off the SimulGrav and whipped off his helmet before his feet even touched the ground. Then he vaulted up the stairs to his apartment and saw Jia at the top of the landing.

"What is it? What is it?" she shouted, her hands covering her ears to block the noise.

"It's okay! It's okay," he replied, but he didn't know that. He stepped over to a wall panel and pulled up the security screen. It showed a breach at the kitchen window by the back deck. Palik bent down and put his hands on Jia's shoulders.

"Jia, go back to your room and close the door. Don't come out until I come to get you."

Jia immediately stopped shouting, and a calm look came over her face. It was scary how quickly she responded to anything that sounded like a direct order. When Jia was in her room, Palik turned toward the kitchen, wondering what he would find.

What he found was more or less what he expected. The kitchen window had been pried off its hinges and was lying cracked on the floor. It was a little more of a shock to see a man tied up in fishing netting hanging upside down from a security hook in the ceiling. The robot had positioned itself right next to where the man was suspended. Palik was worried the man might still have a weapon, so he stayed back by the entryway to watch.

"As by the fires of experience, so by commission of crime you learn real morals."

The robot prodded the man with his intake valve cigar, and the man's body slowly rotated so that Palik couldn't get a good view of his face.

"Commit all crimes, familiarize yourself with all sins, take them in rotation (there are only two or three thousand of them), stick to it, commit two or three every day, and by and by you will be proof against them."

The man hanging from the ceiling spun in a full rotation. When the man's face came back full circle, the robot lowered itself so that they were face to faceplate.

"When you are through, you will be proof against all sins and morally perfect. You will be vaccinated against every possible commission of them. This is the only way."

Palik stepped into the kitchen and cleared his throat. Even though they had never met, and the man in front of him was upside down with his face pressed into the mesh of the net, Palik knew who he was.

"So, you must be Joshua Martin."

• • • • •

OF COURSE, PALIK had expected that Joshua Martin would try to take back Jia, so he had upped his security protocol, like anybody would have. The surprising thing was that Joshua Martin had come alone and that he'd been so sloppy about things. He didn't try to cut power to the house first or send an electromagnetic pulse into the house's computer banks. Not that either of those things would have worked. Palik had been prepared for those kinds of attacks as well. But still, it was hard to respect someone who didn't think enough of you to break into your house properly.

Not that there would have been much to respect about Joshua Martin anyway. As soon as this Joshua started talking, he tried to deny who he was, which only worked until Palik took the digiwallet out of his pocket (who brings ID to a break-in?). Then he got all blustery and said Palik had no right to hold him like a prisoner, but that line only held until Palik offered to call the police in. And then Joshua actually started crying—big, rolling-down-the-cheek tears—claiming Palik would ruin his life and to please show some mercy. It almost killed Palik not to bring up the condition of Jia, but he thought it best if she stayed out of the discussion.

Palik checked back in on Jia, and, fortunately, she had fallen back asleep. If he was lucky, he'd be able to take care of all this before she woke up again, but he didn't have long before morning. Palik went back to the kitchen, detached the netting from the hook, and put the trussed-up Joshua Martin onto a transit cart. He decided to bring the robot along since Joshua really seemed to despise it. The whole trio moved down to his workshop, Joshua complaining the whole way that the netting that was keeping him trapped was hurting him.

"I'm starting to lose feeling in my limbs. If anything happens to me, you will be held responsible by people who know how important I am," Joshua said, his whining quickly escalating into an empty threat. Joshua twisted around, which had the effect of pressing his face into the net and creating a waffle pattern on his skin.

"Okay, I'll try to keep your importance in mind," Palik said. He pulled Joshua off the transit cart and leaned him up against the bench, then straightened him into a sitting position against the wall across from his workbench. "I'm going to take you out of the netting, but don't try anything."

"Make it quick. I'm starting to have trouble breathing."

"It's a net, not a bag. I think you'll be able to get enough air."

Palik released the fastener on the netting, and it fell from Joshua like the petals of a flower. Joshua immediately sprang up and ran for the door. But Palik had set the transit cart in capture mode, so the cart immediately blocked Joshua's path, causing him to trip onto the cart's platform, where he was doused in a generous dose of HypnoMace, generous enough that Palik had to cover his mouth and nose, punch in a deactivation code on the cart and run out into the hallway, all without taking a breath.

When the air had cleared, Palik stuck his head in and saw that the robot was perched over the prone body of Joshua Martin.

"A person that started in to carry a cat home by the tail was gitting knowledge that was always going to be useful to him," the robot said, looking up at Palik.

"Very true, my friend."

Palik grabbed a link of nanotube composite from the workbench. He fashioned it into a crude cord, wrapped it around the limp ankles and wrists of Joshua Martin and secured it around a magnalock. Once the man on the ground before him was tied up, Palik got a chance to examine him more closely. He was going to have quite a bump on his forehead from falling into the cart. Otherwise, Palik guessed him to be in his mid to late fifties. He must have been in good shape at one time, judging from the definition in his shoulders, but he had extra weight that showed in his jowls and gut. His skin hung loose against his face. He drooled and snored slightly. Palik pressed a piece of Chameleon-Putty to the tip of Martin's index finger. Then he looked around for a clean rag to use as a gag. He saw the diaper that Hamdani had left for him. It was close enough. He grabbed a laser blade from the bench and sliced the diaper in half.

"My friend," Palik said to the robot as he fastened the diaper section around Joshua's mouth. "Your book, *Following the Equator*, how long is that?"

The robot hesitated for a second. "*Following the Equator: A Journey Around the World*. 712 pages. The starting point of this lecturing-trip around the world was Paris, where we had been living a year or—"

"Yes, very good. When Mr. Martin wakes up, I would like you to begin reading it to him. Keep going until you finish."

Palik tripped the SimulGrav switch, and Joshua Martin slowly rose off the ground. Joshua's feet floated toward the ceiling so that he now looked like one of those whole chickens that hung in the front windows at some of the traditional markets in Labicittá. Palik returned to the kitchen to see what he could do about the broken window. His eyes still stung from the HypnoMace, and he rubbed them. When he looked up at the window, he thought he saw the angry face of the doctor staring back at him. He rubbed his eyes again. Yes, it really was her. What was she doing here? It was barely dawn.

"What's going on?" she called in through the broken frame. "Are you crying, for chrissake?"

"Crying? No, it's—it just has been more complicated than anticipated." Palik went to the door and opened it so that the doctor could come inside.

She walked in and slammed the door behind her.

"I don't want to hear about your problems, mate. You were supposed to bring the girl to me two days ago. Jia needs regular care, and you know I can't take the risk of messaging you."

Palik sat down at the table and gestured for the doctor to join him. He apologized and then caught her up on Jia, his experiments and now Joshua Martin. There was a lot to cover. It might not have taken as long as reading *Following the Equator*, but it felt like it did.

At first the doctor's reactions ranged from annoyed to impassive. But when he started talking about Joshua Martin, the blood rose in her face and her fingers gripped the tabletop.

"So that's where things stand," Palik finished. "I still don't know what to do about her, and now I don't know what to do about him."

He looked at the doctor and thought at first that she was staring right at him, but then he realized that she was staring past him, or maybe through him. Then she straightened up.

"Do you still have his wallet?"

Palik nodded and pulled it out of his back pocket. He took the piece of ChameleonPutty with the imprint of Martin's fingertip and pressed it against the digiwallet. The doctor took the digiwallet from him, but she couldn't open it initially, as it had a secondary security system. She slid her finger down the screen, and the indicator clicked open.

"How'd you know his passcode?" Palik asked.

"Two-five-eight-zero. He's lazy and sloppy. It's obvious."

Somehow, when Palik had been talking, the doctor had formulated a whole plan. While she scrolled through Joshua's accounts, forwarding messages and transferring files, she told Palik what he had to do and how he needed to do it. Palik listened closely. He couldn't tell if the doctor was joking when she said she could remove one of Joshua Martin's hands so that Palik would be able to have a palm print to access protected files. Palik said he could make a temperature-sensitive mold of Martin's hand that would do the job. The doctor nodded impassively, as if it was all the same to her.

The doctor's plan sounded like it could work. At least, it was better than any plan he could have come up with. And there wasn't much time anyway.

"Jia—the girl—she will wake up soon."

"Don't worry. I can manage her."

"Her breakfast. What she likes. It is in this cabinet."

The doctor smiled. "I appreciate that you're worried about her breakfast." The smile faded. "Now leave."

. . . . .

ON THE DRIVE past where the copra fields had once been and where Joshua Martin's apartment now was, Palik realized he had been talking to himself. Normally, he would have had the robot with him, and talking to a robot didn't seem the same as talking to oneself, though most people wouldn't have made that distinction. Still, there were a lot of details that had to fall into place, and Palik needed to memorize them all. What he was about to do was risky, and if he was caught, he needed to be sure that his actions couldn't be traced back to the doctor or the clinic. That meant he would have to destroy the piece of paper in his hands once he had memorized the information on it. But there were a lot of details and scores of potential passcodes involved.

Palik put the autovan on autopilot, closed his eyes, and began with an old mnemonic device back from when he was trying to memorize physics formulas as a student. He visualized the house where he had grown up as a child, the house his father had built. The rough boards and bamboo planks were perched over a first floor made of stilts. Theirs had been the only house in the neighborhood built with a first-floor platform. His father said he would never be driven from his home by a flood again, and it didn't matter that they were more than a kilometer from the shore.

As he envisioned the house, he saw himself as a boy coming back from school, mounting the steep steps to the back door. He smelled that his mother was making sup kambing, his favorite soup. The aromas of ginger and pepper wafted through the air. As he reached for the door handle, he told himself, "Punch in the same repair access code you used last time," and he watched himself pressing the digits, memorizing them at the same time. He opened the door and saw his mother at the stove. She turned to him, and he saw her as he remembered her when he was a boy, a small, almost slight woman with smooth skin and round cheeks. Her hair was held away from her neck in a bun, but a few strands inevitably fell into her face. She blew them away with a puff and smiled at him.

"Remember, Palik," his mother said, "Joshua Martin is not a thoughtful man, but he is devious. There will be much hidden, but that which he hides will be in obvious places."

"Yes, *Ibu*," Palik said, letting his eyes linger on her young and beautiful face, a face that seemed to have nothing in common with the one ravaged by illness at the end of her life.

"Why are you standing there? Move along," she said, turning back to the stove. "On the table, there's a snack for you. Memorize it and then eat it."

"Yes, *Ibu*." Palik walked over to the table and sat in one of the well-worn chairs. How many snacks had he and his older sister, Alya, eaten in this very spot? On the table, he saw a large cassava cracker, as large as the piece of paper he actually held in his hand. On the top of it, in cramped handwriting that he somehow knew was the doctor's, was the name "Joshua Martin." Under his name was a list of potential passcodes. He committed them to memory, eating each one as it was memorized. At first, the bites tasted of paper, but by the last one, Palik could only sense his mother's cassava cracker. It was as crisp as a cool day.

"Go see your father," his mother said, still turned toward the stove. "He has information for you as well. And make sure you bring some kind of a bag with you in case there is material you need to remove from the apartment of that horrible man."

Palik wanted to ask his mother to turn around once again so that he could see her young face, but he knew he had much to do. He pushed back from the table and exited the back stairs, walking around the house and entering the garage under the house that his father had converted into workspace. His father had always been a tinkerer and occasionally a sculptor, but only the first interest had passed down to Palik. His father had been in the civil service for most of his working career, apart from the years when he had helped to construct the Labicittá base of the Cord. As a civil servant, those skills went unused. The space under the house was where he went to relax, though even in his relaxation his father seemed driven by demons.

Palik stared at the nameplate on the door: "Aditya" it said on the first line. The second line read "Private." Palik knocked tentatively on the door.

"What?" an irritated voice shouted. "Come in, and don't forget to reconfigure the automatic alarm settings on Joshua Martin's apartment."

Palik stepped into a dimly lit and dusty workspace. His father stood with his back to him. He appeared to be chipping away at a large stone.

"Is it time to eat?" his father asked, tapping a chisel with a small hammer.

"No, *Ayah*, not yet. You wanted to see me?"

"Tell me all of the places where you will look and what you hope to find."

"Mattresses, closets, false floorboards, cabinets; passports, money, identification chips, contraband of any kind."

"And do you have much homework today?"

"Yes, *Ayah*, there is much work for me to do at home."

"Well, then get on with it. You may only have one chance."

Palik stared at the back of his father's head, his close-cropped hair and the sweat shining on the back of his neck. His father never turned to face him, and Palik did not ask him to. He looked over his father's shoulder for a better view of what he was working on. In the stone, he saw the face of the doctor wearing a look of impatience.

"You heard your da," the stone doctor said, an impossible furrow appearing in her brow. "Get on with it, bloke."

Suddenly, the autovan lurched to a halt, and Palik snapped his eyes open. The face of the doctor and his childhood home was gone, and he was staring at Joshua Martin's apartment complex. He paused for a moment. That was all a little weirder than he had been expecting.

But the mnemonic device had done the job. He remembered what he needed to do. He grabbed a tool sling from the back of the autovan, detached the transit cart, and passed through the security procedures of the apartment complex. He knew not to be surprised by the hovercams, and by the time he let himself into Joshua's apartment, he sensed everything was going to go smoothly.

He had forgotten about the dog again.

The second he opened the door, he heard the bark from the kitchen. This time, the transit cart was still in the hallway, and Palik had no protection. He turned to see the dog in midair, lunging at him with his jaws open. He had just enough time to put up an arm as the dog latched onto it. The impact threw both of them to the floor, and all Palik could think to do was cover his face.

But then nothing happened. Palik was flat on his back, his tool sling painfully poking his kidneys. The dog had crouched down next to him, looking as if it expected to be hit. Palik sat up. Tentatively, he extended a hand and scratched the top of the dog's head, which caused an eager wag of the tail.

The dog must have remembered him or maybe his scent or maybe just the scent of the HypnoMace, which still must have been on him or the transit cart. Palik wasn't sure which. He was just happy the dog was no longer attacking him. He activated the transit cart, and it slid next to the dog, releasing a dose of spray onto the now-happy animal.

He synced into the apartment system. In his mind he was able to see and even taste the passcodes on the cassava cracker from his mother's table. He entered them in the apartment system and implanted a find/archive/replace protocol. The protocol would take any information of interest off the network and replace it with junk, not unlike the way mosquitoes extracted blood from you and replaced it with whatever it was that made you itch. While the program was running, he searched all the places he had told his father he would look.

As soon as he started looking for hidden items, they appeared everywhere. How had he not noticed them the first time? The mattress was stuffed with money. Chinese, American, New Indonesian, some currencies he didn't even recognize. The closet had a false back with a box containing certificates and fake passports. There were three loose floorboards. Two of them held weapons and ammunition. The third held what looked like drugs or at least chemicals. They were labeled in Chinese, but when Palik ran his scan translator, it came up empty. It was bad, whatever it was. It was much worse than he had imagined.

When his protocol finished running, Palik had almost a terabyte of data and his transit cart was full. The system had spit out dozens of identification chips as well. It was more than he had expected. It was more than enough. Joshua Martin wasn't just a criminal; he was stealing from criminals.

• • • • •

PALIK WAS EXCITED, if a little nervous, to get back to his shop and show the doctor all he had retrieved. Of course, if he had been pulled over for any reason, he had enough contraband on him to spend the rest of his life in jail. He set the autovan for a slow return as he began tabulating the information and preparing what to say.

He was eager to show the doctor everything. He realized he wanted her to be impressed, to see that he was more than just a repairman. In any properly functioning economy, he would have done great things. Maybe he would have gone up the Cord and been someone who really changed this world. Anyway, he at least didn't want her to think he was an idiot.

He punched in the passcode to his kitchen door even though there was still a gaping hole where the window had been. When he walked in, everything looked fine, except for the window frame lying next to a wall.

"Doctor? Doctor, are you there?"

For a second, there was silence, and then the doctor burst into the kitchen. He wasn't sure quite what he had anticipated, but the last thing he was expecting was for her to throw her arms around him and give him a big kiss.

But that's what happened.

When she let go, Palik could see that she had a huge smile on her face. Her eyes were lit up with excitement as she grabbed his hand and pulled him out of the kitchen and down toward the workshop.

"I've got the—"

"Wait, I've got to show you," she said.

"What about Jia? Is she—"

"I said wait."

"And Joshua Martin. Is he—"

"For chrissakes, can't you just hold on?"

She stopped on the stairs and stared up at him, a look of annoyance overtaking her face. This, at least, was more familiar. Palik stayed quiet and followed her down the stairs until they were standing next to the workbench. Joshua Martin was nowhere in sight.

"Where is—" He stopped himself that time.

The doctor let go of his hand and gestured to the petri dishes on the workbench. "Look, number eight."

The workbench was covered in the petri dishes with pig muscle. They had seemed like appetizers before, but now they looked like roadkill. As the pig muscles had grown, they had distorted, bloated, and been shredded by the carbon nanotube cores to which they were attached. All except for the eighth dish. He could see right away that something was different with that one. Instead of tearing, the muscle seemed to have unbound itself from the cord, grown, and then reattached itself. It was an incredible thing to see. Of course, there was bleeding with the process, but a small white fabric square had been placed in the dish, and it had collected the blood, allowing the chemical to do its work.

"I can't believe it," Palik said.

"It's bloody amazing," the doctor agreed. "I hope you don't mind. I ran specs on the agent, and it's clear for children."

"Sure, that's fine. How did you find material to take care of the bleeding?"

"How did I find it?" The doctor looked puzzled. "You had it right on the workbench. I just cut away a small piece to test."

The doctor picked up the fabric from the workbench. Palik looked at it, befuddled, and then he understood. It was the remains of the diaper that Hamdani had given him.

• • • • •

TAKING CARE OF Joshua Martin was as awful as Palik expected it would be. Maybe worse, because the doctor was no help whatsoever. She couldn't be in a room with him for long. That was why she had dragged him into a storage closet when Palik was gone. By the time Palik got him out, he was angry and nursing a deep scratch on his cheek (worse than the one Palik had) from the doctor's engagement ring. Once Palik took the diaper gag out of Joshua's mouth, it all started again. Anger followed by whining followed by pleading. From bluster to tears within the course of a conversation. Palik stayed calm and explained all that he now knew. He showed Joshua the passports and identification chips. He detailed what he knew of the money laundering. He shared documentation that showed clearly how Joshua was embezzling from gangsters. Jia's name never even came up.

"Fine, you've got me." Joshua's shoulders slumped. His clothes were rumpled, and his hair was a mess. "So, what are you going to do?"

Palik flipped open Joshua's digiwallet and swiped at a screen.

"This is a ticket for you on the next blimp off-island. I'm going to take you to the blimpport and watch you board. You're going to leave with nothing but the clothes on your back, and you're never going to return. If you ever do come back, or if anything happens to me, to the doctor or to Jia, all this information will be automatically forwarded to authorities on Labicittá and in several other countries. I never want to see you or hear your name again. I'm going to untie you now. Everything is in place to expose you if anything goes wrong."

Palik could see that the fight was out of Joshua Martin. He looked like the defeated man he was.

"Fine, fine," Joshua said, his head hanging down. "Just don't make me listen to that goddamn robot anymore."

Palik turned to the robot. "From now on, every time this man speaks, I want you to say something to irritate him. And if he moves without my permission, poke him." He turned back to Joshua. "I don't want to listen to you either."

• • • • •

IT WAS AN unseasonably beautiful night, and Palik refused to feel guilty about it. Sometimes climate change had to be on his side, after all. The ocean was calm, and there was the slightest of breezes. He had anchored the boat in a little cove with a natural sand beach. Jia and the robot were on the beach, collecting shells and driftwood while he and Sheila sat on the boat watching them from a distance. Sheila had brought some kluwak nuts, just like she had the first time they had come to this spot, the time he actually found out her name was "Sheila" and didn't have to keep referring to her as "Doctor."

Palik was still a little uncomfortable eating the kluwak nuts. They were, after all, poisonous if not properly prepared, but they did go well with rum, and it was pleasant to watch Jia play, running and jumping with hardly a missed step, this despite all that she had gone through and all the surgeries. Palik had worried a lot about them, but Sheila had told him not to be concerned.

"Children are resilient," she had said.

She was right. Almost a year after those operations, and almost two since he had first taken her from Joshua Martin's apartment, Jia seemed like any other girl. She was even in school now, after some clever manipulation of identity chips so that it looked like Sheila had adopted her in Australia.

There was a lot more to Sheila than he had realized. It was something to see her so relaxed and happy, a lemonade in her hand and her feet raised up on the boat's railing. Her hair was shorter now, and it hung free. It all made her look like a different person than the angry, uptight doctor he had first met.

Of course, he realized now that he had read her wrong initially. She had seemed angry and uptight then because she was scared and felt over her head at the clinic. It was her first job out of medical school, and what did she know about running a clinic? But any girl who grew up in Australia with the name Sheila had to learn to maintain a tough exterior. Really, why would parents do that? Didn't Sheila just mean "girl" in her country? Now, of course, he realized that much of her attitude was an act, like the fake engagement ring designed to ward off unwanted interest.

She had a great capacity to feel for others, and she truly cared about her job. Palik had been impressed by how she handled all of Jia's operations without letting any of her work at the clinic slide. Of course, the automatic triage protocol that he had installed in the clinic's admittance system had gotten her some of the time needed to make all of that possible. It was the surgeries that had really brought the two of them together. All that time watching over Jia, monitoring her recovery, not really knowing if the process would work. Jia needed them both, and they both knew it.

And here they were now, going through a similar experience, all of them joined together in a process and bound to be irrevocably changed by it.

Palik felt the shell of a kluwak nut bounce off his skull, and he heard Sheila laughing. Then she bounced a second shell off his head. Okay, he should keep things in perspective. Sheila could still be a difficult person.

"Should we head back soon?" Palik asked, turning to look at her.

Sheila flipped up her glasses and nodded. She smiled and placed her hands on the perfect round bubble in front of her.

"Still not used to it, huh?"

"You try being pregnant and see if you get used to it."

Palik smiled and downed the last of his drink. He cupped his hands and shouted to shore.

"Jia, it's time to come back."

Jia looked up from the assortment of shells and sticks in front of her, which appeared to have been elaborately categorized by shape and size.

"We can't come," Jia shouted from the beach. "We have to finish our work."

"That's not work, that's play. Jia Chiang, hurry up."

"Work consists of whatever a body is obliged to do," the robot called out. "Play consists of whatever a body is not obliged to do."

"Very good, but I'm obliged to get everyone back before it gets dark. Two minutes."

On the beach, the robot rolled toward Jia and extended its hand, helping her up. Rolph, that was the name of the Australian cattle dog that had once been Joshua Martin's, jumped and yipped next to them.

Palik went to the side of the boat and lowered the dinghy so he could bring Jia, the robot and the dog back from the beach. Then he felt

Sheila's arms around him. She was hugging him, or at least hugging him as much as she could with a pregnant belly in front of her.

"Everything okay?" Palik turned so that he could put his arms on Sheila's hips.

"Everything's great. This has been a wonderful day, and I've enjoyed every moment. I have so much energy right now. I know I'm supposed to be tired, but I feel like there's so much to do."

"I think that's called nesting."

"I don't mean just about the baby. I mean about this island. I've been thinking. A clinic is just a bandage. It's important and necessary, but it can't solve problems. I love this island, but I want it to be better, both for Jia and for her sister, Mega."

"Mega? I thought you didn't like that name. I was half joking when I suggested it."

"It's grown on me over time, like most of your ideas. Like you, actually."

Sheila kissed Palik, then pulled back.

"I'm serious though. I think it's time for me to get into politics. Well, maybe give Mega here a little time first. Are you all right with that?"

Palik thought while he finished lowering the dinghy into the water. "I'm all right with that. Most of your ideas have grown on me, too."

He squeezed Sheila's hand and stepped into the rowboat. On the island, Jia had loaded the robot's arms up with enough driftwood to start a fire. She waved at him excitedly as he rowed toward the beach. The dog snapped at the waves as they broke on the shore. Jia started shouting about a plan she had for the driftwood, and the robot was saying something about building a fire on Jackson Island while Sheila was still talking about her plans for the government on the island. It was a lot to pay attention to all at once. But he was willing to try.

Sheila

It's like flying a kite, Sheila thought, staring up at the Cord. It was a striking view, particularly because the Cord was backlit by spotlights at night. Seeing it up close for the first time, she was surprised by the impossibly thin strand of carbon nanotube stretching out of the launchpad. The tiny thread rose into the sky and continued out of sight, as if the kite at its end was just out of view. But Sheila knew that the Cord reached through and beyond the atmosphere, where it eventually attached to Station in low orbit. Yet that had always seemed an abstract fact, like the knowledge that the Earth revolved around the sun or that dinosaurs once walked the Earth.

Now she was being asked to take it on faith that this flimsy-looking strand would support her and her husband, Palik, on a trip into space. Sheila didn't like taking things on faith. But even though the idea of boarding a climber to ascend the Cord made her nervous, she knew how to maintain her composure. She wouldn't let her nervousness show, partly to maintain her stature as Governor of Labicittá and partly because Palik looked like he was starting to lose his shit. Glancing over at him, Sheila saw that his face was flushed and his hands were trembling, and they weren't even close to boarding the space elevator yet.

"Hold it together, bloke," Sheila said.

"I'm not afraid of heights, and I'm not afraid of small places," Palik said. "But I'm not sure how I feel about the two together. What would that be, acroclaustrophobia?"

"I think I'm suffering from fear of bullshit. Does that have a name? Here, take this. It's a new antianxiety pill. Just don't tell anyone I gave it to you."

"Where'd you get this?"

"I know people."

Palik swallowed the pill and looked relieved. It was only a sugar pill, but Sheila wouldn't tell him that. She appreciated the power of suggestion more than most. Pretending she knew more than she did was one of the ways she had risen from rural Aussie schoolgirl to doctor in a semilegal clinic to being elected governor of this island nation of Labicittá. And it was how she had been able to talk her way onto the space elevator for one of the first trips open to nonmilitary personnel. More importantly, it was how she was able to call in every last favor she had to ensure that her husband could come on this trip with her.

She knew that, despite his complaints, this trip meant everything to Palik. Of course, Sheila was excited to go into space, too. Who wouldn't be? But for Palik, going up the Cord meant much more. She tried to appreciate what it had been like for him, growing up on Labicittá where the economy, the culture and the schools all revolved around the Cord, even though almost no one from Labicittá ever traveled up it to Station. His whole life, he had been staring at this sky-bound string, knowing it went somewhere he couldn't go. It had left a core of bitterness in a man that she knew was otherwise caring and decent. And, at least until the placebo took effect, it also made him a little skittish.

Palik craned his head up the length of the Cord, then tugged at the tie Sheila had forced him to wear.

"It's a long way to go," he said.

"It'll take about five days, they told me."

"No, you and me. It's a long way to go. I never thought we'd end up here." Palik placed his arms around Sheila's waist. "I'm ready to fly, Governor, and I can't imagine what happens next."

Sheila smiled. He was right. He couldn't imagine what he was in for. She hadn't told him the half of it yet.

•　•　•　•　•

TWENTY MINUTES LATER, they had cleared the security screening and were escorted down to the launch bay into a small room just large enough for the flight crew and the half dozen passengers making this trip. The Cord was still a military operation, so no one had put much thought into the niceties that tourists expected. Sheila could tell the travelers who had signed on weren't too keen on being packed into a cramped predeparture room on inflatable chairs. She worried Palik's newfound claustrowhateverphobia might be an issue as well, but he seemed to have calmed down. Still, it was hot and crowded in the room, and everyone was a little unsettled.

They had all been through a training regimen over the past few weeks, so there really wasn't anything more to go over, but one of the soldiers launched into an extended safety lecture anyway. It was word for word the same as one of the videos she had screened in preparation for this trip, only the production values of this soldier's talk weren't as high.

Sheila ignored the soldier. She had bigger concerns. If this trip to Station was a success, it could mark the beginning of a new era on Labicittá. For while the military in charge of the Cord viewed this trip as a necessary PR exercise, Sheila had hopes that the success of this trip would lead the way for transitioning control of Station into civilian hands. Now that the technology for gravity platforms had been perfected, there was no reason Station couldn't be expanded and become more than just a military operation. Energy retrieval, tourism, space exploration, scientific research, it all became possible once you could get a critical mass of people into space. Tourism was what Sheila had her eye on. Not that tourism didn't bring its own problems, but

Labicittá had beaches and fishing and plenty to lure vacationers looking to pour as much money as possible into the island's economy.

Not even Palik knew about her larger ideas. There was nothing to be gained by making her plans known. She would work behind the scenes, figure out how to persuade the powers that be that an expansion of Station into tourism was their idea. That had been the secret to her political success. Well, that and not being afraid to call a grommet a grommet, when necessary. But as far as anyone was concerned today, she was just another excited space tourist, the representative local politician along with her representative native husband. She knew how to play her role, even when she had more than one.

As the safety talk droned on, Sheila sized up her fellow travelers. This was the first time they all had been in the same room together. She had made a point of reviewing the dossiers of everyone who would be coming up the Cord, but people didn't always look like their augmented dossier images.

She first noticed the quadrillionaire, Stefan Odelay, because he, in fact, did look like the image on his dossier (some combination of good living and expensive cosmetic surgery, no doubt). He was the only man not wearing a tie for the event, and it looked like he had just run his hands through his hair this morning, but Sheila understood that being a quadrillionaire afforded one some idiosyncrasies. Or maybe it was just being an American. Even so, she was surprised to see him playing a game on his digivice during the safety talk.

Park Min-Seo was the UN representative on the trip. She was a tall, stately woman with a helmet of dark hair. She wore a traditional Korean outfit, a beautiful dress with a vibrant red panel of fabric. It stood out, but that must have been the point. Sheila had seen her once before at a conference on governance in the Pacific, but that was years ago. Park Min-Seo had given a presentation on the maintenance of traditional cultural practices in the aftermath of Korean unification. Compared to Park, Sheila felt underdressed. As it was, she would be glad to exchange her heels for a set of practical astronaut boots or whatever it was they'd be wearing.

When the safety presentation concluded, they all rose from the inflatable chairs, and Sheila noticed that one of the travelers, a scientist named Hugo Karlsson, was ridiculously tall, well over two meters. Would he even fit into a space suit? Karlsson seemed to recognize how much he stood out. His shoulders were slumped, and his eyes were downcast as he left the room.

Sheila and Palik had been in previous training sessions with the other two travelers. Fritz Steiner was a vice prime minister from one of those tiny European countries with many syllables. He was a slight man who seemed to have no sense of humor whatsoever. Alin Smeeth was a beefy-looking bloke who seemed to crisscross lines between military, business and government. He, at least, did have a sense of humor. When Sheila had asked him how to pronounce his name at their first meeting, he said, "Just like 'Alan Smith.' My parents misspelled both my first and last names, so don't blame me."

Since she and Palik had met Steiner and Smeeth before, they took hands and acted like they were friends. It wasn't that Sheila had anything against these men. She just had no reason to trust them. Palik was less suspicious, which was both a feature and a fault. He struck up a conversation with Steiner about fishing, a hobby they both shared. Sheila asked Smeeth about his blimp ride to the island.

"No blimp for me, lass," he said, with a smug smile on his face. "I came in on a military transport jet. Took a quarter of the time."

And left ten times the carbon footprint, Sheila thought. But she phrased her response more diplomatically. "I thought you weren't in the military anymore."

"Oh, I've got a foot in where I need to be. It's just a sign that this trip on the climber is being taken seriously."

Sheila nodded. By whom, she wanted to ask. But she could wait to find this out. She wished she had better information on everyone involved with this trip, except for Palik, about whom she had too much information. Right now, the conversation had turned toward the varying skills needed for deep-sea fishing vs. freshwater stream fly-fishing. If

Palik kept talking about fishing once they boarded the climber, Sheila swore she would throw him off the space elevator.

• • • • •

THE CLIMBER WASN'T a rocket, which was the whole point. No need for pollution-belching engines, no dramatic liftoff. Just a laser boost to get started, and then the solar panels on the climber did the rest of the work. Payload costs per kilogram were one hundred times less than with conventional rockets. Sheila knew all this, of course. Everyone on board did. But that didn't stop Palik from monologuing about it to that poor scientist, Hugo Karlsson. The man seemed almost twice the size of Palik, but he cowered in a corner in the staging room they had been moved to as Palik explained about the tensile strength of carbon nanotubes and the feasibility conditions for the apex anchor. Sheila took pity on the poor guy.

"Palik, give the bloke some credit. He wrote the paper on transverse wave modulation. He knows how a space elevator works."

Palik smiled sheepishly. "Of course. I'm sorry."

"No apology is required," Karlsson said, standing up to his full height and again towering over everyone else. "Up to this point, all of my experience with the space elevator has been theoretical. The practical application is new to me as well."

They were interrupted by the flight crew, a trio of pilots in whose hands they were all placing their lives. Well, maybe that was a little dramatic. In theory, the flight crew only needed to be there for troubleshooting. They weren't quite glorified elevator operators, but the point was that someday maybe they could be.

"Okay, folks. Listen up." The leader of the pilots, a square-jawed man with matching square hair, was shouting, even though they were in a small staging room. Park Min-Seo shot him a look. Apparently, this wasn't how UN meetings were brought to order. "We've only got a couple hours until sunrise, and we'd like to time our launch to make the most of the day's sun. The forecast is for a bright and sunny day, so it looks like we'll have some great travel weather. But I'm going to need all of you to pass through the doors at the rear of this room, get your flight suits on, and then board the craft for the prelaunch check."

The pilot gestured with two hands to the doors at the rear of the room, which then sprung open, revealing what looked like an astronaut's walk-in closet. Sheila felt a flutter of nervousness, so she took Palik's hand, and they walked into the room. Their suits were labeled with their names. Sheila carried hers into an adjacent changing room.

It took longer to put on a flight suit than one would think, and there was no risk of these outfits starting a fashion trend. The ensemble was bulky and awkward, with layers of stiff gray material, but they were designed for astronauts, not models. Eventually Sheila had everything on, and she waddled her way back into the crowd, carrying her helmet at her side. They all looked like inflated versions of themselves. Sheila had to laugh.

"What's the joke?" Smeeth asked her.

"Look at us in these getups. Pump in some helium and we could float up to Station."

．．．．．

"I STILL THINK there should be a countdown," Palik said through the intracom system in their space suits. He was strapped into his seat with his helmet pressed back against the headrest. "I mean, I understand that it's not necessary anymore, but this seems anticlimactic. All the pilot said was, 'Settle in, folks,' like we were sitting in a dentist chair."

"Darl, if you want me to count backward from ten for you, I will do that." Sheila reached over and touched the arm of Palik's space suit with her clumsy gloved hand. Normally, Palik was a quiet sort. He'd keep to himself, fiddling away on projects in a back room, only to surprise Sheila—and her staff—by having reconfigured the window drapes in the governor's residence with sensors so they would automatically close at sunset. But when he was either excited or nervous, he would talk incessantly, and he was both now. Ever since they had gotten into the climber, he had felt compelled to describe every feature of the small capsule, as if Sheila couldn't see what was right in front of her and as if they hadn't toured the climber a couple weeks ago. But Sheila kept her patience. *Yes, the climber seems smaller now that it's full of people. Yes, the chairs are well designed. No, it doesn't really feel like an elevator.*

"The moment needs some sort of acknowledgment," Palik continued, "some sort of recognition that this incredible thing is about to happen."

It was at that exact moment that the climber started to move with a slight upward jerk. Sheila's first thought was that it did, in fact, feel like an elevator going up. Then Karlsson, the scientist, threw up.

Sheila strained against the seat restraint as if to whisper to Palik, though that was unnecessary with the intracom. "One small puke for man, one giant vomit for mankind. How's that?"

• • • • •

THEY PROBABLY MISSED some of the best views because they were all required to stay strapped into their seats at first. All the passengers had craned their necks toward the nearest viewport, of which there weren't enough. Sheila made a mental note that they'd have to get some user experience designers in to reconfigure these climbers before an operation like this went commercial. The feel of the space elevator wasn't all that dissimilar to riding in a blimp. The ascent was pretty quiet, and they rose up above the cloud line in no time at all. Of course, dirigibles went up and across. It was a little unsettling just to be going up.

By the time they were given the all clear to get out of their seats, they were too high to make out much detail below them. Nevertheless, the passengers immediately huddled around the viewports. Blue for water, green for land, the familiar outline of Labicittá that Sheila knew well from satellite images—the horseshoe with a headache, as it was called. Sheila stood next to Smeeth and Park. She wondered if the two of them had had any dealings before, and now she wished she had checked to see if Smeeth had spent any time in Korea, particularly during the Reunification Years.

Smeeth had his face pressed against the viewport, peering down to the Earth. Park hung back a bit.

"Sorry, didn't mean to take up the whole port with my big head," Smeeth said, stepping back. "Please, take it all in."

Park stayed where she was. "I can see fine from here. We are already pretty high."

Smeeth smiled. "If it makes you feel better, we're not really going up. We're just falling into the sky. It all depends on your relationship to gravity."

"I appreciate the gravity of our situation, Mr. Smeeth," Park said with a smile.

"Ah, good one. Left you an opening there, didn't I now?" Smeeth turned to Sheila. So, Governor, what do you think about our elevator ride so far?"

"Well, this is a lot different than that jet you came into Labicittá on," Sheila said.

"That it is. I was just thinking that I've probably missed my chance to ride in a rocket. If this elevator is all it's cracked up to be, that jet may be the closest I get. How about you, Ms. Park? Think you'll miss the rockets?"

The UN delegate paused, then smiled slightly. "I'm afraid I will always associate rockets with missiles, so I, for one, welcome this development."

"Of course. Of course," Smeeth responded quickly.

Park's response put a damper on that conversation. Sheila knew that Park lived in New Seoul, but the dossier Sheila had reviewed didn't say much about Park's childhood before reunification. Sheila guessed she could fill in the blanks.

From the corner of her eye, she saw Karlsson emerge from the lavatory dressed in regular clothing and looking a little chagrined. It was never easy to be the one who puked. The attendant (or "Mission Care Specialist" by his official title) escorted Karlsson back to the group and encouraged everyone to change out of their flight suits.

"You will, of course, need to wear the suits again when we pass through the Van Allen belt and then again upon arrival," the attendant said. "But feel free to make yourself comfortable for the time being. Relax and enjoy the trip."

Sheila was going to be glad to get out of the bulky outfit, but she also realized that now her real work would begin. She needed to size up everyone on this trip and figure out their agendas without revealing her own. She hoped that everyone else would truly get comfortable and relax, but she suspected most of them were approaching the next few days much as she was.

•　•　•　•　•

SHE STARTED WITH Stefan Odelay, the quadrillionaire. The official line was that he had no financial interest in the space elevator and was just an eager space tourist willing to pay a ridiculous amount of money to fulfill a boyhood dream. Sheila had her doubts about that story. Odelay had huge energy sector investments, and even if this was just a dream vacation for him, he would be unable to ignore the enormous potential for solar generation outside of Earth's atmosphere. As it was, he seemed fascinated by the lasers that were quietly powering the climber upward.

"The laser technology. Impressive enough. But the tracking system. Really blows me away. Got to target the receptor panel perfectly. Else laser just gets shot into space. We stop going up. Adjustments on the microsecond. These new cellular chips. Really change things. You think?"

Sheila wished Palik was next to her at this moment, since this was the kind of tech talk he understood better than Sheila, but he was on the other side of the climber, chatting with Steiner again. They apparently had become fast friends.

"It's the technology that defines our times," Sheila said. She had heard Palik say something like that once.

"Oh, not that far. But changes things. All those years of stagnation. Possibilities, you know. Like this."

Sheila nodded. Apparently, Odelay did not speak in complete sentences. Was this another one of those quadrillionaire quirks, or did it say something about the way his mind worked?

"What kind of possibilities?" she asked him.

"Who's to say? Still early. Energy, of course. Plenty of military contracts. Supplies and the like."

"What about tourism?"

"Tourism? Perhaps. Not the same margins, you know. More labor-intensive."

Sheila knew. In fact, that was kind of the point as far as she was concerned. Sheila tried to get Odelay talking about tourism, but the conversation kept winding its way back to the latest research or next-generation technology. Biofusion. Payskin. Power sticks. Sheila got a crash course in futurism, but she didn't learn much about Odelay. Or maybe she did. Maybe to become a quadrillionaire you had to occupy a unique place in the space-time continuum with a body in the present and a mind that was a decade in the future.

Sheila was grateful when Palik came back over to her and Odelay excused himself to drift over to the other side of the climber.

"You two seemed to be hitting it off," Palik said, giving her shoulder a squeeze. "Under normal circumstances, twenty minutes with Odelay is probably worth a million dollars to someone with an idea to pitch."

"Jaysus, don't you dare try to sell him an invention."

"Oh, come on, Sheila. Everyone here is trying to promote something, or didn't you notice?"

Sheila smiled.

·　·　·　·　·

SHEILA HAD WORRIED that she wouldn't really be able to size everyone up before they reached Station. That was a stupid concern. Five days is a long time, and they were essentially all living in the same room. By the end of the third day, she had had the chance for extended conversations with all six passengers and the three-person flight crew. She knew where everyone grew up and what their family situation was. Hell, she knew the state of most of their love lives, from Smeeth's three marriages to Steiner's forty years with his childhood sweetheart. She talked more about her childhood growing up in the Australian bush than she had at any time except during her first campaign for office. She and Palik shared stories about their daughter, Mega, and she found herself wanting to talk about Jia, but she knew better than to do that in front of Palik.

It's not that there wasn't anything to do during the trip, just that there wasn't enough. The views were spectacular, but there was only so much footage to shoot. There had been training sessions for when they got up to Station, but it wasn't like they were going to the Moon. There wasn't that much they had to learn about being on Station other than how to recognize space-induced nausea. Upset stomach, got it.

Sheila supposed everyone was still holding some secrets, but she felt she had a bead on this crowd now. Park Min-Seo was there to maintain UN control over Station in this new phase of its existence. Fritz Steiner had vague ideas of establishing a research station. Stefan Odelay had his eye on energy transmission. Alin Smeeth seemed to be representing someone with an interest in space exploration. Hugo Karlsson was interested in the mechanics of expanding Station. Palik was really the only one just along for the ride.

By the time they neared the Van Allen radiation belt, Sheila had had enough of talking to people. She didn't mind suiting up with a helmet to keep everyone at a bit of a distance.

· · · · ·

THE VAN ALLEN radiation belt was nothing new. Rings of charged, invisible particles had circled Earth since it was Earth, and even in the period of the early rocket launches, it was a source of concern. But the thing was, rockets moved fast. They hit the edge of the belt and zoomed past it in no time, so even the inadequate forms of protection on those early rockets were good enough. For astronauts in rockets, the radiation exposure wasn't much more than spending some time in the Himalayas.

But for all the space elevator could do, it wasn't fast, at least not rocket-fast. By space standards, the climber was just creeping up the Cord, and they were going to be in the worst of the Van Allen belt much too long to be safe. This meant the suits came back out again, with all the inconvenience that entailed: breathing tanks, gel packs of food inside their helmets, astronaut diapers. That last one was probably the worst.

Sheila had trained for this, though. They all had. So they made the best of it, lumbering into their suits after a last trip to the toilet to try to drain every last drop out of their bladders. The climber seemed a lot more crowded with everyone walking around in suits, kind of like the difficulty of navigating a crowded costume party. More than once, Sheila bumped her helmet on the viewport, trying to get close enough for a look down. They were up high enough now that the Cord seemed to ripple below them, which was a bit unnerving. The curve of the planet was also more evident. It was easy to forget that the world wasn't flat until you were thousands of kilometers above it.

Palik persuaded her to play a game of cards using a ridiculous paper deck he had created specifically for the bulky gloves that came with the suits. The cards were four times bigger than the typical size, and they had Velcro grips on the bottom that made them stick to the gloves. Apparently, Palik wanted to ensure he could still play poker during a space walk.

But as silly as it all seemed to Sheila, as soon as the two of them started playing, everyone wanted in. Though the internal lights in the ship had been dimmed for the night, no one felt tired now that they were above the planet. "Constant day" was the term used on Station, and apparently it could throw off one's body clock. So they all spun their flight chairs to face each other. Palik had to stand up and walk around to everyone to deal cards, and a pouch was passed around for discards. Still, something about this adaptation caught everyone's fancy. They played hand after hand of poker, keeping track of the money going back and forth via the intracom system that allowed them all to voice-text each other messages that screened on their helmets.

The card game was stupid and awkward until Sheila realized that it was actually brilliant. One could learn a lot about people by paying attention to the way they played poker. Some players, like Park, were cautious. She only bet when she had a sure thing, and she was quick to fold when a pot seemed to rise quickly. It was no surprise that Smeeth was a brash player, eager to up the ante and quick to bluff if he thought he could get away with it. But he couldn't get away with much with this group. Odelay seemed to have an intuitive sense of the odds. He folded before he lost a hand and won almost every one he played, like a quadrillionaire, Sheila supposed. Steiner was the one who surprised her. He was a great card player. Even when dealt a mediocre hand, he knew how to play it, and he seemed to be having the most fun of everyone, taking pleasure in the play of the game whether or not he won a hand. Karlsson was an awful card player. He had trouble just keeping the cards attached to his gloves without showing his hand to everyone else. He ended up leaving the game, claiming he was tired, but Sheila thought he had just grown frustrated.

Sheila and Palik were both good at cards and apt competitors for one another. Sheila hated to lose, and when she had an advantage, she played it mercilessly. But she wasn't playing her best cards tonight because she was focusing too much on everyone else. She had been down a little all night until she and Palik went head-to-head on a big pot. He wiped her out, jacks over nines to her three kings.

After all of the years Sheila and Palik had been together, she still couldn't figure out his strategy. He would play quietly, seemingly not having much effect on the game, but whenever there was a really big pot, he was likely to win it. This was true if the two of them were playing cards with friends on Labicittá, and it was true here on the space elevator. In the beginning, when the betting was cautious, he wouldn't have much impact. But as the evening went on and people were willing to take bigger risks, Palik capitalized on them. By the time everyone had finally decided to wrap it up, Palik had quite a virtual pile in his inbox.

Still, it was all in fun. The stakes were low enough that everyone could afford to lose, though Sheila could tell it was all Odelay could do not to notch things up to a level that he could really care about. As the lights rose to indicate dawn had arrived, they all decided to try and get some rest. They spun their chairs away from one another and lowered the visors on their helmets. Sheila, to her own surprise, found she had no trouble falling asleep.

• • • • •

SHEILA WAS READY to scream by the time the radiation indicator said they could take off their suits. She felt disgusting and hungry and couldn't wait to change. There were no showers on the climber, so Sheila did the best she could with a sponge bath in one of the changing stalls. She wasn't quite clean, but at least she felt human again.

When she came out of the changing stall, she saw the rest of the passengers, now arrayed in normal clothes, huddled under one of the upward-facing viewports. She walked over to them and saw why. They had gotten close enough to Station that it was within visual range. It was just a little speck in space, but there was a blinking light on the bottom (or was it the top?) of Station. They could see it clearly now, and excitement was building. The climber had the latest in gravity stabilization technology, but Sheila still felt light, almost buoyant.

She reminded herself that she had a goal. Securing a place for tourism on Station would secure a future for Labicittá. Otherwise the island would become little more than a pass-through site for equipment. It wasn't that there wouldn't be money to be made that way, but it would be a lot of money for a small number of people. The challenge was to figure out how to make the Cord the thing that, directly or indirectly, kept thousands of people employed. To do that, you had to sell dreams, and that might not be too hard because, as she stared past Station at the pinpricks of stars surrounding them, it was all starting to seem like a dream.

Now that they had all changed and the flight crew had placed the suits in a decontamination unit, they were free to bounce around the cabin, which is what they actually did. Sheila had thought she was just buoyant with excitement, but apparently the gravity stabilizers were not calibrated quite right. Everyone was feeling something approaching weightlessness. Smeeth and Steiner leapt onto the walls and half spun away from them. Palik and Odelay were having some kind of contest to see who could jump and touch the ceiling first. Even Park and Karlsson, who were the least adventurous among them, were prancing along the floor, enjoying the bounce effect in reduced gravity. Sheila tried it all and, more importantly, shot footage of everyone enjoying themselves. This was the kind of experience that people would pay a lot of money to have. It was a tourist's fantasy.

· · · · ·

SHEILA COULD BE coldly calculating. She had to be in her position, but that didn't mean she was incapable of awe. And as they approached Station, her earthly concerns melted away. Ever since leaving the atmosphere, when the darkness of space came to dominate their view, the whole climber had grown quiet. The passengers stared silently into the cosmos. Palik took Sheila's hand. The planet seemed to recede, and the horizons began to curve, as if the solid ground was evaporating below them.

As the Cord tugged them closer, she felt a bit of trepidation. She realized that she had been looking at the blinking lights of Station as if they shone from a lighthouse, warning them off from a craggy shore. But those lights were more like beacons, calling them into a last refuge before the cold darkness of space. Station was the largest structure ever placed into orbit, but it now seemed impossibly small and fragile.

The whole trip it had felt like they were climbing to Station, but now that they had left the Earth's atmosphere it had started to feel like they were falling toward Station instead. The Earth now looked less like the mass of land at the base of the Cord and more like a bright blue marble with a string attached to it. If she allowed herself to, Sheila could feel terrified about the tenuousness of it all. The Cord was the only thing keeping the climber in place, and the planet itself was moving all the time. Things never stood still. There was no solid ground. It was a little unnerving.

She glanced around. The passengers were quiet. Park looked a little nervous. Karlsson may have been tearing up around the corners of his eyes. There was a bead of sweat on Smeeth's forehead. Steiner had turned away from the viewports. Only Odelay seemed unfazed. Palik squeezed her hand tightly.

"If only Jia could have seen this," he said, his eyes starting to glisten.

"I know. I know," Sheila replied. She squeezed his hand and then released it. She knew they were lucky to have had Jia with them for as many years as they did. With all the surgeries and the associated medical problems, Sheila had known, intellectually, that Jia would not outlive them. Still, when Jia's time had come, it had been devastating. She told herself to remember the good times. Jia had loved playing with the dog and the robot. She was a wonderful big sister to Mega. And Palik was right that Jia would have loved this trip. She had been fascinated by the Cord, and she loved traveling.

Sheila wanted to say more, but she wasn't sure she could. She knew Palik wouldn't misread her silence, and she loved him for that.

When it was time to once again put on their freshly cleaned flight suits, no one made any jokes. The climber was as quiet as a funeral.

• • • • •

ONE THING FOR the fucking to-do list was to improve the docking. For Chrissake, she practically had whiplash!

Sheila had expected the docking to be as anticlimactic as the launch. No such luck. When the climber neared Station, what had seemed like a slow crawl all of a sudden felt more like an out-of-control plunge. When the flight crew attempted to slow the climber, the brakes engaged in fits and starts, pressing the passengers against their restraint belts and then slamming them into the seats. By the time they finally reached Station, Sheila was ready to lose her lunch. From the sounds she heard through the intracom, Karlsson already had. When the climber finally stopped, she was sore, sick to her stomach and just glad to be still. They didn't mark their arrival, and there was nothing to see. The upper viewports were pressed up against the outer walls of Station, and even the side ports had their views obstructed by Station's exterior scaffolding. It felt more like they had arrived in an interstellar repair shop.

After the safety check, and double check, and triple check, they all finally got to stand and line up at the base of a ladder that would take them through the roof of the climber. Sheila and Palik were toward the middle of the pack. They heard a *whoosh* of pressurization, and they awkwardly made their way up the ladder in their space suits.

This was another thing that would have to change. Why did they have to climb a ladder? If it wasn't for the gravity stabilizers, they could just float up into Station. That would be easier. Or maybe they could have just put the exit on the floor level. Who the hell designed this? Space engineers. They couldn't care less about convenience. Sheila took a deep breath. There was a lot of work that needed to be done.

Eventually they left the narrow metallic tube at the top of the climber to enter an even smaller passage on Station. She only knew that they had entered Station because the color of the metal showed more signs of wear. A paint job would help. And maybe a welcome sign. Bloody engineers!

But then they passed into a larger, still-metallic, room where they could all stand side by side, though it was cramped. She could see now why she and Palik had had to pass a claustrophobia test before being cleared for the flight. When they had all crowded in, Sheila saw that there were other people in the room with them. Leaning against the far wall was a tall, broad-shouldered man wearing a military jumpsuit. A smaller, stouter man in a matching jumpsuit stood next to him. Sheila found herself gawking at them and not just because they were the only ones not wearing helmets.

"Keep coming in, people," the man said, waving the passengers along. "If we can't fit you all here, we'll have to send a few of you back. Take my hand, sister."

The man smiled and extended an arm Sheila's way. She was in no danger of falling, but she grabbed the man's wrist anyway in appreciation of the traditional Labicittá greeting. Then she realized why she couldn't stop staring. These men were relaxed, and she hadn't seen a truly relaxed person since she had left Labicittá. Sheila released his wrist and fell back into the nervous scrum of passengers, a buzz of shuffling and scraping.

"If I could have your attention. Well, you've made it. Welcome to Station." The man cupped his hands around his mouth as if he needed to shout, which he did not. "I'm Colonel Levi Johannson, Station Commander, and this is Dr. Carlo Abrazzo of Station's medical team, though we are also apparently tour guides, since you are our first tour group. You are now in geosynchronous orbit approximately forty thousand kilometers above Earth, with everything depending on the strength of that nanotube you just rode in on. Good thing it's the strongest material we've got. Your comfort is also due to the gravity plates keeping your feet on the floor. Station is the culmination of years of research and engineering, not to mention billions of whatever currency you've got. All of this is a way of saying that we're all fortunate SOBs just to be here. We're going to let you get to your quarters now and get acclimated. Then we'll meet up and give you the grand tour. A bit later we'll see if we've got any chess players among you. We play a lot of chess up here. Follow me."

Colonel Johannson led the group out of the small room into—if it were possible—an even more cramped metallic passageway. Sheila had to duck not to bump her helmet, and she wasn't sure that Karlsson would even be able to walk upright. Sheila was beginning to have some doubts about this whole project. How could you persuade anyone to spend days in astronaut diapers just to wind up shuffling through a series of tiny metal rooms? None of this was any fun.

At the end of the passageway, Colonel Johannson turned back to them and smiled. "Now, I could have had you all take off your helmets already, but I'm guessing this crowd is pretty ripe. So when we step into the next area where we've got a little more circulation, I'll give you the go-ahead. Any questions?" He did not wait for any. "Good, we've got plenty of time to talk. Don't worry about it. Okay, you ready for something special?"

He waited. "Well, just because you've got helmets on doesn't mean you can't nod." They all nodded.

"That's better," he continued. "Here we go."

Colonel Johannson had been standing in front of a hatch door and now he leaned back against it, letting his weight push it open. Sheila stared through the hatch. He wasn't kidding.

The view was disorienting at first. Of course, they had been looking at stars the whole trip up the Cord, but only through tiny viewports in the climber. But this room was spacious, and its walls and ceiling were all made out of some kind of glass. All around was an uninterrupted canopy of stars. Sheila took off her helmet and immediately whipped out her digivice to start recording. She wasn't the only one.

"This is the first section of Station to use andioglass," the colonel informed them. "You'll notice if you look to your far left-hand side that there is a cover that we put up to protect this room from space debris. According to the specs, the cover shouldn't be necessary, but we don't like to take chances up here. Okay, I'll shut up and let you all look around now."

Sheila wanted to get Palik's attention so that she could take some footage of them together, but he still had his helmet on. When she had taken hers off, the automatic communication link went off. She tried to give his arm a squeeze, but the suit was too thick for that. Finally, she had to whack the back of his helmet just to get his attention.

"Hey, what the—" Palik said, removing his helmet so he could speak to Sheila.

"I... This is such a nice moment. I wanted to capture it," Sheila replied, feeling silly now.

"Yeah, I'm glad you didn't want to tell me you loved me or you might have broken one of my ribs."

"Fine, fine, just ruin it."

Sheila didn't want to squabble in front of everyone, but even in this confined space, it didn't seem like anyone was paying attention to them. There was something eerie and a little terrifying about being able to walk right up to the edge of space. Even though they had been told that the andioglass was sturdy enough to keep them safe, it didn't seem like much of a barrier, particularly if it was vulnerable to space debris.

Smeeth and Odelay had their noses pressed right up against the glass. Sheila wasn't surprised to see Park and Karlsson hanging back a bit from the edge. Palik had joined his new best friend, Steiner, who gestured over in the direction of the moon. Sheila wondered if they'd be able to see the old European moonbase from Station.

"Hey, look right over there." Smeeth turned and gestured to the whole group then pointed off into the distance. "Follow my finger, right there. Look ahead and keep going for about two hundred or three hundred million kilometers. There it is, Mars."

Smeeth had a big grin on his face, which was flushed. "That's what it's all about. Everything else is just window dressing."

"What are you talking about?" Sheila asked.

"Astronomy, solar power, whatever else you lot have on your minds for Station, you're just wasting your time. It's all about Mars. The people who can make things happen will ensure it."

It was Steiner who responded next. "I believe, Mr. Smeeth, that we are all here representing interests."

"Represent all you want, mate." Smeeth was shouting now. Sweat had matted his hair to his head. "The people who want to get to Mars don't take no for an answer."

"And who might these people be?" Sheila prodded.

"Bugger off, Doctor Governor, I've had it up to—"

Suddenly, Smeeth grabbed his head with his hands. He let out a moan.

"Let me through, let me through," Dr. Abrazzo said. The doctor placed his hands on Smeeth and lowered him to the floor.

"I can assist. I'm a doctor," Sheila said.

"Thank you, Doctor. I should be fine. He just needs to get to the infirmary." Dr. Abrazzo had his fingers on Smeeth's wrists, taking a pulse. "This is not uncommon. It's a pressurization issue. Not unlike the bends for deep-sea divers. He'll be fine as long as we take care of this quickly."

Dr. Abrazzo spoke into his communication bracelet. "Nurse, I need you to prep the depressurization chamber. Patient arriving in two minutes. You two"—he pointed to Odelay and Karlsson, the two tallest men left standing—"get on either side and help walk him over to the infirmary. Right now."

Sheila could tell neither Odelay nor Karlsson was used to being ordered around, but they snapped to attention anyway, got on either side of Smeeth, and hauled him out of the room, following Dr. Abrazzo and led by the colonel, who was opening hatch doors ahead of them.

The remaining members of the group were left alone, staring at one another.

Steiner spoke first. "Well, that was unexpected."

"Yet revealing…" Park commented.

"I believe," Sheila said, "that after a shower, we will have a lot to talk about."

• • • • •

AFTER A SHOWER, they did have a lot to talk about. Smeeth's outburst had made all of their careful politeness unnecessary, and it gave their deliberations a measure of urgency. Their grand tour had been postponed until Smeeth was released from the infirmary, so all the remaining passengers met in the mess, a featureless and windowless room with a table and chairs and enough chess sets that they each could have had one. It was time for negotiation.

Park was used to such settings, and she seated herself at the center of their small group. Sheila made a point of sitting right next to her, with Palik at her side and Steiner next to him. Odelay and Karlsson sat on the other side of Park. Sheila had feared that Park would run things like a UN meeting, and they would all be asked to make opening statements, but, to her relief, Park got right to the issue at hand.

"I have spoken with Dr. Abrazzo," Park began. "He has assured me that Mr. Smeeth will fully recover. It is also unlikely that he will remember what he said during his outburst, which gives us a temporary advantage."

"This is what I feared when I saw that Mr. Smeeth would be joining us," Steiner said. He apparently had access to intelligence reports on Smeeth that Sheila did not. "Smeeth works for very wealthy, very dangerous people who are much more interested in Mars than they are in Station."

"I have read about this group," Park said, apparently also having access to better intelligence than Sheila did. "What is it they call themselves?"

"Marsites," Odelay answered. Wow, him too? Sheila really needed to be getting better information from her people. Everyone else seemed to know more than she did, which was not a comfortable position for her to be in.

Sheila knew this was a time to speak rather than remain silent. "I haven't worked with Smeeth before, but I'm familiar with the type, as well as the type of people he represents. They will seize control of Station unless we can stop them."

"And do you have a proposal for how to do so?" Steiner asked.

"Well…" Sheila took a moment, making sure she had everyone's attention. "I believe the saying goes that we can all hang together, or we can hang separately."

· · · · ·

NEGOTIATIONS WERE NEVER fun, and these were no different. Nevertheless, Sheila found it easier when all involved were negotiating against people who weren't at the table. They were still jockeying for position, but they were all riding the same horse. And, to extend the metaphor, there was no time to waste because the faster horse was still in the stable recovering from the bends. Okay, metaphors were never Sheila's thing, but basically, after a few intense hours, they had hammered out a framework. It would all need to be approved by the powers that be, but it was in everyone's interest to do so, so she was confident the agreement would hold.

Station would stay under UN control. Exploration would remain ostensibly a military operation, but it would be defunded. Instead, resources would first shift to the science and energy projects. Tourism would build gradually, but it would be developed alongside the science and energy sectors. If that process was demilitarized and the expectation was that spouses and families traveled to the Cord, then Sheila was satisfied. Well, that and she secured an agreement that Labicittá residents would be at the top of the queue to fill support positions. Everyone got a little something—except Smeeth, of course.

They agreed that nothing would be said about this arrangement after they arrived back on Earth. By then, it could be run through channels on the planet. They would say nothing to Smeeth about the arrangement until it was too late for him to stop it. All they had to do was act friendly and play tourists for the rest of the trip.

"In fact," Steiner noted, "it would be a nice gesture for all of us to check in on Mr. Smeeth. Just to see how our friend is doing."

Even Park smiled at that one. It was a conspiracy, for sure.

$$\bullet \quad \bullet \quad \bullet \quad \bullet \quad \bullet$$

THE DOCTOR WAS right. Smeeth didn't remember anything of his outburst. In fact, he didn't seem to have any memory of leaving the space elevator. He was pretty disoriented, and he never did seem to catch up with the rest of the group. Throughout the rest of the trip, he constantly seemed a half step behind. Or maybe it was just that he kept waiting to get down to business, not realizing that all the business had already been conducted. Whenever Smeeth tried to venture into a discussion of the future of Station, perhaps looking to find allies for the Marsites, he was put off. Sheila guessed he must have thought them all a rather dim lot because they were just behaving like a bunch of space tourists.

They spent a lot of time shooting footage of space, getting tours of the technical sections of Station, playing long games of chess with the crew. Sheila and Palik took many walks along the outer perimeter of Station. It wasn't a very long perimeter, but the view compensated. In some ways, it reminded Sheila of the walks they took along the beaches on Labicittá, only with deep space instead of an ocean on the horizon.

Each day Sheila was here, she got more excited about the possibilities for Station and Labicittá. She, as well as the others, practically skipped through the passageway, and not just because the gravity controls could be erratic. Odelay was impressed by the efficiency of solar arrays. Park thought the command structure on Station was sound. Karlsson couldn't be kept away from the astronomy sector. And Palik, who would have guessed it? All his talk with Steiner about fishing? Not only had they figured out a way to draw tourists to fish the waters of Labbicittá, but they played around together at the space debris station, using their fishing skills to clear space junk with lasers.

On the last night, she and Palik snuck into the zero-gravity room when everyone else was asleep. Palik had joked about joining the forty-thousand-kilometer club, but Sheila didn't need persuasion. She wanted to experience everything Station had to offer, and weightless sex was one of those things. It was as awkward as you'd expect—easy to lose orientation and hard to stop moving once you'd started—but it was also as exciting, an experience all about the body while also feeling out-of-body. They left the chamber breathless and slept the sleep of the innocent.

As they readied to leave Station, the weight of responsibility settled itself on Sheila's shoulders once again. There would be a lot of work to do as soon as they arrived back on Earth. In fact, Sheila was sure that they hadn't heard the last of Smeeth or his patrons. They weren't the type to give up.

When they boarded the climber once again for the descent to Earth, Sheila's distraction was apparently evident, at least to Palik.

"You did some great work, lass. Put a smile on your face."

Sheila did. "I know. It's all I hoped for. I just wish I could be sure it would last."

Palik placed an arm around the bulk of Sheila's suit. He squeezed her tightly enough that she could feel the pressure through the thick material. "We can't be sure anything is going to last. We just try to set the right things in motion and hope that others can keep them moving ahead."

"So you going in for philosophy now?"

"I'm just an honest repairman, ma'am."

"Right, and I'm just a country doctor."

Joshua

A nother one of those bitches, just like her mother. I should have said it to her face, but that would have blown my cover. Not that I did the best job staying undercover, but it's not easy to trail someone. There's a lot of running, then stopping and pretending like you're just standing around on a street corner. This is harder than you'd think when there is no reason whatsoever to be standing around on the streets of the disgusting slum that Labicittá has become, with begging children and garbage on every corner and probably open sewers, judging by the smell. Labicittá has really gone to crap since the last time I was here. This place had been booming then and even more so once the Cord got opened up to tourism. But what a difference a generation can make.

This is one of the downsides of being immortal. I get to see everything that was once good go bad.

Another downside about being immortal is that I thought I knew Labicittá because I had lived here years ago. I thought I knew how to follow someone on the streets without being noticed. I probably should have gotten suspicious when that bitch circled all the way around a block for no good reason, but how was I supposed to know she was carrying a surveillance app? It's impossible to keep up with new technology. Hey, mate, here's a new app, and there's a new digivice and, look, still another new blood filtering protocol. It's too much.

Anyway, here I thought I was following her on the sly, and the next thing I know, there's a police hovercam floating next to me, giving me a retina scan while I get remotely interrogated by a cop via a video uplink. Meanwhile, that bitch is standing there glaring at me while a crowd forms around us looking for a free show.

Fortunately, my passport was precleared, and my account is in the black, otherwise it could have been a short trip to Labicittá for me. As it was, I got a citation on my account and a canned lecture from the hovercam cop. Meanwhile that bitch was just standing there with her rollup, accessing my public profile and putting in for a restraining order, no doubt. It's a good thing I had thought to scrub my data before making this trip.

"I know your type," she says, pointing her rollup at me once the hovercam was finished with me.

"You know nothing," I tell her. I aim to sound badass, but I'm off my game. My voice is too high. I may sound whiny. But there's something disconcerting about her eyes that unnerves me. Even with her hair covered from view by her hijab, it's obvious that she looks like her mother. And apparently, she is just as nasty as her mother, too. Still, I know what I need to do. I pull up her sleeve, grab her arm, and squeeze.

Then I feel this shock and I'm on the ground. When I look up, everything is a blur for a second. When the world comes back into focus, it's just the hovercam and a screaming cop threatening to haul me in. I put my hands up to show I've got no more fight left in me. But it doesn't matter that she's won this round. This is the upside of being immortal. There's no rush.

I'm probably lucky that the hovercam cop just doesn't want the hassle of having to run me in. He makes me sit on the curb with my hands behind my head, waiting for that bitch to walk away. I get more of a lecture via hovercam, and I say that I must have had too much to drink. Apparently, that is the right line, or at least a line that the hovercam cop has heard before. Eventually, the hovercam flies away, and I push through the crowd and out onto the main road. When I get far enough away, I sync in to flag an autocab and slouch against the wall of a building to wait for it. A headache starts coming on. That dull, insistent throb that is too deep in the skull to massage away. Where the bloody hell is that autocab?

By the time the autocab shows, the headache has gone from throbbing to pounding. I need to get back to the hotel and take some serious meds. I hop into the cab and mumble the name of the hotel. Then it's like needles and a dark black cloud at the center of my vision spreading out, and I hear a voice *don't deserve to live what you've done she's just a child* it comes over me enveloping me like a *keep you in this net like the fish you are* it is another one of those it is another one. Another. Other—

· · · · ·

AND SO NOW I'm in my hotel bed. What the hell happened to me? I've had bad headaches before but never one that knocked me out. And how'd I even get here? Last I knew I was in the autocab. I guess the hotel is used to guests arriving passed out. I'll have to tip pretty well. Wow, I'll have to get a doctor to take a look at me once I get back to Australia. I grab my digiwallet off the bedside table and see that it's intact. Then I look at the time and realize that I've been out for fourteen hours. I've never slept that long in my life. Maybe there's some kind of blimp lag from the flight to Labicittá from Perth. Maybe. Who knows? Living forever can be damn tiring sometimes.

The headache is gone, but a bad headache leaves its own special kind of hangover. I punch in for room service and end up talking to an actual person, one of the valets who wanted to make sure that I was okay. The concern is nice, but he's probably more worried about a tip. I thank the valet and sync in a tip with my order—need to keep these people on my side, after all—even if they are going to nickel-and-dime me to death. No, not to death. There is at least that satisfaction.

After room service brings me some breakfast, I get some calories into me and start coming around. I open the blinds in my room and get to look out the window to where the Cord hangs in the distance out over the water. When the Cord catches the sunlight, it seems to blink, like it is flashing some kind of signal. And when one of the climbers starts ascending, it looks like a comet rising slowly in the air.

It's still quite a view. That hasn't changed. Although back when I was first on the island, living over on the far side and hustling to try to make a living, I hadn't had much time to appreciate it. I wouldn't have been able to afford to stay at this hotel back then. Of course, now that I can stay anywhere I want, the nicest hotel on the island is run-down, like everything else on Labicittá these days. This hotel still shows the signs of the boom-era. All the walls were made with local bamboo, and there were windows wherever you could catch a view of the Cord. There was plenty of carbon nanotube as well, but that was just decorative, playing off a time when the Cord still drew tourists to Labicittá. It doesn't look like anything has been updated in a generation, probably not since that bitch was the governor.

It had been a horrible thing to have to witness, even from a distance. The doctor who had helped to ruin my life for a time getting elected governor, and Labicittá becoming the biggest tourist attraction on the planet. This place was so popular that people came here without even planning to ride up the Cord. Blimp after blimp of people coming to spend their money on Labicittá. How many nights had he lay awake plotting his revenge against the doctor and the repairman only to find out that they had both passed away. And of natural causes! Where was the justice in that?

Say what you will about the Marsites, and no doubt they are total shits, but at least they put an end to Labicittá's Golden Age. What the hell do they care about tourism? For them, it's all about getting control of the Cord and getting off this planet. Everything else is just a warehouse to them, so I won't be surprised if Labicittá becomes even more of a shithole in a few years. But in the meantime, there's money to be made off an area in decline, and I know how to make money. Besides, being immortal is expensive.

• • • • •

BY THE TIME I take a shower, my head has cleared and I'm ready to get to work. I sync in to see what's happening, and I've got a message from one of my investor goons, impatient for an update about the meeting, which he knows isn't scheduled until later in the day. Such idiots I have to do business with, barely worth the time it takes to send back a comforting message. Then I see the notification about a restraining order. I knew that daughter of a bitch would file one! I appeal, which will stall for a while, by which time I plan to be off this island for good. I'm not looking to spend any time in front of a Marsite judge. Still, that means there is no room for error.

I consider forgetting all about her. I could just make the deal that got me here and go back to Australia. But that would be wrong. After all, getting to Labicittá and taking my revenge was the only reason I started this whole process in the first place. I will never forget about her parents and how they humiliated me, sent me off this island with nothing more than the clothes on my back after stealing everything I had. To live forever with regrets is unbearable. I need to win, even if I'm competing against the dead.

Despite the headscarf, this daughter, Mega, looks just like her mother, and if my revenge has to skip a generation, so be it. I take some pleasure in knowing that after the island was taken over, that whole family lost everything they had. And the daughter will have less than nothing when I'm done with her. It's good that she and I had had an encounter where she thought she had bested me. It will make what happens next all the sweeter. Me, Joshua Martin, who was forced off Labicittá with nothing—with less than nothing—now returning as a friend and ally of the new rulers. And, of course, I will live forever, though that's not something I will share with her.

After all, just because I can live forever doesn't mean I will. The procedure was a complete success, that I'm sure of. In the years since, nothing has changed. Aging is a thing of the past for me. It's just that I'm still as vulnerable as anyone else to blunt force trauma or injury to major organs. The success of the procedure means that my cells will continually renew themselves. So maybe it is more accurate to say that I will live forever as long as I don't die first.

I think of that as I look out my window onto the busy streets below. I don't like walking about in crowds or dealing with traffic. Maybe that's why I did such a bad job following that bitch around. I'm just not comfortable in situations where there's too much going on to control. Even with hovercams on every street corner, what's to stop some criminal or a misprogrammed autocar from taking me down? Accidents can happen.

• • • • •

MY APPOINTMENT IS for lunch, which isn't that far away even though I've just finished breakfast. I decide to walk over along the beachfront to stay out of the crowds. My headache has returned a little bit—not much, just like a persistent pressing on my scalp, which beats the hell out of yesterday's sledgehammer to the brain—but I'm hoping a little ocean breeze will help.

I head out the back exit of the hotel so I don't have to meet another valet, and wrap around the hotel to get to the beach. It's a weird experience being here. This whole tourism/beachfront section is new to me, but it's already becoming dilapidated. People think they know what they're doing when they build these attractions, but I've seen it before, a big plan that will only work if everything goes right. Well, guess what? Things go wrong. And then what? You wind up with a whole section of the city devoted to tourism and no tourists because the Marsites have invaded and taken over the island. People are idiots.

From the beachfront, I can see the ruins of the old capitol building. It was on a peninsula sticking out into the bay. I had vague memories of it when it was intact from the last time I was on the island. It was inspired by the old Sydney Opera House and echoed those huge intersecting curves. I'd never got close enough to see it up close, and now it is just a pile of charred and rusting beams. The Marsites must have liked to keep it that way, just to remind the natives. Apparently, it was the first building the Marsites took out during the invasion. D'Onforio had been the pilot of the lead plane, if you can believe the official history. I'm not sure I can, but it's good to play along, particularly considering I'm meeting with D'Onforio in about half an hour.

As I pass out of the downtown area, I approach the Marsite government zone. At first I wonder if I will recognize it. That's silly. The whole sector is surrounded by a six-meter-high wall topped with razor wire. There is a constant whirring sound in the air from the drones circling the perimeter, no doubt equipped with lasers.

But I don't have anything to worry about. My meeting is precleared, and the guard at the sentry post just retina scans me and waves me through. Inside the sector, things are a mess. Wow, these Marsites really don't care much about aesthetics. They just walled off an old section of the city for their own use and changed it as little as they could. If a building was destroyed in the invasion, they just fenced it off and didn't even bother carting off the rubble. All the business storefronts are abandoned or have office cubicles pushed up against plate glass windows. I guess the upper levels of buildings are used to house soldiers in what used to be apartments. A former school seems to have been converted into an armory, and military-looking vehicles are plugged into chargers on every corner.

At least the signage is good. That makes sense. There's no way my digivice is going to give me directions in a restricted zone. Signs have been hammered into the ground on almost every corner, telling you where to go, what not to do and even how you should feel—*Administrative building 50 meters left* and *Spitting spreads germs!* and *Look up to your future.* The last sign featured a full-color representation of a Martian sunrise. It is the only new-looking thing in the entire restricted zone. The Marsites have made their point—fuck Earth.

• • • • •

D'ONFORIO KEEPS ME waiting, which I expect. What I don't see coming is that the reception area outside his office is the nicest room I've seen since leaving Australia. The bugger has his own Ottoman oasis right in the middle of the filth of Labicittá. The room is lined with all these tapestries hanging behind overstuffed sofas. And he's got a real human receptionist. I had been expecting one of those awful robot receptionists like in Australia, but, of course, the Marsites have this whole thing about human purity, so robots are out, which is probably the best thing they have going for them. Technology, sure, I'm all for technology; it's the thing that has made me immortal. But there's a huge difference between a robot and a human. At least Marsites appreciate that. And, look, they didn't need robots to take over this island. Yeah, I think I can do business with these people.

Finally, the receptionist gets a flag on her screen that tells her D'Onforio will see me, and I get to go into his office, which is even more lush than the waiting room. Same decor, the only difference here is, wow, this bloke has a thing for guns. He's got them mounted behind glass and in display cases. The base of his desk is actually an old cannon. Crackers, if you ask me, but it makes an impression.

I see D'Onforio in profile, staring out the window into the sky. He has sharp features and a Roman nose. And though he's not that tall, he's been putting some time in at the gym (or maybe undergoing muscle supplement treatments), so that makes an impression, too. In fact, when I realize that there's a ceiling light focused in front of the window, I begin to wonder if he posed there on purpose. He's a playwright after all, or at least he was back before becoming a Marsite commander, so maybe he thinks of his office as a stage. Kind of pretentious, if you ask me, but it's his stage.

"Commander D'Onforio, thank you so much for seeing me."

D'Onforio turns from the window with a look of surprise as if I have disturbed his meditation on the meaning of life. I have to pretend that I am interrupting him even though the bloody oaf just told the receptionist to let me in.

"Ah, Mr. Martin. It is good to meet you in person."

We shake hands, and D'Onforio gestures to the upholstered chair in front of his desk, and then he sits down behind the cannon desk with a glass top. We make some small talk. I compliment the mild weather, as if D'Onforio is personally responsible for it, and he accepts the compliment as if he is, in fact, the God of Climate.

"So, tell me what brings you to Labicittá, Mr. Martin," D'Onforio asks, as if I haven't had this meeting set up for months. We're here to talk money. We both know that.

I lay out the proposal again even though it was all in the encrypted document transfer. It's always good to explain everything in a negotiation as if you're talking to an idiot, because most of the time you are.

D'Onforio nods as I speak, but I don't really think he's paying attention to me. At one point I swear I catch him admiring his profile in the reflection from the window. This bloke is full of himself, which I note to make sure to take advantage of.

"And so, Commander D'Onforio, as you saw in the proposal that I sent, the profit margins are astronomical. Everyone will want to drink water from Mars. There is more than enough interest in this commodity to provide substantial funding for the Mars project, while making us both very wealthy men—well, wealthier than we both already are."

D'Onforio smiles at that bit. I think I've got this bloke figured out.

"Yes, Mr. Martin, there is great interest in all things having to do with Mars. That is one reason we have been able to recruit the best and brightest to our cause. But my concern remains one of, let us say, propriety. I have read your proposal, and it makes a certain...practical sense. If you pay what you propose for water from Mars, then, yes, the logistics could work. But, you understand, our goal is one of independence, and if we are dependent upon water from Earth to replace that which is shipped from Mars, then our mission suffers."

"I understand, Commander. But if, let's say, the water harvesting efforts on Mars exceeded expectations. If the mission was able to report that there was, in fact, more water than the mission needed, then that would be a sign of the mission's great success."

"True enough, but why should we expect to find more water than scientists predict?"

"Ah." I paused briefly and lowered my voice. "I do not think the important thing is how much water you find. The important thing is that you have more water than you need. Then you can make an announcement to that effect—"

"Yes, I see, and certified water from Mars becomes the medium of advertising our success. You have made your point. It is better for the mission if we exceed expectations. After all, who expected that we would so easily take control of this island and the Cord?"

"Well, I for one have long admired the great successes of your movement. I only wish I was still young enough to be able to dream of a life on Mars." Okay, now I was laying it on a little thick to a mortal, but you do what it takes to seal the deal.

"Yes, I sometimes wish I was younger myself, and perhaps that accounts for my impatience with our colonization efforts. After all, the first landing on Mars took place decades ago, and it is outrageous that there is still no permanent settlement on the planet. Things take so long that I sometimes flirt with the idea of one of those immortality treatments for myself, but, of course, if they really worked, we would all be immortal, eh? No, their track record is so poor I might as well go to a voodoo priestess."

D'Onforio laughs broadly at his joke, and I'm sure I blanch. What the hell does he know, the old bludger? I haven't aged for decades, and my treatment has been flawless.

I gesture to the water pitcher on his desk and fill myself a glass. I drink slowly, settling my emotions. I can feel a headache start to come on.

"Are you well, Mr. Martin?" D'Onforio asks.

"Yes, I'm sorry. I have been traveling a lot lately, and it seems to be catching up with me."

"Ah, not a traveler, are you? Well, perhaps you were not meant for Mars after all. It may be best that you live out your remaining days during the decline of the planet, no?"

This is a tougher smile to put on, but I do it. Still, I don't like where this conversation is heading.

"Well, it sounds like we have an agreement then, Commander?"

"I believe we have reached an understanding."

Now my smile is authentic. I just have to get this egomaniac's retina scan synced on a contract, and then everything else will take care of itself. I have presold options to Martian water rights from now until the end of the universe. Once this deal is done, I never have to deal with this arse again.

"But there is one thing." D'Onforio taps his hands on his desk, and the entire desktop activates, transforming itself into a giant screen. He flicks his wrist so that the files on the desktop one-eighty around to face me. My name is on the top of the screen along with files about my companies, my more recent personal history—and that bitch! Her picture is staring up at me from the corner of the desktop.

"Due diligence, you understand," D'Onforio says, looking away from me. "We take the necessary precautions in all of our dealings."

The throbbing starts again. D'Onforio begins droning on. Concerns about my past connections. Concerns about the bankruptcies. The likelihood that I will sell the water rights. And, of course, the restraining order. Am I someone he can trust?

I have answers to all of it, except the restraining order, of course. I hadn't anticipated that. I give him assurances; however, I sense he doesn't want explanations. After all, he had this information before he agreed to meet with me. No, he just wants a better deal.

But what more can I offer? With the water rights presold, I can't move much on the price. I have to think fast, but it's hard to think when my head hurts. *My head, it hurts. Make it stop.* Of course.

I look right into D'Onforio's gray, watery eyes. "What you need is someone you can trust. Not just in this situation, but in all situations, yes?"

D'Onforio looks back at me, puzzled. For the first time in this meeting, I have the upper hand.

"As you know, Commander, many people, though I know you are not among them, trust robots."

D'Onforio stiffens up. "It is trust in robots that has brought the human race to its current pathetic, dependent state."

"Yes, I understand. I understand completely. Putting our trust in robots comes with a price. But if you have to rely on people, you also pay a price. I have to imagine that some of the people, even in a committed organization such as yours, have disappointed you. Is that not the case?"

D'Onforio's eyelids flicker, and he nods. I have him wrapped around my finger like a cord.

"What you need is someone who can only be trustworthy, and I can provide you with someone like that." I lean in closer to him so that I can speak in a whisper. "You need a transhuman."

D'Onforio pulls back.

"They are not robots. There's a big difference. But just think of what this means. Someone you can trust. Someone who is dedicated to your vision. Someone who is programmed that way."

I take out my digivice. Fortunately, I have a hologram of the latest Jia version. I project it above D'Onforio's desk; a list of specifications scrolls down next to the image of her body.

"I can provide you with the full specifications, if necessary. But I have worked closely with this model, and I can speak personally to its reliability, its utter trustworthiness. This model is cloned from a single source, which ensures continuity across generations. The newest models also have a much longer life span, and they can be given enhanced digital components as they become—"

D'Onforio cuts me off. "I am aware of the concept. This is a subject that I have some interest in." D'Onforio walks around his desk, sizing up the hologram as if it is a work of art, which in some ways it is. Each Jia has been a triumph of aesthetics and science and, of course, commerce.

"How soon can you get it to me?"

"I can have her—I mean it—on the next blimp over from the continent. This model will pass standard security screenings."

D'Onforio smiles. But it's not a smile of happiness. It's just a sign of greed. I know it well.

"Mr. Martin, I believe we have a deal."

• • • • •

EVEN WITH A deal in hand, it still takes forever before I get to leave D'Onforio's office, and the success of the negotiations can't take away the pounding in my head. The shot of syrupy liqueur D'Onforio insisted I drink didn't help any. When I leave the office, all I want to do is go back to the hotel and lie down, but I know I have to take care of business first.

Once I get into an autocab, I sync in and contact the investor goons, letting them know the deal is in place. They'll get their damn contracts, and hopefully they'll get off my back now. Then I sync in for home and call up Jia. Her face appears on the screen of my digivice, the same face from the hologram, the same child's face I have seen in so many generations of Jias that I've begun to lose track of them.

"Mr. Martin, it is so good to see you."

"Jia Chiang, I need you to pack up immediately and come to Labicittá. I'm forwarding directions for you to follow."

"Will I be joining you?"

"That is still to be determined. For now, just follow the orders I'm sending."

"Yes, of course."

"That is all for now. Though you are free to smile."

"Yes, Mr. Martin."

Jia's face dips down so that she is not making eye contact, and a grin appears on her face. Then I can just close the connection. I've been down this circuit before. No explanations. No goodbyes. That makes it easier all around. It's so much better than having an actual child. I'll never make that mistake again.

When I get back to Australia, I'll have to put in for another Jia. At least they last longer now than they used to. It's an expense, but I can afford it now. With this water deal, I've got enough to live on for decades. If I ever took vacations, I could become a tourist now. But where would I go? Someplace like Labicittá? As the autocab speeds by the empty beaches, I can see what good that does. I'm not the sort to relax. I just wish this headache would go away.

And I can't forget what I came here for. The water deal is just a pretext. It means nothing. It's just an excuse to get to Labicittá. What matters is what happens next.

• • • • •

WHEN I GET back to the hotel room, I order the biggest meal ever, and I eat every bite of it. In fact, I'm so hungry the waiter's arm starts to look pretty appetizing. The throbbing hasn't quite gone away, but I'm so used to it by now that it's just like a buzz in the background. Jaysus, I can't wait to get off this island.

But now that I'm fed, I'm ready to do what I came here for. And, I have to be honest, I'm a little nervous. There's risk involved. I could have just contracted a hit, but some things I just have to do myself. In a world full of idiot mortals, I can only trust myself. Well, myself and the Jias, but they've been programmed for trust.

I just need to wait until nightfall, when everyone is asleep. Then I need to cloak into whatever security system they have and set up my equipment. A modest explosion, followed by a fire. My hope is that this will echo, at least psychologically, the attack that brought this island under Marsite control. I'll be there to see her face if she runs out of her house. If she gets caught in the explosion, so be it. It's a simple enough plan that all the equipment passed through the screening check when I blimped in. It won't take much to reroute the house's electricity through a dynamo. I'll be in and out in ten minutes and can trigger the explosion by remote control.

I sync into my digivice and check for the address of the nanochip I had put on that bitch's arm. That had been the trickiest part of the whole plan, making physical contact, and though it got me tased, once I could track her, I'd known I'd be fine. There's not much to do other than stay awake. Part of me wouldn't mind sleeping off this headache, but there will be plenty of time for sleep once this is over.

Headache aside, I feel good. Yes, revenge is a dish best served cold. Ice cold.

• • • • •

AT FIRST, I don't notice anything about the house. Just another old Labicittá building with a commercial storefront and a residence up on the second floor. It was ramshackle a generation ago, never mind now. But then it all starts to come back to me, and I'm stunned, shocked. It's the same house! Even under the dim streetlights, I recognize it. The same place where this whole thing began, when they stole my Jia and kidnapped me, and I was tortured by that damn robot and that original bitch. I didn't even think that the place would still be standing. Why would they have even held onto such a dump after becoming governor and chief bottle washer, or whatever that repairman became? Mortals are sentimental about some things. Idiots.

What a pleasure this will be! And how easy. With the cloak program, I can override any security system. A backwater like this doesn't even know about the kind of technology I have access to.

I ease up to the side of the building and walk up the steps to the back entrance. As I'm coming up the stairs, I wave my digivice, and there's a brief flicker of power. I check the display and see that I now control the security system, the house's power, basically everything. I'm not really even breaking in. I'm just walking into a home that now recognizes me as the owner. And it will continue to do so until I blow the place up.

I wave the digivice in front of the door and it swings open, lights dimly rising to meet me. I'm in the kitchen. I was expecting to see the same downscale appliances and furniture that I remembered from before. But, of course, some things change. Too bad they bought a nicer oven just so I can destroy it.

The protocol is set to run. I open the oven and place the dynamo inside. The timer is all set to let me walk away and watch the blast from down the block. Such a simple—

What the hell! My head! What just happened? My arms are pinned, and my face is pressed into something, into—oh no!

"Concerning the difference between man and the jackass: some observers hold that there isn't any. But this wrongs the jackass."

That voice! It can't be! Even though I'm upside down, I can see it. It's an antique now, but it's that same robot from before with the stupid mustache! The robot rotates on its sphere so that it's right in my face.

"Let me out of here!" I scream.

"The trouble ain't that there is too many fools, but that the lightning ain't distributed right."

"You've got no right to do this, you damn robot!" I twist in the net to get my hands free. But the robot pokes me in the ribs with a metal pipe.

"Ow! Stop it!"

The lights come up, and someone sweeps into the room.

"Suparman, did you let this robot out?" a female voice shouts. Then she sees me and stops in her tracks. "Oh!"

It's her. Just perfect.

· · · · ·

AT FIRST I don't say anything and just let the three of them run around me like they've never seen a man hanging from a net in their kitchen before. The bitch apparently has a brat with a ridiculous name—Suparman—and he's as excited as a kid on Christmas, running around me and shouting things to the robot. The robot just spins around awkwardly on its ball, tipping off-kilter as it circles me. The bitch isn't much different, only she runs around while tapping into her rollup and shouting into the screen, showing the dynamo she took from the oven like it's a prize piece of evidence, which I suppose it is. She's screeching, the brat is yelling, and the robot keeps whirring around. I'm still upside down, of course. After hitting my head, the throb went straight to eleven, and now it feels like I'm being beaten with a PVC nanotube. I can't take it anymore.

"Shut the fuck up!" I scream, trying to twist to face them.

That quiets everyone down for a second. Then the robot spins over to me and pokes me in my ribs with its pipe.

"Under certain circumstances, urgent circumstances, desperate circumstances, profanity provides a relief denied even to prayer."

"Oh, Jaysus," I mutter. I reach through the net and try to grab its stupid mustache. The robot shifts out of my grasp and then jabs me in the cheek with its little pipe again.

"Call off that robot and let me down. I'm injured. And please make that robot be quiet."

"The unspoken word is capital. We can invest it or we can squander it."

This can't get any worse. Then it gets worse.

• • • • •

THE BITCH MUST have posted something to a network because it only takes minutes before the whole neighborhood comes into the kitchen. Men with long beards, women with headscarves, some of them speaking a language I can't even understand. All of them talking at once about what I'm doing there and what to do with me. But there aren't any cops, and I can't decide if that's good or bad.

I complain that I'm dizzy from hanging upside down, but they ignore me. I really am dizzy, and I've got a pounding headache to boot. And somehow I'm hungry, desperately hungry. Every time I try to shift positions, that damn robot pokes me with that pipe. When one of the longbeards tries to push the robot away, it locks itself in place.

"Mega, call off this bot."

"I can't," she says. "It was my father's, and its command board is frozen. Every time it's a sunny day, the robot still expects to go out fishing."

The man bends down, flips a plate on the back of the robot, and starts fiddling with it. I hear a playback of a voice that sounds familiar.

"From now on, every time this man speaks, I want you to say something to irritate him. And if he moves without my permission, poke him."

"That's my father's voice!" she screams, running over to the robot.

"Something must have triggered an old command," the longbeard says, placing his hand on her shoulder. "It's been a long time since I've heard Palik's voice." He reaches down again and deactivates the robot, which allows him to push it away.

"Don't turn him off," the brat calls out. "He doesn't like being turned off."

The bitch whispers something to the longbeard. I hate secrets, and now that I don't have to worry about this robot poking me, there's no reason I can't find a more comfortable position. I squirm around and try to right myself.

"Hey, stop moving!" the longbeard shouts.

"I'm injured, and I'm having trouble breathing, and you will be held responsible. Get me down from here!"

"We'll get you down when we know what to do with you."

"I'm a personal friend of Commander D'Onforio, and he will hear about this."

At the mention of D'Onforio's name, things get quiet.

"Mega," the longbeard says, "let's at least set him right side up while we figure out what to do with him."

She nods, and the longbeard pulls a chair over by me. He stands up and reaches to the ceiling. The next thing I know, I've fallen on my head. I see stars, actual stars, like the ones in the sky.

The longbeard laughs, but he steps off the chair, then lifts me up onto it. I'd like to say being right side up is better, but I feel awful. Worse than I've felt this whole trip.

Then the longbeard pulls up another chair next to me. "So, now that the world is right side up, you want to tell us what you're doing here? Why are you following this woman around and breaking into her house? Rich man like you with a nice suit and important friends."

I stare straight ahead and don't say anything. I feel dizzy. The whole crowd in the kitchen is silent now, staring at us. The longbeard reaches over to the robot and grabs its pipe, which I can now see has been shaped to look like a cigar. He pokes me in the ribs with it.

"Ow!" I shout. "No speak anything to you." That's not what I meant to say, but my brain and mouth don't seem to be communicating. What is going on?

"You know, when Mega first saw you stalking her, she thought you may be one of those wannabe Marsite vigilantes that's always causing trouble, but you're something different. Most vigilantes aren't adept enough to use cloaking tools and dynamos, but it's a good thing Mega is a security expert, which I guess you didn't know."

Something's not right. I should have known that information. Who did the preliminary research for me on this project? I can't remember. My head hurts so much. It's those needles again and the black cloud blocking out my vision. *Don't cry. It's just a scratch. Next time I take your whole finger.* Finger. I reach out my finger. She comes toward me. I can smell her. I smell. I leap from the chair, but the net holds me back. So hungry. Must eat. Eat brains. I scream. Roar.

"Brains!"

Prologue

Aditya

At first, Aditya took the bucket and bailed out the bottom of the boat in a relaxed manner, much like he would have done back home after a day of fishing. His main concern was not to upset his wife, Nisrina, or their baby daughter, Alya, or even the members of the other family on the boat with them. But there shouldn't have been water collecting on the deck, and he knew it. Then as the rain picked up, he began bailing faster and faster, trying to stay ahead of water falling from the sky in torrents and washing over the side of their boat. Then he stopped once he realized that the boat must also be leaking to be taking on so much water. It was too much. It was all too much. There was nothing he could do but hold on to his wife and child. He could not even join Nisrina in prayer.

After a week, Aditya decided that there was no God on this ocean. On this ocean, in a small boat that had almost capsized twice, the second time washing away the chest with most of their food, they were alone. Even when a fish was caught by Farel, one of the boys from the other family, he could not celebrate with the rest. In fact, he could not even look them in the eyes anymore because he knew that they all would die here on this ocean. He knew that they would never reach Labicittá, and it was all his fault.

He was more sure of this now as the cresting waves made it difficult for them to stay seated. Water streaked across Nisrina's eyes. She blinked it away, both her arms firmly gripping their child. She looked like a little girl cradling a doll. She was too young to be here, too young to be a mother and now pregnant again with the son who was to be named Palik after his own father. She was too young for all the responsibilities that Aditya had thrust upon her.

There was a shout from the bow. Aditya looked up to see a large wave approaching them. He threw himself around Nisrina and Alya, grabbing the deck rail around them as firmly as he could. But doing so put him off-balance. As the wave swept over the deck, it knocked his feet out from under him. His hands slipped, and his jaw came down hard on the metal edge of a seat. He felt the water carrying him away, and for a moment, he was disoriented. Then there was a sharp tug on his waist and the pressure of water rushing by him, sucking away his soul and leaving his body behind.

The next thing he knew he was lying on the deck of the boat at his wife's feet. She was screaming his name. He reached down and felt the cord around his waist. This was the second time it had saved him from being washed overboard.

"It's okay," he said to Nisrina. "Stop screaming."

"You weren't moving. I thought you were dead."

"It's okay."

Aditya stood up. He felt dizzy, and his jaw was sore. But he was okay. He quickly scanned the deck. All eight of them were still on board, and everyone from both wretched families was staring at him. This trip had been his idea. This boat had been his purchase. This route was the one he had chosen. He was responsible for everyone, and he had failed them.

"It's okay," he repeated.

They never should have left Indonesia in this boat. He knew it was not designed for an ocean crossing, nor for this many people. But he had been desperate to leave, and he had insisted that they depart immediately. He couldn't bear to stay in Indonesia another day, waiting for another island to sink into the sea. It had seemed like everything was coming undone. But was it? Was it actually any worse now than in the past? He knew the history. There were always catastrophes. War, typhoon, tsunami, islands sinking under the rising ocean. He had heard the stories from his parents and grandparents. Maldives, Aceh, East Timor. He had thought he was brave to insist on leaving, but now he wondered if that just made him more of a coward.

Alya was crying, upset by her mother's screams, and she was not to be soothed. Aditya could not blame his daughter. He wished he could cry along with her. Instead he stepped over to kiss the top of her head. Nisrina pushed him away.

"Don't. You're still bleeding," she said.

Aditya touched his face. His hand came away damp, a mixture of blood and ocean water. He pressed his palm against his sore jaw, hoping to stem the flow. He looked around the deck for a rag of some sort, but anything that wasn't tied down had long ago been washed overboard. It was a sad sight, the two families—wet, tired, hungry—in this pathetic boat, with no idea anymore where they even were, no idea if Labicittá was even close. The navigation system had not worked properly the whole trip, and the electrical system had shorted after the first storm.

He had been such an idiot.

There was a tap on his shoulder. It was Johan, the father of the other family, and he silently handed Aditya what looked like a child's shirt. Aditya took it from him and pressed it against his aching jaw. Johan was a good man, a good friend, and he had every right to hate Aditya right now. Three, four days at most was what Aditya had promised. Instead they were now on their second week adrift, with no end in sight.

Then Johan said, "We must be closer now."

Aditya said nothing. He did not even nod. He could not pretend.

· · · · ·

THE SKY WAS the color of ashes, and the rain continued to fall in shards. It was impossible to see more than a few meters ahead of them, difficult to even know when a big wave was approaching. There was nothing to do but hold on and wait for the inevitable disaster. Even his daughter had stopped crying. Aditya could not look anyone in the eyes, least of all Nisrina.

The boat continued taking on water at the ebb of every wave. Aditya joined the other men and boys who were futilely continuing to bail. But it was useless. If the boat did not capsize, it would sink, and then they would all die.

Suddenly, Aditya was thrown off his feet. The air was expelled from his lungs, and he knew the moment had come. He heard screams and looked frantically for Nisrina and Alya. They had not moved. Aditya could not comprehend what had happened. The boat seemed simply to have stopped. It must have struck something.

There was the sound of a *whoosh* behind him. He turned to see that Johan had launched a flare into the sky. It was their only one. A foolish gesture at best.

"It's no use," he shouted at Johan.

"Land," Johan shouted. "Look!"

Johan gestured behind Aditya, who turned to see the faint outlines of what was in fact an island. They had practically steered into it, but the visibility was so poor that they couldn't see it until now.

A big wave hit the boat, this time sending the stern into the air. They must have struck rocks close to shore. Aditya got to his feet and ran to the front of the boat to inspect the damage. Whatever they had struck was big enough to ground them, and it had breached the hull.

"We're going to have to swim," Aditya screamed up to Johan. "The boat won't stay together much longer."

He could see the hesitancy in Johan's eyes.

"The current can take us in," Aditya insisted. "The waves are going toward the island."

Johan grabbed Aditya's arm.

"Are you mad? We have children. Your wife can't swim to shore. Be quiet."

Aditya knew Johan was right. What was he thinking? He left Johan's side and went over to Nisrina, but he could see in her eyes that she knew what he did not. She clutched Alya tightly.

"I'm sorry, *cintaku*. I'm so very sorry."

For a time, they waited, bracing themselves in anticipation of every wave that threatened to knock them to their knees.

Then a shout erupted from the other side of the boat. Had a child from Johan's family been swept overboard? The boys were jumping and pointing to the island. Aditya squinted and saw a light where there had been none before. Was it a ship? He couldn't be sure, but Johan gestured for him to come forward, and he joined the boys in waving and screaming frantically, even though he knew no one could hear them.

They stood together in the bow. It was the part of the boat closest to the island and what might have been an approaching ship, but it also was where the boat had run aground. The deck was no longer level, and he could see that the bow sat dangerously low in the water. The whole boat began to pivot near the gunwale, and he had to hold the rail just to keep his balance. He tried to make out if a ship was in fact coming toward them, but the sky was so dark it swallowed everything but the sea.

When the next wave hit, it was followed by a cracking sound. He looked down to see the deck splintering at his feet. "Nisrina!"

He pivoted and leapt over the widening crack. He felt a shudder as the deck below shifted, and he was flung off his feet, across the deck, and overboard.

The silence was what he first noticed, even before the water. For hours the sound of the unrelenting pounding of rain loomed over everything, and the first sensation of not hearing it anymore was relief. Of course, in an instant, he realized what had happened. He was underwater. He could not see. He could not breathe. But then the tug of the cord against his waist reminded him that he was still attached to the boat.

He swam blindly upward, kicking with all the power he had as his lungs burned to breathe. Finally, he broke the surface and opened his eyes to chaos.

The boat had broken in half. The bow section was still teetering on the rocks, and the children clutched to its high side, screaming. But the stern had detached and overturned. The fragmented hull, the underside chipped and worn, was all Aditya could see, and it was starting to float away, with Nisrina and Alya attached to it.

The cord tugged again at his waist. Aditya took a breath and dove beneath the splintering wreckage, swimming until his hands collided with the stern of the boat. He surfaced again, taking a breath then screaming Nisrina's name. He could see nothing and no one, the hull of the half boat now blocking his view. He could only assume Nisrina was still tied to the rail, as he was, but this section of the boat was sinking quickly, and it would take them all down with it. He kicked as hard as he could with his feet to keep his head above water while he grabbed the knife from his pocket and pulled the cord at his waist. He began sawing. Another wave hit and took him under, but he kept kicking, kept cutting, until he felt it give, releasing him from the cord. The knife slipped from his hand, but he was free.

He kicked to the surface again, returning to the chaos. The hull was already lower in the water. Holding onto the only exposed section of the boat's rail, he took as deep a breath as he could and submerged himself. He forced himself to open his eyes in the sharp, biting salt of the ocean water. But he could see nothing. He pulled himself underwater, hand over hand, along the rail, fighting the current, toward where he hoped Nisrina would be found. He wasn't even sure if he was on the aft or starboard side of the rail. He pulled and pulled, fighting the buoyancy that wanted to pound his head against the deck. But then the pulling got easier, and soon he was approaching the surface of the water. He ascended again out of the ocean, having found nothing.

"Nisrina," he screamed. He had lost her. He was sure of that now.

"Aditya," a voice called.

He turned toward the sound and couldn't believe what he saw.

It was a ship, perhaps not much bigger than theirs had been, but he could see instantly that it was one of the new search-and-rescue ships he had read about. It had robotic arms extending from it like some kind of sea creature, grabbing and pulling bodies from the water.

There was a figure on the deck, hands cupped at their face, and Aditya heard his name being shouted again. The figure waved for him to swim toward the rescue ship. But he couldn't leave Nisrina and Alya. He tried to take another breath, but a wave hit and he choked on water. Suddenly, he felt himself being attacked, and he instinctively struck out with his hands, feeling his knuckles collide with metal. His body was jerked away from the hull.

It was a rescue arm. It had him in its grip and was pulling him away. He tried to struggle against it, but he felt so weak now, coughing up water.

He thought about Nisrina and Alya as he was taken even farther away from them.

Waves crested over him as the arm retracted, pulling him closer to the rescue ship. The arm slowed as it approached the ship, and he could make out the figure of Johan standing next to the man who had called his name.

Aditya struggled to free himself from the arm, and he pointed back to the hull.

"My wife," he screamed. "My child!"

Then, with a jerk, the retracting robotic arm stopped meters from the ship. Even over all the noise, Aditya heard a sound he recognized as a motor burning out.

The man next to Johan vaulted over the rail. Holding onto it with one hand, he landed on the now-jammed rescue arm. The man extended his free arm toward Aditya and shouted back toward the ship, "Release the arm grip. Turn the damn thing off." Then he extended his hand farther, shouting, "Aditya, take my hand."

"But my wife, my child."

"Brother, take my hand!"

The voice, it was familiar, and in the recognition, Aditya did as he was told. He reached his arm up toward the deck of the ship. The man grabbed his wrist tightly, and Aditya felt the tension of the rescue arm release. As he felt himself yanked over the railing of the ship, Aditya realized something impossible.

Hamdani.

The man was Hamdani, his childhood friend from his home village, perhaps his oldest friend.

He collapsed into the strong and powerful arms of Hamdani, and they both fell to the deck.

"Nisrina," Aditya said, his face pressed up against Hamdani's ear. "Nisrina and the baby are still out there."

"She's here," Hamdani said. "And we have the child. I think we have everyone." Hamdani steadied his feet and pulled them both up, holding Aditya as if he were a child.

"What's the count?" Hamdani screamed over the thundering of the rain and waves.

"All accounted for, sir. We need to get to shore now!"

Aditya turned and saw a man in uniform standing next to Johan, and behind them, Nisrina and Alya! Aditya couldn't believe they were still alive! He reached toward them, needing to touch them, but he slipped on the wet deck and fell. He tried to rise but fell again. He was too exhausted to even walk. He crawled to his wife and child, pulling them close, collapsing into their tears.

"Safe," he heard himself whisper.

$$\cdot \quad \cdot \quad \cdot \quad \cdot \quad \cdot$$

OF COURSE, ADITYA had known that Hamdani had immigrated to Labicittá. But he had known it in that abstract way one follows old acquaintances on social media without ever expecting to see them again. Once islands began to sink into the sea, the ties that bound people together frayed. Friends became acquaintances, and acquaintances became people one read posts about.

Aditya would not let go of Nisrina and Alya. Nisrina insisted that she and the baby were okay. She had cut the cord that bound them to the boat as soon as it began to break up. They were the first ones the rescue arms had found. Aditya hugged his wife and child. He stroked his wife's belly. He wore the remains of the cord around his waist like a belt. He was not ready to take it off.

And Johan would not stop talking.

"I couldn't believe it either! Hamdani! I thought maybe I had already drowned, and this was some kind of vision in death. I have heard of such things. And this rescue ship! Have you ever seen anything like it? It plucked us all out of the water like petals on a flower. And look, there is Labicittá!"

Johan gestured to the approaching island. Even in the rain, it looked beautiful, majestic.

"And over there, that must be where the Cord will be built. You and I, my friend, we will build it."

Aditya smiled weakly. He did not know where Johan found the energy. He only knew he would need to find it himself. There was much to be done. This was only the beginning.

About the Author

Jim O'Loughlin lives in Cedar Falls, Iowa, where he is the head of the Department of Languages & Literatures at the University of Northern Iowa. His creative and critical books include *The Last Caucus in Iowa*; *Kurt Vonnegut Remembered*; *Dean Dean Dean Dean*; and *Daily Life in the Industrial United States, 1870-1900*, the last of which was co-authored with Julie Husband, with whom he also co-authored Nic, Devin and Ian.

CPSIA information can be obtained
at www.ICGtesting.com
Printed in the USA
JSHW042326150422
24958JS00002B/103